Secrets

and

Charades

by

Cindy Ervin Huff

SMITTEN
HISTORICAL ROMANCE
LIGHTHOUSE PUBLISHING OF THE CAROLINAS

SECRETS AND CHARADES BY CINDY ERVIN HUFF
Published by Smitten Historical Romance
an imprint of Lighthouse Publishing of the Carolinas
2333 Barton Oaks Dr., Raleigh, NC, 27614

ISBN: 978-1-946016-14-0
Copyright © 2017 by Cindy Ervin Huff
Cover design by Elaina Lee
Interior design by Karthick Srinivasan

Available in print from your local bookstore, online, or from the publisher at:
lpcbooks.com.

For more information on this book and the author visit:
https://jubileewriter.wordpress.com.

Brought to you by the creative team at Lighthouse Publishing of the Carolinas:
Eddie Jones, Shonda Savage, Kathy Davis, Andrea Merrell, Molly Realy, and Brian
Cross.

Library of Congress Cataloging-in-Publication Data
Huff, Cindy Ervin
Secrets and Charades / Cindy Ervin Huff 1st ed.

Printed in the United States of America

Praise for *Secrets and Charades* . . .

I have watched Cindy at conferences, laboring to perfect her work and honor our Lord with her writing, and I am proud to introduce her published book, a delightful, tender story of honesty and integrity that demands truth before passion. Two wounded people learn to love, and thus to trust, to build a beautiful marriage.

~ **Charlotte S. Snead, Author**
His Brother's Wife, Invisible Wounds, and *Recovered and Free*

Secrets and Charades by Cindy Ervin Huff is an engaging post–Civil War Western that captures a reader's interest from page one. Author Huff does an excellent job of weaving complexity into the simple life of the rugged Texas terrain. A captivating novel of the Old West, *Secrets and Charades* should find itself on the bookshelves beside many long-loved Western classics.

~ **Elaine Marie Cooper, Author**
Saratoga Letters

As a man who writes for men, I'm not one to pick up a romance book. But this one had plenty of hair on its chest. Huff is a superb storyteller. She does a marvelous job capturing the moods and actions of pioneer men and what it must have been like for folks in a world not quite ready for strong, godly, educated women. Adventurous, humorous, and filled with tension so strong I was pulled in and often spoke aloud to the characters on the page.

~ **Tez Brooks, Author**
The Single Dad Detour (Kregel)

A mail-order bride. A marriage of convenience. Jake is determined to find a woman to be a mother figure to his young niece. He gets more than he bargained for in Evangeline. Filled with all the adventures and struggles of the West during the post–Civil War years, *Secrets and Charades* is an engaging read. Most striking is the reliance on God each of the main characters display in all circumstances, both good and bad. Cindy Huff is an author to watch. I look forward to reading her next work.

~ **Rebecca Waters, Author**
Breathing on Her Own

Fans of Western Historical Romance have a fantastic new author to love. Cindy has woven delicate threads of authentic human emotion into the sturdy fabric of high-tension action. A must-read.

~ **Linda W. Yezak, Author/Editor/Speaker**
Triple Edge Critique Service
The Circle-Bar Ranch Series: *Give the Lady a Ride* and *The Final Ride*

I thoroughly enjoyed reading Cindy Huff's *Secrets and Charades*, her wonderful historical romance set in Texas. How Cindy wove together the lives of her story's characters and the challenging threats they faced captured my interest and held me to the end. Exceptional debut novel.

~ **Beth Ann Ziarnik, Author**
Her Deadly Inheritance

Cindy Huff's amazing ability to bring to life her characters, attracted me to her debut novel first off. I could see them in my mind's eyes: Jake's slow-moving, thoughtful speaking and actions and Evangeline's determination to make her own decisions. I particularly liked the way she created their responses to each other. Scene upon scene, chapter upon chapter, Huff built the confidence and trust Evangeline and Jake found in each other. *Secrets and Charades* is a lovely story for all those who adore historical romance. Huff has a wonderful writing future ahead of her.

~ **Carole Brown, Author**
Hope Shining Through the Shadows of Suspense

Dedication

In memory of my little sister, Carol Ervin,
who read the very first rough draft of this novel and pronounced it good.
If she can watch this world from the next, I'm sure she is smiling.

Special Thanks To ...

My mom, Audrey Ervin, who always told me I could do anything
I put my mind to.
My sister, Linda Ervin, who also read the rough draft and believed in me.
My awesome husband who corrected grammar, asked helpful questions,
and listened to me talk about my imaginary characters as if they were real.
Beloved, without your support this novel would still be images in my head.

CHAPTER 1

Missouri
March 3, 1873

"Young lady, my marital status is none of your concern." Evangeline Olson paced about her medical clinic. "What possessed you to answer an ad in the *Matrimonial Times* on my behalf?"

"Aunt Evie, please," Maggie said.

Evangeline steeled herself from Maggie's doe-eyed pleading. "No." She waved a dismissive hand. "You got yourself into this mess, and you can get yourself out." Her heart was beating a tempo perfect for flight, and she reached the door to her bedroom at the back of the clinic before Maggie could respond. Without a backward glance, Evangeline slammed the door. The pounding in her head muffled Maggie's pleas through the closed door.

"Aunt Evie, I have all of his letters. Read them."

Evangeline slid to the floor, back against the wall, forehead in her palms. At twenty-eight she had chosen a career over marriage. A headache thumped in her temples. *Deliver me from interfering family.*

"Are you listening? Please, I'm begging you. Just read them. If you don't like what you read, I'll write him an apology."

Evangeline remained silent.

"They're on your desk. Mother says the truth is easier to remember than a lie. You'll find a journal on the desk where I copied all my correspondence to Jake."

* * *

Charleton, Texas
March 8, 1873
From his bedroom window, Jake Marcum could see the sunlight spill down the hillsides. His body dripped with sweat from another battlefield nightmare. He massaged his forehead, attempting to dislodge the visions of cannon fire and the echo of screams. Bending over the porcelain basin to wash his face, he touched the jagged scar across his left cheek.

The clanging of the oven door and the aroma of coffee pulled him away from his haunting memories. When he reached the kitchen, the housekeeper was already busy with breakfast. "Mornin', Selena."

"*Buenos dias, Señor* Jake." She pulled steaming-hot biscuits from the oven.

Cookie Slade's morning ritual of humming did nothing to ease Jake's restless thoughts. "Want some coffee, Boss?"

Jake took the cup and headed outside. Cookie limped along beside him.

The porch stretched across the front of the house, unprotected by the overhanging roofline. Cookie lowered himself to the top step, careful not to spill his coffee, and Jake plopped down beside him. They gazed for several moments at the mountainous vista before them. Jake appreciated Cookie's patient silence. Both men faced forward—their usual position for serious conversation, something eye contact tended to obscure.

"Ever since you sent that proposal to Miss Olson, you been off your feed." Cookie tasted his brew and waited.

Jake watched the soft, billowy clouds move across the morning sky. "It's in the Lord's hands now."

"Sounds like you need a mite a convincin'."

Jake studied an ant crawling across his boot. "You know I gotta do this for Juliet. She needs more book learnin', more genteel ways."

"It ain't like you jumped into this." Cookie adjusted his stiff leg. "You been writin' this woman for a year. Why her? You had a passel of desperate gals respond to your advertisement."

"Right enough. But Evangeline was the only one who wanted to write for a while. She wanted to get to know me first."

"Speaks kindly of her character."

"Yeah, it does." A familiar longing deepened his heartache. "Life in this place took my family, Cookie. Juliet's all I got. My brother and his wife woulda wanted their daughter raised like a lady. They'd want her to get a better education."

"True. And neither of us wants to see Juliet sent off to boardin' school."

"I'm not ready to have more family taken from me, not even for boardin' school." Jake savored his cooling coffee. "What if Evangeline hates it here?" He pulled her picture from his pocket. "I been lookin' at this picture of her and her niece every day since she sent it." He'd memorized her features: high cheekbones, full lips, taller than her niece. In her letters, she'd described her eyes as green that changed with her moods, and the color of her hair as not red, but burgundy. Jake turned the picture slightly for Cookie to see before securing it in his shirt pocket once more.

"She's a looker." Cookie's eyebrows lifted, and his smile revealed a missing tooth.

"Makes me wonder why she ain't married. Her letters are cordial and friendly. Her writin' don't tell me if she has a disagreeable nature. I hope marryin' her makes things better for Juliet." Jake stared into his coffee mug as if searching for confirmation he was doing the right thing.

Lord, I can't turn back now. Either she says yes, or she don't. I'm trustin' you.

Jake's eyes drifted toward the grove of trees shading the cemetery.

Maybe this ain't in the cards for me. You know I only loved one woman, and that be Nora. It hurt to have that love throwed away. But if it's Your will for this woman to become my wife, help me truly learn to love her.

***

Jordan, Missouri
March 12, 1873
Evangeline knelt at a simple wooden cross marking the grave of her dearest friend. Fiona MacDougal had been her comforter, healer, and faith restorer. But most of all, she knew the truth and loved her anyway. The dear woman often said Evangeline's past had no hold on her future.

"Oh, Fiona." Evangeline's voice broke.

The Irish brogue whispered through her memories, taking her back to their last bedside conversation. Fiona seemed to have drawn closer to her Lord near the end. Her eyes had sparkled with heavenly light.

"Evangeline, I have seen a vision."

"Yes, Miss Fiona?" She perched on the edge of the bed, giving her full attention.

"I saw ye in a new place with large mountains and wide plains, and the wind was blowing ye hair. Thy face be more serene than I ever seen it afore. Ye seemed younger, and love glowed from thine eyes, the love a woman has for a man."

"Ha!" The word flew from Evangeline's lips before she could check it.

Fiona's scowl rebuked her. "Don't be like Sarah and laugh at a word from the Lord."

"Please forgive me." Evangeline touched Fiona's cool, thin hand. "Are you sure this isn't your wishful thinking?"

"No, lass, I had the *feelin'*."

Evangeline stayed quiet. Her friend's sincere belief in the *feelin'* and the visions that accompanied it were discounted by some as a symptom of old age. Fiona's *feelin'* had always been on the mark. But maybe this time ...

"In that new place, lass, the Lord promises healing and wholeness. The thing ye have been resisting, the gift He desires to give, is there. Open the eyes of thine heart and the ears of thy spirit and be prepared when the call comes. I know in me spirit it will be soon."

Evangeline patted Fiona's hand. "We will wait and see."

"Evangeline Felicity Olson, don't patronize me."

"Forgive me. I meant no offense."

"Please, child, I have such an urgency in me heart for ye to understand that this vision is truly meant to be. Promise to keep thine heart open."

Evangeline kissed her cheek. "I promise to try."

"I will pray it will open very wide to His will."

The memory of Fiona's intense look lingered as Evangeline gazed at the grave. Moisture trickled down her cheek. "Miss Fiona, I need you so much. I'm scared. Whether I like it or not, your vision may be coming true." She wiped her face with the back of her hand, then traced the deep grooves forming Fiona's name. A shiver of loneliness coursed through her body. Her legs cramped from kneeling. "I've been reading the rancher's letters. Perhaps this is the answer to my dilemma. Maybe a new start is the right thing. He is a man of faith. At least he writes of faith." She sat upright and began pulling weeds from around the tombstone.

"Yesterday, I compared the date on Maggie's first letter with the date in my journal where I recorded your vision. The dates match. Maybe that's why I am drawn to his letters. You told me to keep my heart open. You know too well my resolve never to marry. Going West to find love, is that even possible for me? Jake wrote that he needs someone to help his niece Juliet become a lady. I think I could be a good mother to a twelve-year-old, but a wife is another matter entirely."

The approaching night air chilled her as she gazed at the sunset between the trees. The shadows and light blended together to form what looked like a cross between the branches. Evangeline felt peace wash over her as Fiona's words filled her heart.

Lass, the Lord will guide ye. Don't forget that wherever ye go, He will go with ye.

CHAPTER 2

Charleton, Texas
March 15, 1873

Jake Marcum stood outside the Charleton General Store envisioning Cordelia Hanks watching for him. His letters to Evangeline had become the talk of the town thanks to the nosy woman.

The store was long and narrow, stocked from floor to ceiling with a variety of goods any rancher, farmer, or miner might need. Like a cat about to spring on a mouse, Cordelia always guarded the door.

Jake felt foolish staring into the window waiting for the right moment. Jedidiah Wood and his daughter, Bertha, had entered the store only moments ago. He hoped the additional customers would distract Cordelia so he could take care of business with her husband, Angus.

The tinkle of the doorbell was drowned out by Cordelia's caustic words. "Jedidiah Wood, I hope you don't expect Angus to extend any more credit to you and your half-wit daughter."

Bertha appeared oblivious to the insult as she greeted the proprietors in her usual repetitive manner. "Howdy, Miss Cordelia. Howdy, Miss Cordelia. Me and Pa come in to get a few things." She handed the proprietress her list with an innocent smile.

Jake removed his Stetson and smacked it against his leg to remove the dust. He wiped his boots on the mat near the door. Discomfort wrapped around his gut as he waited. *Get your business done and get out. Don't look her way, just …*

Cordelia gave the Woods a dismissive nod as she handed their list to her husband and turned her full attention to Jake. "My, my, I like a man who is considerate of others. Most men just track filth all over my shop." She ambled toward him, managing to maneuver her round body and billowy skirt down the narrow aisle to greet him. "You've come for your mail." She lowered her voice, obviously for effect. "You've received more than usual—a telegram from your lady friend." She extracted the letter and telegram from her pocket and handed them over.

Nosy biddy. Jake felt his eye twitch, a clear sign his patience had remained outside with his horse.

"So, Mr. Marcum, your lady friend is coming April fifteenth— at least to Hardyville. Will you be going for her or have the stage bring her to Charleton? She can always wait right here for you, if necessary." She stood close, a hungry look in her eyes while Jake read the telegram. The smell of her toilet water assailed his nostrils, and he stepped back two paces.

"I need to send a reply."

Cordelia escorted him to the postal counter. "Here is the telegram form. Can I help you write the message so you can use the fewest words? My son, Horatio, says I'm good at that."

"No need." Jake placed his Stetson on the counter and wrote his message. He passed it back to her without looking up. "Where is Horatio?"

"We have a mare about to foal. I think he prefers working with horses over being a postal clerk. I don't suppose you prefer the company of horses. You apparently enjoy the company of a refined lady like Miss Olson or you wouldn't have been corresponding for a year."

Jake retrieved his hat. "When will it go out, and how much do I owe ya?"

"Let me see." She read the words out loud. "Meet you in Hardyville STOP Preacher there STOP Jake." She looked up at Jake, her pencil poised in the air. "That's one dollar and fifty cents. So, you've decided to pick her up in Hardyville. I haven't been there in over a year …"

Her chatter sounded like a dull saw on a log. Jake reached into his pocket for the money without offering a reply. He tipped his hat and headed toward the front counter.

"Don't worry," she called after him. "Horatio will get this out right away."

Jake headed toward Angus. "Here's the list." He unfolded a sheet of paper. "I was wantin' to order somethin'."

Angus Hanks, as round as his wife but six inches shorter, offered a pudgy hand in greeting. Reaching beneath the counter, he pulled out the mail-order catalog. "What is it you want?"

"A sewin' machine," Jake said low, hoping Cordelia wouldn't hear.

Angus turned to a well-worn page. "Your new wife will be the envy of every woman around. They swear this top one's the best. Cordelia has had her eye on it for ages. Says her old machine needs replacing. I know she just wants to be the first one to have the newest model."

Jake swirled his hat as he stared at the picture. "Kinda pricey."

"This one below it is also an excellent choice. We could ask my wife what she thinks."

"No thanks." Jake grabbed Angus's arm and lowered his voice even more. "I'll take the first one."

"I'm placing an order tomorrow. It should be here soon after your wife arrives."

"I got twenty dollars to put on it, and I'll pay the rest after the cattle drive."

"I'll get your things together and add your payment to your account."

Jake waited as sweat formed under his collar. Glancing over in Bertha's direction, he inadvertently caught her eye.

She flashed her version of a coy smile, albeit awkward and large. With voice booming, she greeted him as she greeted every male in the area. "Why, howdy, Mr. Marcum, it's a real delight to see you. How have you been?"

"Just fine. And yourself?"

"Mighty fine. Mighty fine. Thanks for asking." Bertha batted her eyes. "I must be going now." She gave a clumsy curtsy to Cordelia, then Angus, and finally to Jake. "My Pa instructed me not to dilly-dally, but wait for him in the wagon." The child-like woman marched out the door swinging her arms.

What if the reason Evangeline ain't ever married is because ...

Jake felt his neck redden.

God forgive me.

***

Jake arrived home in time for dinner, still nettled by Cordelia's prying.

Whole town probably knows 'bout the telegram. That woman seems to know who died before they're dead.

His irritation compounded his already anxious thoughts. After a year of writing, she was finally coming. He pulled the picture from his pocket and studied her image.

"Evangeline Olson, you seem like a fine woman—maybe too fine for me," he said aloud to the picture. Now that she had agreed to come, he could barely breathe.

Standing before the washstand mirror in his room, Jake stared at his face—darkened and weathered by the sun—as he dried it with a towel. What would she see? Would the scar frighten her? Smoothing his shirt and tucking it into his pants brought his mother's words to mind. *Jacob, coming to the table disheveled is disrespectful to the cook.* He could hear her laughter.

I hope Evangeline laughs.

"Uncle Jake, it's time for dinner," Juliet hollered.

Jake left his anxious thoughts as he followed her voice to the dining room.

"Did ja get another letter?" Juliet's sing-song voice was light, like Nora's had been. It pierced his heart. She ran to hug him. "I want to read it. Did she say yes? Did she?"

"I received a telegram today, said she was comin', so I s'pose the answer's yes."

"Hurrah! I can't wait." Juliet danced around the room, her black braids bobbing up and down in rhythm. Jake could see his brother Robert's carefree ways sparkle in her brown eyes.

He took his place at the table and smiled at his niece. "Well, you're gonna be waitin' a mite longer. She won't be comin' for a month."

"A whole month?" The girl's face sagged. "I think I shall just die."

"Sit down and eat," Cookie chided as he carried a plate of beef to the table.

Juliet flopped onto her chair.

Cookie dragged his leg, extending his right arm for balance. Even after stampeding cattle threw him from his horse, the man wouldn't quit the ranch. Jake admired his determination. He'd stepped into his new role with ease, helping around the house and mentoring the cowhands.

Selena followed Cookie from the kitchen. "*Mija*, you're going to break the chair. Stop sitting like a boy and try to sit like a lady." She placed a bowl of beans on the table. "No man will want to marry a girl who acts like a boy." Selena's deep-brown eyes twinkled as she teased Juliet. She grasped the side of her dress and, rising on tiptoes to appear taller than her five-foot-two-inch frame, glided gracefully back into the kitchen.

Jake grinned as Cookie observed her movements with admiring eyes.

"Who says I'll ever get married?" Juliet turned in her chair, raising her voice so Selena would hear her. "There's no one here to marry anyway, 'cept your son, Manny." Her nose crinkled as she spoke. "An I ain't marryin' him anyhow, so I can sit how I like."

Selena's knowing laugh drifted from the kitchen. She brought out the tortillas and grinned at Juliet. "You will be sorry you did not try. Someday there will be someone special, and it will be too late to learn how to be a lady."

"Uncle Jake, why's Selena always tryin' to marry me off? I don't wanna get married. I wanna be a rancher like you."

"Say grace, Juliet," Jake said, trying to keep laughter from seeping through his lips.

***

Jake removed the letter and telegram from his pocket and seated himself on the parlor chair that had belonged to his parents. The floral upholstery was worn and faded now. Juliet sat on the arm of the chair to look over his shoulder while he read the letter.

He then placed the telegram in her outstretched hand. She studied it for a long time. "I ain't never seen a telegram before," she said, then began to read. "Mr. Marcum I will be arriving fifteenth April taking train to Hardyville STOP Please advise how to proceed from there STOP Miss E. Olson STOP. Why does it keep sayin' stop?"

"That's how the telegraph operator knows it's the end of a sentence."

"Ain't that somethin'?" Juliet's eyes lit as she kept up her barrage of questions. "How far is Hardyville from here? Why can't she go to Charleton? It's closer."

"Hardyville is where the train goes. Charleton has only a stagecoach stop. I sent a response tellin' her I would pick her up in Hardyville."

"You sent a telegram, a real telegram?" Her eyes sparkled as she listened.

"I certainly did." Jake marveled at his niece's fascination with trivial matters.

The smell of hay and sunshine surrounded him as she hugged his neck. Juliet looked sweetly at him and asked, "Can I go with you?"

"No." His answer was sharper than he meant it to be. "I figure

I'll go alone."

Her smile melted as he disengaged her arms from his neck. A pout replaced the smile, and Jake softened his tone. "Besides, there won't be no room for you on the buckboard for the return trip." Seeing an argument forming on her face, he added, "And no, you can't ride in the wagon bed. It'll have her trunks in it."

Plus, I will be nervous enough meeting her without having you talk her to death.

"Can I show the telegram to Manny?"

"I reckon so, but don't lose it."

Just as the words were out of his mouth, Juliet vanished in search of Manuel, taking her joyful anticipation with her. Dread filled the void as he stared at the worn curtains. The last rays of sunlight fought with shadows.

Cookie eased himself onto the chair across from Jake. "You seem adrift somewhere."

"Now that she's comin' … *really* comin' … I'm plum scared."

"Well, women do that to a man. They scare all the courage right outta him. Turn him to mush. Explains why I never married. 'Sides, I got me a nice deal here—shelter, grub, and good company. Whadda I need a wife for?"

"I've no regrets keepin' you on when I inherited the place, so don't make me start now. It was your idea I take Juliet when Robert died. Your idea I place an ad for a wife." He sure hoped Cookie's instincts were right about Evangeline. "Maybe I don't need a wife either."

"Just 'cause I don't want a wife don't mean you shouldn't have one. Anyways, you said Juliet needed a woman of refinement around to trim the rough edges offa her."

"True." Jake's forehead furrowed.

"Pray on it. The Lord knows all about this here situation."

"Yep, He does."

"I'm off to bed. I'll pray on it too."

As Jake listened to Cookie's footfalls, each step reminded him of his own crippled soul.

Lord, You know I'm anxious 'bout a lot of things. Things I never wrote in those letters. Things only You know. When the time's right, I'll need to tell her. And please, Lord, help me do right by her.

CHAPTER 3

MacGregor Home
Jordan, Missouri, late March 1873

Evangeline's bedroom was cluttered with trunks and crates. Dresser drawers lay open like stair steps, and piles of books were strewn about. Glancing up at the mirror on the opposite wall, she could see her sister's face streaked with worry lines. Although Katie MacGregor had their father's Swedish blond hair and blue eyes, Evangeline was convinced Katie inherited the majority of their mother's Irish stubbornness.

"Evangeline Felicity, I still do not see what you are trying to prove." Katie maneuvered through the packing maze.

"I am not trying to prove anything." Evangeline stooped over the closest pile of books, her worn black skirt's loose hem catching the toe of her high-button shoe and causing her to stumble.

Katie grabbed to steady her, then ripped the rest of the errant hem from the dress. "Yes, you are. You're trying to make some kind of statement to Shamus because he hired Dr. Marshall." She shoved the strip of fabric into her apron pocket.

Evangeline kept what she hoped was a calm appearance. "Why should I care? He's a competent doctor." Acid formed in her stomach with the lie. She leaned into a trunk with a stack of books.

"You're angry Shamus gave your rooms in the clinic to Dr. Marshall." Katie tapped her foot. The clicking of her sister's shoe on the wood floor vexed Evangeline. "You're taking this on like one of your causes—like temperance and women's suffrage. That's it … just another cause." Katie removed clothes from one of the trunks and refolded them.

Evangeline yanked a blue floral gown from her sister's grasp and stuffed it back into the trunk. "I don't know why you insisted on sewing me these new gowns—especially with all your objections to my leaving. My things barely fit in the trunk as it is."

"Throw out those matronly rags. You don't need all those black dresses. You're not in mourning." Katie retrieved the wadded gown.

"According to you, I *am* in mourning—mourning over a dying career." Evangeline's irritation grew as Katie folded the garment and set it aside.

"Evangeline, there are certain things women shouldn't do." She folded another blouse before placing it on the refolded gown.

"Being a partner in a medical practice is one of them." Evangeline finished the familiar statement. "My moving has nothing to do with Shamus's decision."

Katie placed the two folded garments in the trunk. "You know how the community is. Every time you attend one of Shamus's patients, they run back to him to confirm your diagnosis. The Duncans blame you for Woodrow's death."

Evangeline fought the desire to flee the room. The memory of her biggest medical disaster taunted her. "Dr. Marshall could not have saved Woodrow Duncan, and you know it."

"We know that." Katie lowered her voice as if speaking to a child who had blurted out some inappropriate question. "But the Duncans don't believe it. If Shamus had been there, they wouldn't have questioned his death."

"How can you calmly fold my unmentionables while insulting me?" Evangeline turned away.

Katie's voice softened. "But you're a great help to Shamus—he values your gifts."

Please stop! she wanted to shout, trying to block out her sister's nagging words. Katie's anxiety only made things worse. Evangeline's resolve to not become angry weakened as Katie wore her down.

"You're only upset. When you calm down, the regret will come." On and on Katie pressed, her words sounding like a swarm of bees in Evangeline's head.

Exasperated, Evangeline slumped as she sat on the bed. "Enough." The pile of books in her lap teetered.

"Oh, dearest sister ..." Katie paused, sadness filling her countenance, "why can't you just stay here?" She joined Evangeline on the edge of the bed. "You are an heiress now. You can buy a house. You don't need to practice medicine."

"Heiress is a wretched title for what that money has brought me." Tears threatened and anger clutched her heart. "We've had this discussion before. I've made my decision." Evangeline emphasized her point by sending a book banging into her trunk.

Tears formed in Katie's eyes. She rose from the bed and turned to face the window. "I worry. What if something awful happens to you?"

"You worry about everything." Evangeline watched her sister staring at the sunset, the shadows of the approaching dusk resting on her shoulders. "You even worried about Maggie's marriage, and you adore Dexter."

Katie turned as she pulled a hankie from her sleeve to dab her eyes. "You're right, I needn't have worried. She has married well. Dexter's family is a pillar in the community. He has loved her for years. I am relieved he came to realize it when he did. Honestly, I worried she would marry below her station, or worse, be an old maid."

"Really? An old maid at seventeen? I would think you would be relieved I'm ridding myself of the title."

"You're different. You're a doctor—doing noble things." Katie replaced the hankie up her sleeve.

Can you not hear yourself, Kathryn? First, you tell me being a woman limits me as a doctor, and now you say I'm noble. "So, marriage cannot be part of female nobility?"

"No, I didn't say that. This rancher is ... well ..."

"Below my station?"

"Maaaybeee," Katie said, dragging out the word. "I mean, he

is a total stranger."

"Momma and Papa were total strangers."

"That's different."

"They were strangers when they met. Other than your daughter writing Mr. Marcum as me, how is it different?"

Katie's eyes were full of sadness. She sat down beside Evangeline and took her hand. Her voice softened. "You know why I don't want you to go."

"Yes." Evangeline squeezed her sister's hand. "Please understand. I don't blame Greta, Heidi, or you for insisting I go to New York to live with Uncle Carl's family. How could you have known what New York City held for a motherless child of thirteen?"

They locked eyes for several seconds, not daring to say more. Katie's voice quavered. "This time it's different?"

"Yes, this time I want to go. It's my choice." Evangeline patted Katie's shoulder. "Ever since our parents died, all my precious sisters have been telling me what to do. Everyone seems to feel they know what's best for me. I'm a grown woman, Kathryn, I can hear from the Lord."

"If something happens to you, I shall never forgive myself."

Evangeline cupped her sister's face in her hands. "I cannot promise you nothing will happen, but if it does, you are guiltless. I'm the one deciding to go. After much prayer, I feel this is God's direction."

Silence fell between them as Katie resumed refolding. Evangeline closed the lid on her trunk of books.

"Besides, dear sister, I can defend myself. Remember, I learned to use a rifle in the war. Anyone tries to hurt me, I'll shoot them in the foot."

Katie laughed. "I'm sure you will shoot more than a foot. You have the O'Malley temper, don't forget."

"And you don't, I suppose?"

"Of course not. I inherited the nagging quality of Aunt May." Katie smoothed a neatly folded green gown.

"You'll get no argument from me."

"I'll not try to persuade you any more to stay. I realize now your mind is made up. Besides, I knew what Maggie was doing. I discovered her journal."

"Why didn't you stop her?" *You couldn't say no to Maggie, could you?*

"Perhaps I hoped something good would come out of it."

"Like Dexter becoming jealous enough to propose to your daughter, no doubt." Evangeline added another book to her growing pile of leave-behinds.

"Yes, but on some level I was hopeful for you as well," she quipped. "At least let me throw out those ugly clothes. That rancher will take one look at those hideous things and run for the hills."

"There you go ... nagging again."

"I promised I would not nag you anymore about going. Your clothes are another matter."

Evangeline took the pillow from the bed and heaved it at her sister, hitting her square in the face. Katie gave her a feigned look of shock and wrapped Evangeline in a strong embrace.

"I'll miss you so much, my little Evie."

"I'll miss you too, my Katie."

CHAPTER 4

Double M Ranch
April 6, 1873

J ake could depend on Traveler more than on any man. The tall,
gray stallion knew the pace needed to approach the cattle.

Scanning the area, Jake could see his foreman, Kent Walters,
and Manny herding some strays on the east slope. They were
moving the cattle near the branding area. As his eyes moved along
the ridge westward, he spotted a cow grazing with her calf. Taking
out his lariat, Jake directed Traveler toward the two. He swung his
rope, lassoing the calf before the cow realized it. Methodically, he
pressed the horse forward, drawing the calf toward the fire while
his mind rehearsed his greeting to Evangeline.

Nice to meet you, ma'am.

Too dull.

I've been lookin' forward to meetin' you.

Traveler whinnied and reared up, moving out of the way of the
bawling cow, her horn inches from impaling Jake's leg. He gripped
the reins as his whole body maneuvered in the saddle, trying to
avoid a meeting with the ground. Tony Sanchez and Duke Arnold
quickly lassoed the mother.

"That momma cow don't want you takin' her baby." Artie
Weaver's youthful laughter started the banter.

"*Amor* has you distracted, *Jefe*." Tony leaned on the saddle horn
and winked.

Jake reeled in his lariat and tried to ignore them.

Duke joined in. "Maybe you need to go back to the ranch and
find somethin' safer to do. Don't want you to lose a leg before you
see your lady love."

"That's enough." Walters approached with another calf. "You

fellas are just jealous."

Jake took the good-natured teasing as he headed out to find another calf, but also wondered if they were right. *What was I thinkin'? This is the busiest time of the year. In two months we'll have these cattle on the trail to Abilene. I shoulda told her to wait until after. Well, what's done is done.*

His throat constricted. Next week he'd be a married man. How would things change when she came? Jake didn't have time to formulate an answer. Traveler whinnied, drawing Jake's attention back to the grazing cattle.

"Boy, what would I do without you?" he said to the stallion. The next few days would be intense, and he couldn't afford to lose focus. *Quit actin' like a schoolboy. You've been around women before.* But being around them and knowing how to talk to them was …

No matter how determined he was to stay single-minded, Jake couldn't push the nervousness of their upcoming meeting out of his mind.

***

Hardyville, Texas
April 15, 1873
Jake stood on the train platform, hands on his hips, staring eastward at the empty tracks. Heat waves appeared, reminding him of the train's later-than-desired arrival. The sunlight distorted his vision and its heat matched the burning in his stomach. He removed his hat and mopped his brow with his suit sleeve. Store-bought suits never fit right. He unbuttoned the front and tugged the jacket in a futile attempt to make it more comfortable.

His boots made heavy strides as he walked across the platform, remembering the disasters of the previous week. The branding had taken longer than planned, partly due to Artie's and Duke's constant bickering. The two had almost come to blows. Jake left instructions with his foreman to give them their walking papers if it happened again. That's all he needed, to lose two more men. Actually, a man and a half. Artie was still wet behind the ears, but a quick study.

He recalled the events that carved a full morning out of a branding day. Bo's horse had stepped into a hole and broke his leg. The horse had to be put down. Bart was almost too willing to do the deed. Bo, crying like a baby, stormed toward Bart, fists flying, only to catch his foot in the same hole. It took time to dispose of the horse carcass. Not to mention, Bo's injury left Jake one man short. Another reason to confirm his timing was bad.

Jake's late departure resulted in driving through a rainstorm for a day and a half. He'd led the horse and wagon through the swollen river. Then the wagon stuck in mud. By the time he arrived in Hardyville this morning, the sun had dried his clothes and baked mud into every seam. Jake had just enough time to secure rooms, bathe, and don the suit. He'd have to buy a new set of clothes for the return trip with money he hadn't planned on spending. Glancing down at his boots caused a groan as he saw mud still clinging in the crevices.

The shrill train whistle brought his mind back to the present. He wished he had thought to get flowers, something to keep his hands still. Jake took out his handkerchief and wiped the sweat from the inside of his Stetson again. Realizing he'd done this not five minutes ago irritated him. Nothing he could recall had ever set his nerves on edge like meeting his soon-to-be wife. As he placed the handkerchief back in his pocket, he rubbed his boots on the back of his pants, hoping she wouldn't notice the mud. It took a bit of time to properly clean it off. Unfortunately, time had run out. He walked with measured steps toward the slowing train.

CHAPTER 5

Hardyville, Texas
April 15, 1873

Evangeline gazed at her reflection in the train window, noting the perspiration trickling down her cheek as she adjusted the limp feather on her hat. The heavy petticoat under the velvet frock hid her dowry and absorbed the heat. Her equally limp lace hankie served to dab the moisture from her neck and brow. Gathering her carpetbag, satchel, and valise, she rolled her shoulders and exhaled a slow, even breath before heading toward the door.

Their eyes met at the same moment. A tall man with a nervous look came toward her. She had no picture of Jake, but she could have picked him out anywhere. His tanned complexion and determined gait told of hours spent in the saddle. The well-worn Stetson contrasted with his suit. Obviously, the suit was meant to impress.

She took in his features. Despite the scar across his cheek, she thought him handsome. She returned his nervous smile with one of her own. The sparkle in his blue eyes caused her face to warm. How she wished he were homely.

He removed his hat, revealing neatly cut, jet-black hair.

Embarrassed at her own inability to take control of the awkward situation with some appropriate greeting, Evangeline stared.

The man gave a slight nod and fidgeted with his hat as he spoke. "Miss Evangeline?" His baritone voice suited him.

"You must be Jacob." She placed her carpetbag and valise at her feet and extended her hand. Jake's firm grip caused her to wince. He dropped her hand and hid his momentarily behind his back.

"Jake's fine, ma'am."

"Very well ... Jake."

"Can I take your bags?" He took them before she could object.

Being accustomed to carrying her own things, she felt strange holding only her handbag. "Thank you."

"I'll take these to the hotel, and you can get settled in while I come back to the station for your trunk." Jake's long stride put distance between them.

"Trunks," Evangeline corrected, hurrying after him.

He stopped to stare at her, giving her time to catch up. "Trunks?"

"And boxes." Her voice softened. "I hope you don't mind. My sister Katie insisted I come prepared. She will ship more if I need them."

"More?" He adjusted his grip on her bags.

"I'm sorry if it's too much." Evangeline felt the warmth rising again. "You said in your letters some things are difficult to get out here. My sister found an article about others who have come west with a list of what to bring. You described your house as large."

"Don't fret, we can make room." Jake looked amused. "Whatever makes you comfortable."

Evangeline stopped walking. No one had ever suggested making *her* comfortable before. Her guard went up. Was he sincere? After all, she had only his letters to judge his character.

Jake turned back to her. "Is somethin' wrong?"

"No, not at all, just taking in the scenery." Evangeline hated her constant blushing at his boyish smile.

"Yes, ma'am, take your time." He turned toward the hotel and waited.

"Let us continue." She motioned with her hand, keeping her tone even. "I really need to freshen up. I must be a sight."

"You look real fine to me." His remark caused her to focus on the storefronts and narrow walkways rather than his grin.

"I'm sure you're tired from your trip. I got us both rooms for the night. You can wash up before we have dinner in the dinin' room. Hear the food's pretty good. Thought you might want to rest a spell too." Jake shifted the bags to one hand and opened the door with the other.

* * *

Three hours later, Jake paced the lobby. He'd secured her things on his wagon in the livery. Once that was done, he had headed out to buy some traveling clothes—a simple task turned complicated. Evangeline looked like a sophisticated lady when she'd stepped off the train. Feeling like a country bumpkin in her presence, he found himself debating between a pair of brown trousers or blue work pants. Then between a blue shirt or a red plaid. Once he'd made his choice, he bought a new white shirt for the wedding. Never before had Jake taken this kind of interest in his appearance.

The trunks and boxes both encouraged and disturbed him. Did she think he couldn't provide for her? Or was she really that practical? Her letters didn't come anywhere close to describing the lady who was about to become his Mrs.

Evangeline seemed well above his class. Yet she didn't appear to put on airs. Trying to rest in his room while resisting the temptation to knock on her door had made the last hour agonizing.

Seeing her at the top of the stairs caused his chest to constrict. Her still-damp burgundy hair was coiled in a braid on the top of her head. Her blue gown complemented her curves, and a small handbag hung from her wrist. She lifted her skirt as she maneuvered the staircase, revealing a bit of ankle.

Jake took off his hat, circling it between his fingers. The schoolboy jitters he had been fighting since receiving the telegram came back in a rush.

As she descended the stairs, her eyes seemed focused on his boots. Good thing he'd taken the time to clean them before dinner. His broad shoulders wanted to flee the confines of his store-bought suit. "Ma'am, don't you look fine."

Evangeline bit her bottom lip before she answered. "You are very kind."

"Only speakin' the truth."

Her brows formed a frown. *Did I say somethin' wrong?* Jake wondered. "Are you hungry?"

He offered his elbow and escorted her to the dining room where the waiter showed them to a corner table and pulled out Evangeline's chair. Jake felt foolish not holding her chair himself. He placed his hat in one of the empty chairs and sat opposite her.

The mustached waiter handed them menus. His satin vest had seen better days, and his trousers wore a patch on the left knee. "May I recommend our specials? The roast beef melts in your mouth and the fried chicken is the best this far west of the Mississippi." He held his order pad with pencil poised.

Jake ordered for both of them. "We'll have the roast beef and some coffee."

"Very good, sir. That is served with potatoes, green beans, and fresh bread."

"Sounds fine."

Evangeline fidgeted in her seat and patted her hair.

"You alright, ma'am?" Jake studied her face. She seemed to be catching her breath.

Evangeline fanned her face with her hands before answering. "I'm fine. Just a little warm is all."

"I could open the window. Might be a breeze." Jake started to rise.

"Please, let's just wait for the waiter to return."

Jake sat back, feeling like a rube. A gentleman would ask the waiter to do it, but it seemed rather silly when he was perfectly able to do it himself. The sooner they were on their way to the ranch, the better he'd feel.

"I apologize. I didn't mean to imply ..." Her eyes traveled around the room, and her hands pulled the linen napkin into her lap. "What a lovely restaurant. The waiter seems nice."

"Yes, ma'am."

"Have you been here before?"

"No, ma'am."

The awkwardness grew heavy. Being a man of few words wasn't serving the situation. And staring at this beautiful woman made words stick to his tongue.

Evangeline laced her fingers together and placed her hands on the table. "Jacob, there are a few things I must say, and I need to say them now." She sounded very formal.

"Go ahead." He hoped his face appeared calm. "And it's *Jake*, ma'am." His voice came out stern, not at all what he wanted.

"Very well. Then I would appreciate it if you stopped calling me *ma'am*. I have read your letters over and over again … *Jake*. In them, I saw an honest and good man." Again, she looked down at her hands before gazing into his eyes.

A nervous tic began in his jaw as he waited for her to continue. There was something in her voice that was setting off alarms.

"There are a few things I hope you will understand."

He motioned for her to go on. He brought his chair closer to the table, an action which caused her to sit straighter.

She withdrew an envelope from her handbag as her words rushed out. "Here is the money you sent for the ticket. I prefer to pay my own way. I came by choice. Even though it is customary for the prospective husband to pay, I would rather not take your money." She slid the envelope across the table.

Jake shifted in his chair and stared at the envelope, searching his mind for an appropriate response. He made no attempt to retrieve the envelope.

Evangeline fingered the cameo pinned on the collar of her dress, straightening the already upright brooch. "I would like to explain some untruths about the letters you received."

Jake's nerves tingled as he focused on her rosy lips. His hands steadied the table as he waited. Her cleansing breath was audible. His mouth went dry as the moments ticked by.

"The first thing I must tell you is … I did not write those letters. I knew nothing about them until six weeks ago."

Jake gripped the table even harder. "Pardon me, ma'am, did you say six weeks?" His mind raced to find an explanation. She certainly wasn't after his money, not that he had any. He was "cash poor and land rich," to quote Cookie. He thought of Juliet's tear-streaked face if Evangeline changed her mind. *Lord, what's your plan in all this?*

"Yes, six weeks. For an entire year, my niece Maggie has been writing you as if she were me." She paused and took another breath. "Maggie is not a wicked girl. She had two reasons for writing those letters as me. The first was to make her gentleman friend jealous enough to propose, and the other to find me a husband."

"Were you lookin' for a husband?"

Evangeline held his gaze. "Truthfully, no."

Jake fixed her with the look he used when questioning his men after they'd done something stupid. "Then why did you come?"

Evangeline looked away. When she refocused on Jake, her green eyes held a determined glint. "Your proposal seemed more in regard to being a mother to your niece than a wife to you. I was impressed with the devotion you have for her. Every letter was filled with references to Juliet and how much she needs to learn more feminine ways. You told stories of her tomboy antics. Not to mention your references to her need for more education."

Can't argue with her logic. You certainly don't know how to court.

"I liked what I read in your letters, which says a lot." Her voice quavered. "I certainly don't impress easily."

He placed his elbows on the table. "I reckon my proposal did sound that way."

"Maggie copied her correspondence to you in a journal. When I read it, I realized she wrote based on her observations and left out details she thought would not appeal to you."

"What details?" Jake straightened up as the waiter came with their food. "Would you mind opening the window? The lady's a mite warm."

"Certainly, sir." The moments it took for the task to be completed grated on Jake's nerves. The waiter bowed his head slightly toward Evangeline before leaving. Her eyes followed his exit before they rested once again on him.

"Maggie wrote about all the social functions we attended together. I rarely do those things. When I'm not working, I prefer to relax at home with a book or sewing. Honestly, I don't care much for parties."

Jake was relieved. "You stay busy nursin' people?"

"That's another falsehood. I'm not a nurse. Maggie thought that sounded more palatable to the male ego than the truth."

Oh, God, please don't let her be a—

"I am a doctor."

"A real, honest-to-goodness doctor?" Watching her eyes flash at his question made him wish he'd held his tongue.

"Is there any other kind?" Her words were prickly. "Your response is quite typical." An angry edge seeped into her words. "I studied medicine under my brother-in-law." She shifted to a professional tone. "It took a while to find a medical school willing to accept a female student. By the time I entered Hastings Medical Institute, I had learned so much from Shamus it was easy to stay at the top of my class." Her eyes and body language challenged Jake to say more. Her voice had risen a bit with each declaration. Patrons at neighboring tables turned their way.

Jake felt heat under his collar. He nodded at the gentleman seated nearby, and the man turned back to his food. Jake searched his mind for a way to calm Evangeline down. Keeping his voice low he said, "You were never a nurse in the war?"

"Yes, I was." She adjusted the napkin in her lap, allowing time for gapers to lose interest. "My sister and I accompanied her husband as his nurses. I worked both in the hospitals and on the battlefield. The experience gave me the desire to become a doctor."

Jake let her words ruminate. *God, when I asked you to provide an educated woman, this is not what I had in mind.*

"If this is too uncomfortable for you, we can call off the marriage and part friends. I will hold no ill will toward you." Evangeline looked down and focused on slicing her roast.

Jake found reading this woman more of a challenge than reading a man. If they were playing poker, he'd fold just to be on the safe side. He'd read Nora wrong and look where that got him. How uncomfortable was the idea of marrying a doctor?

What if I take my hat, give a gentlemanly bow, and leave?

But how would he explain it to Juliet?

Jake, you're a bigger man than that.

"May I ask why you came all this way to tell me the truth rather than writin' a letter?" That old feeling of betrayal clutched his heart. He studied this woman closely, her head bowed as if in prayer.

She twisted her napkin and looked up. "No one should hear such things in a letter. That would be cruel." Her voice caught. "I speak from experience. I was engaged before. His sister wrote to tell me he had married someone else." She took her napkin and dabbed at a crumb. "Truthfully, the Lord directed me to come to you."

"How?" Jake leaned forward, his food untouched, his fists clenched in his lap.

"You mentioned several times in your letters about your faith. So, I'm hoping you find my explanation encouraging rather than crazy." She shared the account of Fiona's vision and the events that led up to her coming. "And when I realized the date on Maggie's first letter matched the time Fiona told me her vision, as much as my logical mind wrestled to deny it, I knew it was the direction of the Lord. I had been praying for a change. After reading your letters, I knew only God could put such a thing together. Once I sent the telegram, His peace filled my heart."

"Does God often give you visions?"

"No." Her smile was endearing. "He never gives me visions. Whenever I think I hear the Lord's voice, it sounds like Fiona."

The candlelight created golden flecks in her eyes. *Lord, what have you gotten me into?* Realizing he had been staring tongue-tied for too long, he searched his mind for a response.

"For me, the Lord sounds like my old friend, Ben Mitchell." Jake scratched the back of his head. "So, the Lord directed you, but you weren't seekin' a husband. I won't hold you to somethin' you don't wanna do."

"I didn't say I wasn't willing. I felt you needed all the facts. This mail-order bride arrangement is difficult enough without misrepresenting myself." She shifted in her chair. "I made a commitment to come west and marry you, and so I shall."

"I don't shirk on my commitments either." Jake placed his hand on hers, feeling a slight shiver. He put the envelope in his jacket pocket with his free hand.

Evangeline extracted her hand. "I assume you've never been married. Which makes one wonder why?"

Her question caught him off guard. "I musta left that detail out." His thoughts took on Cookie's voice. *Reckon you can't call the kettle black about secrets, now can ya?*

Her eyebrows lifted in question.

"I was married for only two months, a long time ago. Mary died of consumption." He looked up to see sadness in her eyes.

"I'm so sorry. You must have loved her very much to have remained single for so long."

"Yeah, guess I did." He gulped his lukewarm coffee, forcing the guilt of the half-truth down with the liquid.

Evangeline picked up the conversation with a forkful of potatoes. "Then we can go forward with the marriage with some … reservations."

"Reservations?" *Now what?* He tried to eat, concentrating on his food and away from those probing eyes.

"Jacob, I mean Jake, you agree we are strangers?"

"We are that."

"As strangers, I'm not comfortable being *intimate* just because a preacher says the words. I would prefer to … wait." She stared at her food.

"Well, one thing your niece wrote is true. You shore do speak your mind. My response to your honesty is, take all the time you need. You're right, we're strangers. Waitin' makes sense."

Her face visibly relaxed with his words.

"You do realize there won't be no time for courtin'. There's no minister in Charleton. We'll get hitched before we head to the ranch. As you said, Juliet's the most important thing in my life. She needs a woman of refinement. I ask you to keep our confidence about those letters. Juliet don't need to know. She read each one over and over ever day until the next one come. Promise me you won't hurt that girl. She's hung a lot of hope on havin' herself an aunt who she can be like."

Evangeline's eyes glistened with unshed tears. "Rest assured, our secret will remain between us."

They picked at their now cold food.

"I want this to work, I really do," Evangeline said.

"So do I." Jake took a sip of his coffee and grimaced at the cold contents. "But if we're bein' honest, I'm not sure how I feel about being married to a doctor." He wondered if the community would refer to him as the doctor's husband. Or worse … the doc's wife. He could just picture Thomas Farley's smirk.

"Are you saying I can't practice medicine if we marry?"

"No, ma'am, I'm sayin' I gotta get used to the idea." Again, the sound of forks scraping plates dominated the space between them. "Do you plan to keep doctorin'?"

"Not right away. Getting married, making a home, and teaching your niece—all these new things. It's a bit overwhelming." Evangeline wiped her mouth with the corner of her napkin. "If it's in God's plan in this new place, then surely I will." She took another bite. "Perhaps you would prefer we not mention it to anyone at first."

Jake kept the uncomfortable feeling covered as he spoke. "Maybe. We have enough things to learn about each other right off."

"Promise me you won't say no when, or if, I decide to take up my practice again."

Jake fished for words to make his promise truthful. "Fair enough—if you promise to give me plenty of time to get used to bein' married to an educated woman." He went back to eating.

"Let me assure you, I may be educated in the medical field, but I'm ignorant of ranching and all that it entails. I'm confident you will have much to teach me."

They chatted further over dessert, keeping the conversation light. When Evangeline's head began to droop from fatigue, Jake escorted her to her room.

"Thank you for greeting me so warmly. I will see you in the morning, and I promise to be better company."

"I figure we can take a day here to let the horses rest, and you can see if there's anythin' in the stores you might want. They have more choices than in Charleton."

"Walking sounds wonderful after sitting for days." Evangeline extended her hand. "Thank you again. You've been ever so patient and kind."

Jake wrapped both his work-worn hands around her slender, soft one. Her lovely eyes flickered a moment at his touch.

"As I said, take all the time you need." He tipped his hat and bid her good night.

CHAPTER 6

Evangeline smoothed the creases of her mother's wedding gown. Katie had helped her lengthen the hem and widen the waistline. Her mother had been a girl of sixteen when she married, but Evangeline's womanly curves needed more room. The dress was out of style, but it brought her mother close. Katie had managed to find a white hat to embroider with the same bird design her mother had stitched on the collar of the gown. Her sister's ability to pair the old and the new pleased her.

Lord, this dress reminds me how You are bringing together all the wonderful things in my past with the new joys yet to come.

At least that was how she chose to look at this marriage.

Father, please keep the sorrows of my past locked away from this new chapter of my life.

A gentle rap caused Evangeline's stomach to clench, but with a determined gait, she crossed the room and opened the door. Jake stood before her, his fingers rotating the hat in his hands.

"Evangeline, ma'am, you look mighty fine." He placed the hat on his head and offered his elbow.

"Thank you, kind sir. You look very dashing yourself." She took his arm and closed the door behind her.

The time spent in town the day before had been pleasant. The area surrounding their hotel was a little too rowdy for her taste, but they'd found a lovely park for a stroll.

"What do you think of having our picture taken to mark the day?" Jake's smile brought out one of her own.

"You did purchase that silver frame I admired so much." Her stomach lurched. A photo seemed so permanent. "A wedding picture would look lovely in it."

I wonder how well fear looks framed in silver.

37

The morning air was crisp with the heat of the day still hours away. The street had quieted considerably from the evening before. Evangeline pushed away the nightmare all the noise from the surrounding saloons and gambling establishments had dredged up in her mind.

"Would you like to catch a ride on a buggy?" Jake asked. "I'd hate to see you ruin your lovely gown."

Walking would allow more time for her nerves to settle and delay the inevitable, although Jake's observation was not only considerate but correct. Ruining this heirloom was not in her plans.

"Yes, let's do."

Once inside the carriage, she took in the scenery as it passed from dilapidated to freshly painted buildings. These storefronts held a grocer, baker, and millinery shop. Next to the parsonage was a photography shop. Evangeline pointed as the buggy stopped. "How convenient."

"The parson's wife runs it. Heard she's a right fine photographer." Jake helped her down and paid the fare.

"Imagine … a female photographer. How progressive."

Jake chuckled. "I figured you'd be impressed." He placed his hand on the small of her back and escorted her to the door.

***

Jake was carefully wiping his feet when a tiny middle-aged woman opened the door and greeted them with a broad smile.

"Come in, come in. What a wonderful day for a wedding. I'm Loretta Norton, the pastor's wife." She waved them into the parlor.

Pastor Norton came down the hall buttoning his vest. A single hair stood at attention on his bald pate. "My, my, I do appreciate punctual people. Although today I am not one of them." His left hand smoothed the errant hair as his right hand extended to welcome Jake.

"Before we begin the ceremony, I would like to take some

time to share a few marriage insights my lovely bride and I have discovered over our thirty years of marriage."

Evangeline and Jake sat as Mrs. Norton set tea and cakes before them. Jake took a deep breath. *So much for gettin' this over with quick.*

Pastor Norton settled in the chair across from them, holding his Bible. "This, my friends, is the key to a successful union. Read it, apply it, and you'll get through all the rough-and-tumble parts of your marriage to enjoy the sweetness beneath." He turned several pages as he spoke. "Ephesians tells us the wife is to submit to her husband. Everyone knows that verse. But there's another one far more important that we husbands often forget. It's a hard chore to join two lives together as one when you're in love. It's even harder when your bride gets off the train, and you see her for the very first time."

Jake squirmed, unable to look at Evangeline.

"When I was told I could not pastor a church without a wife, I felt God directing me to propose to this tiny creature." He glanced at Loretta, who ducked her head like a shy schoolgirl. "After a lot of prayer, she agreed to marry this prideful seminary graduate. But I was so determined to make a success of my ministry, I ignored her. When I found her bags packed one day, she had my attention, and I begged her to stay. I got down on my knees and asked God to show me the way. This was the verse he led me to, Ephesians 5:25. 'Husbands, love your wives, even as Christ also loved the church, and gave himself for it.'" He looked solemnly at Jake. "That, my friend, is the real key. Marriage takes sacrifice. Every day, I ask Jesus how to love Loretta like He does. Each couple is different, so Christ's love is manifested in a different way."

Jake found the pastor's words a heavy weight on his shoulders. It was so easy for him to put the ranch and whatever needed doing before the Lord, but now he had to try and put his wife's needs first. Sweat formed on his palms.

"Are you both Christians?" the pastor questioned.

"Yes, we are," Jake said.

Pastor Norton turned to Evangeline. "Young lady, I imagine you can speak for yourself. Have you accepted Jesus as your Savior?"

"Yes, of course."

"Good. That's the first step." He gave a satisfied nod before flipping the pages of his Bible once again. "Now, let's look at a few other verses."

The pastor continued with his instructions as Jake stared at the clock on the wall. Each quarter-hour chime made him more anxious. They could be married and on the road, and yet here they sat. Seeing Evangeline poised and attentive brought conviction to his heart. *God forgive me. I know this is important, and if we weren't in such an all-fire hurry, I'd ...* He set his teacup on the table and tried his best to focus.

"There you have it. My advice for a peaceful, happy marriage." Pastor Norton rose from his place. "Now, if you two will join me before the fireplace, we'll get on with the ceremony."

CHAPTER 7

Evangeline's Journal

April 17, 1873

Here I sit in the lobby of the hotel, waiting for my new husband to bring the wagon. I'm still nervous, but now that the wedding is over, my stomach aches less. We spent yesterday exploring Hardyville. That day is a fog in my mind. The long silences confirmed my suspicions that Jake is a man of few words. Nausea threatened to embarrass me all day. God graciously answered my petitions in that regard, and I managed to keep meals down. Nightmares sent sleep far from me. I rose early this morning to watch the sunrise and had a few hours for a good cry. I managed to deposit my bank draft in the Hardyville Bank my first day here while Jake retrieved my things from the train depot. I know providing my own way of escape is not very Christ-like.

This morning I became Mrs. Jacob Marcum. I take comfort from the scriptural account of Rebekah, who went to a distant land to marry a stranger. Wearing my mother's wedding dress made her seem close. I imagined her smiling at me. At least I hope she was smiling. Katie's worried expression haunted my vows.

Jake insisted we have our picture taken to commemorate the day. He purchased a lovely silver frame as a wedding gift. He has been very thoughtful and kind. I find it strange to look down at my hand and see a gold band there. He thought I would want a ring. We will soon be on our way to his ranch. Perhaps my anxiety will lessen as we travel. God is showing me many of his good qualities. He doesn't smoke or drink or swear. He is slow to speak, which is unnerving at times but, overall, shows a man who is thoughtful with his words. I need to focus on those things. Fiona said my past can only affect my future if I let it. I pray daily I might overcome.

* * *

Evangeline took note of Jake's brown trousers and a blue cotton shirt with a neckerchief. He sported the same familiar Stetson. This is how she had imagined he would look from his letters. It suited him. She had chosen her green calico dress and had on as few petticoats as society deemed decent, along with a simple sunbonnet. She debated about wearing a corset, recalling Katie's thoughts on proper female apparel. But the corset had chafed on the long train trip, and two days in a wagon confined in that contraption seemed ridiculous. She plaited her hair into a long braid that hung just above her waist, rather than putting it up. Jake helped her into the front seat of his over-filled wagon.

"Guess I don't need to worry none. I figure you must be pretty serious about stayin' with all this baggage."

She appreciated the fact that Jake made sure her skirt was tucked into the buckboard before he climbed into his seat. His close proximity caused a shiver Evangeline held in check. *Lord, help me. Give me peace.* They rode in silence through town. Out on the open road, she ventured to speak.

"In my whole life, I've only made two choices on my own. The first to become a doctor, and the second to marry you."

"Are you sayin' that to ease my mind?"

"I suppose." *Mine as well.* Silence fell once more between them. Evangeline gazed at the prairie that spread out toward the mountain vista, almost forgetting her traveling companion until his voice caught her attention.

"What was medical school like?" His eyes lingered for a moment as she gave him her full attention, then he focused once more on the team of horses.

"The studies weren't hard. I love to learn new things. However, a professor at medical school believed women were too weak-brained to be doctors."

"Is that true?"

"You think because a male professor said it makes it true?" Her nerves prickled and her voice rose with her answer.

Jake pushed his hat toward the back of his head. "Sorry, didn't mean to offend." He nervously adjusted the reins in his hands. "I meant, is that what they taught you in medical school?"

Still slightly peeved, the words came unchecked. "Only ignorant people would believe such a thing." Evangeline immediately regretted her retort and placed her hand over her mouth. "I'm so sorry. That came out wrong. I meant the professor was ignorant, not you."

"No offense taken." Jake's smile reached all the way to his eyes as he laughed at her discomfort. "As I said before, I appreciate you speakin' your mind."

"Most people don't, especially men."

"If you have a mind to say somethin', do it. Juliet's always sayin' what's on her mind. Guess I'm used to it."

"I'm sorely rebuked being compared to a child. Now it's my turn to apologize. We certainly aren't getting this conversation off on a pleasant road."

Jake turned his head in her direction. "I'll admit, until I took on the responsibility of Juliet, I had no idea how to care for a young'un. I sorta figured it out as I went along. I'll have to figure out how to care for a wife, as well, 'specially such an educated one."

"The fact you are raising your orphan niece shows a good heart. I'll take a man with those qualities over a well-educated, impeccably dressed know-it-all any day." Evangeline surprised herself with her declaration.

Jake remained silent a moment. "Thank you, ma'am. You can keep speakin' your mind anytime if it's of a complimentary nature."

The twinkle in his eye unnerved her.

"Raising a child is nothing like living with a wife." She turned to face him, daring that twinkle to reappear. His brows rose and disappeared underneath his Stetson. His hand adjusted his bandana before he faced forward.

"Of that, I have no doubt." His voice was laced with a chuckle.

The majestic mountains appeared close enough to reach out and touch. The vista spread out like a soft blanket. The quiet kept them company for a time.

* * *

Jake enjoyed her nearness as they rode along, making the quiet ride pleasant. She smelled of lavender, and the wind blew tendrils of her thick hair loose from her braid. He wondered how she would respond if he ran those strands between his fingers. But the daydreams were interrupted when Evangeline began to ask questions. Several hours passed while he answered her many inquiries about life on the ranch. He couldn't believe how much he was talking. It seemed like he spoke a month's worth of words during their journey. He found her easy to talk to, at least about his ranch.

After a light lunch on the trail, they traveled a few more hours. Determined to reach their evening lodging before dark, he pressed the horses hard. He had added a few hours to the return trip by skirting the river crossing. The thought of embarrassing himself in her presence if the wagon got stuck weighed heavily in the decision.

Near dusk, Jake pulled the wagon to a stop. Before them, two sod walls protruded from the hill with a wooden framed window and door on the third wall. A chimney rose above the grassy roof. The soddie appeared to be one with the hill.

"A house made from the earth, how ingenious."

Her attempted enthusiasm wasn't lost on Jake. "Hope this'll do. It's a little rough." Jake waited for a reaction, but her face revealed nothing but fatigue. "This is one of my line cabins. My men use this place when they're too far to get back to the bunkhouse before nightfall."

"It will be fine. As long as it has a bed, I will be happy."

"It has bunk beds. Can't say how comfortable it'll be for you," Jake said, beginning to regret his choice for the evening's lodging. He retrieved the provisions from the wagon.

"As long as it doesn't move, it will be heavenly."

"You'll find a rain barrel over yonder. There's an empty bucket too. You can wash up," Jake said as he entered the soddie and placed a box on the table. "Time for me to get a fire started."

***

Evangeline scanned the dimly lit room. The lantern revealed bunk beds built right into the dirt wall, inhabited by insects. "That bed might move after all," she muttered under her breath. "Would you prefer I cook?" She hoped her reluctance wasn't obvious in her voice. "Show me what supplies you have."

"I generally keep a few things on hand, but there's other provisions in that box on the table. I'm gonna tend the horses. Watch the damper on the fireplace. It has a mind of its own."

Evangeline's hand trembled as she began the simple meal preparation. After placing two potatoes to bake in the hot ashes and securing a pan of beans on the fire, she set about cleaning the table with the underside of her dress. A spider met its demise as it crawled across the table.

"God," she whispered. "I asked for a change. Help me make the best of it."

As she reached into the box for the tin plates, she gave thanks for one blessing. "This is the least romantic place I could imagine. I hope Jake agrees."

* * *

Jake unhitched the horses from the wagon and led them to the creek for water. He allowed them time to rub their backs in the grass before staking them out under a nearby tree to graze, smiling as he thought about sharing a meal his wife had prepared. "My wife," he said out loud, liking how comfortable the words felt on his tongue.

He turned toward the soddie to see smoke billowing from the door and window.

Racing to dip his neckerchief in the rain bucket, he tied the dripping cloth around his face. Through the smoke he spotted Evangeline, desperately searching for the damper. Even though he'd opened the damper, it had apparently chosen to close. In two steps, he reached her and guided her outside. She gulped in the fresh air as Jake returned to open the damper wide. Once it was securely open, he removed the pan from the flames and headed back outside.

The vulnerable look on Evangeline's sooty, tear-streaked face moved him. He wanted to kiss her tears away but, instead, removed his neckerchief and used it to wash her face. "Are you sure you're okay?" His fingers lingered a bit longer after the task was done.

Her chin quivered beneath his touch. She moved, placing a few feet between them. Her hand went to her throat. "I apologize. I should have watched the fire while setting the table. I have ruined dinner for you." Her faltering words were suddenly joined by heart-wrenching sobs.

Jake closed the gap between them and patted her awkwardly on the shoulder. "It'll be fine. I've done the same thing a time or two."

"Cry?" Her voice squeaked as she wiped her nose.

The sound of Jake's laugh seemed to help Evangeline gain her composure. It took several minutes for the smoke to clear.

She washed her face with water from the barrel before entering the soddie again.

"The table looks real nice." Jake took in the green shawl covering the dirty table. A jar of peaches sat in the center between two tin plates.

"Thank you." Evangeline sniffled. "I'm not much of a cook anyway. At least we can blame the bad taste on the damper."

The food was burnt but palatable. The peaches were the only redeeming part of the meal.

Jake helped with the dishes and brought in more water. "You can get ready for sleep while I tend to the horses." He left, closing the door behind him.

He curry-combed the horses and moved them to another area to graze after watering them again. His mind focused on his new wife. This was the only night they would be completely alone. Tomorrow, they would reach the ranch. The surroundings were depressing, and after that damper disaster, Jake doubted the evening could get any worse. Why hadn't he taken her in his arms instead of lamely patting her shoulder? What man does that?

One trying to keep his promise. And that was going to be fairly easy tonight thanks to his poor choice. *Lord, You knew I needed to be so thick about my plans to help Evangeline get comfortable. I suppose I should thank You for that.*

Jake knocked before entering. His throat constricted at the sight of Evangeline under the ragged blanket of the lower bunk, her dress draped over a chair. She fidgeted and adjusted her blanket without turning to acknowledge him. He removed his boots, socks, and shirt, then climbed into the upper bunk, placing his foot cautiously on the lower bunk as he hefted himself up. Dirt filled the air as he wiggled down under the cover. A soft cough drifted up.

"Sorry." Jake wished he had asked some of his men to clean the soddie.

"As long as no creature joins me under the covers, I can manage a little dust." Evangeline stood and shook out her blanket.

He rose up on his elbow to watch, and his eyes widened. Her

petticoat showed off her figure, and Jake almost hoped some critter *would* invade her bed. Then maybe he could rescue her again.

Her own eyes widened as she turned to see him watching. She scrambled back into her bunk. "Good night."

"Good night, Evie."

"Evangeline. I prefer Evangeline."

"Yes, ma'am." Jake turned toward the wall with a grin.

* * *

In the darkness of the early morning hours, Evangeline's foggy brain awakened to noise in the room. Forcing her exhausted mind to full alertness, she recognized Jake's voice.

"Johnny, stay back!" His voice rose. "Keep your head down!"

Evangeline had seen her brother Charley have these nightmares. Rising from her bunk, she peered at Jake in the top bunk and spoke softly. "Jacob, are you alright?" When she touched his shoulder, he sprang upright, banging his head on the wooden ceiling beam. A moan of pain escaped his lips.

"Oh, my stars, are you alright?" Evangeline ventured closer. "You were having a nightmare. I attempted to wake you. I'm so sorry."

"I'm awake now," Jake growled, holding his head.

"Let me have a look." She lit the lantern, helped him climb down, and guided him to a chair. His face was streaked with blood, and his eyes reflected both embarrassment and frustration. Sweat trickled down his bare, muscular chest. The darkness and his half-naked presence brought back her own nightmare. Terror tried to force its way into her heart, but her mind schooled the emotion.

I can do all things through Christ who strengthens me.

Swallowing her urge to flee, she assumed her professional manners and examined the wound. "I don't see any splinters. Let me get my bag and clean this up. You'll need a few stitches." She tore off several lengths of material from the bottom of her petticoat and handed him one to apply pressure to the wound. "Hold this. Don't move while I get my bag."

With the light of the full moon, she climbed up into the wagon and found her bag in the first trunk she opened. Gripping the handle, she headed back to the cabin, confidence rising in her heart as the familiar pushed away the strange. As she set her bag on the table, Jake's grin reminded her she was only in her undergarments. *I can do this. Lord, help me.*

"Now I know why women wear so many petticoats. Never know when they'll be needin' a bandage."

Evangeline ignored his attempt at humor and poured antiseptic into a bowl. She filled another with clean water and used another piece of her petticoat to cleanse his wound, examining the cloth for dirt before she began. If Katie hadn't insisted that her medical supplies be packed in the trunks, the bandages would have been more readily at hand. Once the wound was clean, she began stitching, focusing on his wound rather than his nearness.

"Ouch!"

"I'm doubly sorry. I caused you to injure your head, and now I'm hurting you again."

"It's not that bad." The higher tone in his voice told a different story.

"This is the last stitch. There you are." Evangeline moved efficiently as she wrapped his head. "After I finish, stay seated. You need to drink some chamomile tea. It will help you rest. And I want you to sleep in the lower bunk."

"I can't let a lady sleep up there," Jake protested.

"But I insist. Besides, I'm not prone to nightmares." *Well, at least I don't cry out in the night.* Evangeline carefully adjusted the damper before stoking the fire for the tea.

* * *

Jake's head throbbed as Evangeline moved about. The firelight glistened in her hair. He was fascinated by her methodical motions as she placed the pan, adjusted the handle away from the fire, added a few tea leaves, then a few more.

"It shouldn't be long now." Evangeline dug a tin cup from the box, took yet another piece of petticoat to strain the tea leaves, and poured him a cup. "Hope I got all the leaves. It's hard to tell in this light." She placed the tea on the table and sat down next to him.

"Think I'll sleep on the floor." Jake took the cup from her. She looked so beautiful, even in the dim light.

"That is probably a better idea. I'll fix your pallet while you drink this."

She gathered the bedding off the top bunk and arranged it on the floor as he drank the tea. He admired her, hoping she didn't notice him staring. Her graceful movements stirred him as the firelight complemented her curves. *So much for rescuing her again.*

"How's your head? Any blurred vision?" She appeared unaware that her ripped petticoat—revealing her calf—had his full attention.

He had to focus on her words. *What had she asked?*

"My head aches like the Devil. But my vision is just fine." Jake tried to keep his words matter-of-fact. "Sorry I scared you."

"My brother Charley woke with nightmares after he returned from the war. If you didn't wake him, he would be in a foul mood in the morning. When Shamus tried, he got a bloody nose, and Katie was almost strangled. My voice, however, would bring him back peacefully." Wiping stray tea leaves from the table, she smiled. "Obviously, my voice does not have the same effect on you."

"Obviously." Jake groaned. "Best to leave me be. I generally wake up by myself, but it's nice to know you understand. I was afraid it would scare ya."

"As a nurse on the battlefield, I saw horrific things. It takes a lot to scare me now."

"That's an answer to my prayers."

"You were concerned I would be afraid of your nightmares?"

"My neighbor's wife went back East 'cause of his nightmares."

"How sad. Whatever became of him?"

"Sold this soddie and his claim to me and went further West. Heard he died of influenza out in California."

Jake's words seemed to cause her to scan the interior. He wished he could read her thoughts. Her hand rested near her throat, and her lovely eyebrows were furrowed. But the expression fled in an instant.

"I promise never to wake you from your nightmares again. I'm sorely grieved I caused your injury. You need something for the headache, but I would have to search through boxes."

"I'll be fine. How was your brother about you leavin' to come here?"

"Charley didn't have anything to say about it."

"What about the rest of your kin?"

"Katie and Shamus worry this was an unwise decision. Maggie thought it sounded romantic."

"But Charley had nothin' to say?"

"He died two years ago."

"Oh, sorry. Was he ill?"

Tears pooled in her eyes. "My baby brother used to be so much fun. Everyone loved him. The war changed him. He brooded a lot, drank too much, and saw things that weren't there. Shamus found him hanging from a rafter in the barn."

Jake found himself startled by the depth of her emotion. Again, the thought of embracing her took a front seat in his mind, but it was soon booted out once she'd wiped her tears.

"That's enough gloominess for one night. We have another weary day on the road tomorrow."

"We should try to get more sleep before the sun comes up. Everyone will be expectin' us by suppertime."

"Let's not be in a hurry if your head is hurting."

"We'll decide in the mornin'. For now, if you'll help me to my new bed, I'll try to get more shut-eye." Jake knew he could have moved to the bed himself, but he couldn't resist having her close a little longer.

As she helped him across the room, he breathed in her lavender scent and felt the softness of her burgundy hair against his hand as it rested on her back. Her closeness stirred up longings long buried. They began to overwhelm his resolve, but she released him before he could act on them. She covered him with the blanket and rose to her feet. Jake admired the curve of the now-exposed leg from his pallet.

"Should I turn out the lamp or leave it low?"

"Turn it out." She extinguished the light and Jake's eyes followed her silhouette in the moonlight. She banked the fire once again and crawled back into bed as the moonlight touched her face.

"Night, Evangeline." His tender voice produced a brief smile from her, barely visible in the dim light.

"Good night, Jake. Don't hesitate to call out if you need anything."

Her words made him chuckle.

CHAPTER 8

Jake finished hitching the wagon as the sun rose over the horizon. When he peered in the door of the soddie, Evangeline stood before him trying to press the wrinkles out of her green dress with her hands. She'd re-braided her hair and had managed to set the small space in order. Her medical bag rested on the table with her valise.

"Ready to leave?"

"Yes." Her flat tone reflected the fatigue etching her face. "Let me look at your wound before we get started."

"No need." Jake's tiredness matched hers. He grabbed her bags. She stepped between him and the table.

"How are you feeling?"

"Fine." Jake turned to leave. *Don't have time for this.*

"I am not going another step until I get a good look at your head."

Some women can be so stubborn. "Fine." He took off his hat.

"I see you've removed the bandage." She pulled his head down to get a better look. "I need to clean it before we go. It looks much better in the light of day." She directed him to the chair. Even the smell of lavender and her close proximity could not distract him from his searing headache.

In a few moments, she'd cleansed the wound. "I still have a few pieces of petticoat left to bandage your head."

"It ain't necessary." Jake rose from his place as he secured his hat on his head, giving her his no-nonsense stare.

"You need a bandage to keep it clean."

"No time for that." Jake strode toward the wagon, his head throbbing with every step. "Gotta get a move on, missy."

Evangeline's voice caught up with him before she reached his side. "You need to cover that with something."

"You need to get in the wagon."

"Your hat is filthy."

"Your petticoat any cleaner?" Jake spat the words out before he could take them back. "I mean ..."

Evangeline raised her hands in surrender. "I'm sure you'll be fine."

Silence fell between them as the sun climbed higher in the sky. Sweat trickled down Jake's back, making him even more uncomfortable.

"How long before we get there?"

"Late afternoon, unless somethin' happens."

"Unless something happens ... what does that mean?" Evangeline snapped.

Jake glared at her. "'Cause out here things happen." He winced as the jolting of the wagon beat a rhythm in his head.

"What kind of things could happen?" Her voice became shrill.

"Horse could go lame, wheel could break, outlaws, Injuns, mountain lions, snakes, thunderstorm." Jake's voice rose with each addition.

"Enough."

"Didn't mean to *scare* ya." Jake knew his response was tinged with sarcasm.

"Please stop saying that. Why do men always assume women are afraid of everything?" She crossed her arms and looked away.

* * *

The creaking of the wagon wheels on the uneven terrain filled the silence. Guilt from her harsh words grabbed Evangeline's conscience. The fault for his poor night sleep lay with her, and she intended to claim it, starting with a more civil tone and careful words.

"Please forgive my wicked tongue."

"You're tired. I should apologize to you." Jake reached over and covered her hand with his. "I don't know what I was thinkin' when I decided to use that old soddie for the night."

Evangeline removed her hand from his. "I imagine you were being practical. I doubt I would have slept any better in the finest hotel in New York."

The wagon hit a deep rut, causing Evangeline to slam into Jake. She scooted toward her side of the seat, uncomfortably aware there were just inches between them. She caught a glimpse of pain on Jake's face once she repositioned herself. The words *how are you feeling* perched on her tongue. Instead, she searched her mind for conversation. "Where did you honeymoon?"

"What?"

"I was asking about your late wife. Where did you honeymoon?" Once she repeated the question, it seemed inappropriate, but it was too late to take it back.

"We didn't." Jake's short response was followed by a long silence.

Evangeline wondered if he, too, felt the question was out of line.

He shifted in his seat and rearranged the reins in his hands before speaking. "You might as well hear the whole story. Mary was very ill when we wed. Her pa, Ben Mitchell, wanted to make me his heir. His sons had died in the war, and his brother had no desire to own the ranch. Ben figured if I married Mary, his will wouldn't be questioned. His brother in England is quite wealthy, I understand." Jake turned to face her. "Mary was like a sister to me. I refused at first, but she convinced me it would make Ben happy after losing her brothers." Jake straightened his shoulders and focused forward. "I owed Ben my life. And before you ask, I did care for Mary. But the town gossip painted me a no-good gold digger at first."

"At first?"

"You know gossip. It hangs on till a juicier bit comes around."

He readjusted his hat.

"Be careful. Don't dislodge your stitches."

"I am *very* aware of them stitches." Jake rubbed his temple.

She responded with her doctor voice. "Being aware is good. But with no bandage, the chance of infection is greater."

"Well, we don't have no bandages handy, and before you suggest it, I'm not diggin' through all them boxes to look."

She crossed her arms and stared at the side of his face. "And my petticoat is no longer an option?"

A weary sigh escaped his lips as he kept his eyes on the road ahead. "Exactly. And no naggin' on your part will change that."

"Fine. Be bullheaded then." Evangeline adjusted her bonnet to block her vision of him, but not before she saw him scowl. "I'm sorry." Her tone was soft as she placed a hand on his shoulder, then quickly removed it, turning her focus to the mountains before them. "I must admit I'm a bit overwhelmed by ... well, by everything."

Jake shifted again, jostling the seat and causing Evangeline to look his way. "No need to feel that way. Juliet'll make you feel right at home. I'm sure you'll get along with everyone. I think you'll surprise 'em."

"How?"

"Other than bein' a mite naggy, you don't seem prissy or stuck up." Jake glanced back at the road as his smile broadened.

"If I was not so tired, I'd be offended."

She heard Jake chuckling under his breath as she tried to hide her own amusement.

* * *

The sun's rays became more intense as the day lengthened. Evangeline adjusted her bonnet to shade her face. Conversation was sparse. Her eyelids drooped, but the bumping of the wagon kept her awake. Her mind wandered in the silence.

She'd passed the night relieved Jake had kept his promise.

Evangeline wasn't naive. She'd seen the longing in his eyes. His confession about Mary spoke a lot to his desire to do the right thing. But Evangeline was healthy, so his only barrier was his promise. She took sly looks at her husband on occasion and sensed he was doing the same. As she turned to watch the passing landscape, her bonnet shielded her face, giving her a feeling of privacy.

Her thoughts went back to her childhood home. Visions came to her of innocent times when Charley's hijinks caused their father to laugh and their mother to fuss. Remembering Charley made her wonder just how hellish Jake's war memories might be. Were nightmares only a part of the burden he carried from the war?

Approaching the top of a rise, Jake stopped the wagon.

Evangeline stared. "Is that—"

"The Double M."

Her eyes traveled over the large adobe ranch house with long verandas, two additional wings on each end, massive chimneys, and tiled roof. There was a barn with a large garden behind it, stables, a chicken coop, and several other buildings. A whitewashed fence surrounded the whole area and from her vantage point, she could see horses in the corral and figures moving around the compound.

"This is your ranch?"

"*Our* ranch."

"It's quite large. Your description did not do it justice."

"It ain't so big. I mean, the Triple Diamond is twice the size of mine."

"The Triple Diamond? Where is that?"

"Farley's spread is up the road nearer to Charleton. Farley's goal is to have the biggest ranch around here. But I'm content with the Double M." Jake removed his hat and ran his fingers through his hair, wincing as he touched the stitches. Gingerly, he adjusted his Stetson back on his head.

She saw pride in his eyes as he gazed at the view before them.

"If you're not too tired, I have somethin' to show you before we go home. It's up ahead a piece."

"Certainly."

***

After a short detour, Jake stopped the wagon in front of a small, deserted cabin nestled in an oasis of overgrown greenery.

"This is the family homestead. Pa got gold fever in forty-nine, but we never made it to California. Wagon broke down near here, and Ben Mitchell and his wife came to our rescue. He talked Pa out of his foolish venture. Pa built a soddie the next day." He helped Evangeline down from the wagon. Stretching their legs gave a respite from the bumpy ride.

Standing in the ruins of his past, Jake shared his history. "Ben taught my pa everythin' he knew about ranchin'. They became good friends."

"When did you move from here to your ranch?"

"After the war, I came home in pretty bad shape. The girl I'd hoped to marry had married my little brother, Robert." Jake tried to sound matter-of-fact even though raw emotions lingered near the surface with his fatigue. "My pa died while I was off fightin'. I couldn't bring myself to live in the same house with Robert and Nora, so I hired on as foreman for Ben."

Evangeline nodded for him to go on.

"I was drinkin' and carryin' on, tryin' to forget the war, not proud of my actions back then." He removed his hat and wiped the sweat from his forehead with his sleeve. "Ben took me under his wing and showed me the light. Helped me forgive myself and receive God's forgiveness. Came to Jesus because of Ben. I owe him my life."

Her eyes never left his.

"I'm sorry ... I'm ramblin'," Jake said. He saw a single tear fall down her cheek.

"Your story reminds me of my brother. I wish Charley had found the Lord."

Again, he resisted the urge to pull her close and comfort her.

Evangeline removed an embroidered handkerchief from her sleeve and dabbed her eyes. "Please, finish your story."

Jake cleared the lump fighting for a place in his throat. Something about this woman brought out his gentler side. "I married Mary. She was real frail. Consumption took her from me two months later. Ben died the following spring." His voice caught at the telling. She touched his shoulder in sympathy. The warmth of her hand radiated through his shirt.

"That was a bad year. Nora died in childbirth the same summer. The baby boy was stillborn. Robert got thrown from his horse that autumn. The only good come from all the hurt was Juliet comin' to live with me. She's been a healin' thing."

"This is where Juliet was born, and you grew up?" She pointed toward the weather-worn cabin. "How old were you when your family built this place?"

Jake knew her question was meant to take his mind to happier thoughts, and he took her hand. Her palm was clammy, and she was trembling. Standing side by side, he kept his focus on the house. "My brothers and I helped Pa build this place when I was eight. Ma had a fine garden."

Evangeline released his hand as they explored the house. Jake tried not to notice her abrupt motion or the emptiness of his hand. "At seventeen, I went off to the war. Pa had sent me to find my brother Clevis. He was s'posed to be attendin' college with my cousins back in Kentucky. Clevis wanted to be a lawyer, go into politics. I preferred ranchin' to schoolin'. He quit school and joined up and talked me into doin' the same. Clevis believed the foolish talk of the Confederacy whippin' the Union in six months. In six months he was dead."

"How awful for you." Evangeline reached for his hand. "War has a cruel price."

Jake found immediate comfort in her touch. He'd forgotten how healing a simple touch could be. His mother's hand had always soothed his aching heart. His wife's hand remained in his as they left the house. Sadness and sympathy were not his goals in bringing her here, even if she seemed more relaxed as a comforter.

They faced the dilapidated barn. A tornado had aged it. The walls leaned, and the roof was half gone. Its desolation reflected Jake's mood.

Evangeline dropped his hand and peeked in the barn door before turning to take another look at the abandoned house. Her weary eyes sparkled. "Why don't you fix up this place? It seems a shame to let it fall to ruin. I can almost imagine the happy times you had here growing up. Perhaps Juliet would like to live here someday when she marries."

"You and Juliet think alike. We come here for a picnic once a year and visit the graves over yonder. She said the same thing a time or two, except for the marryin' part." He took one more look around. "Are you ready to go, or do you want to linger?"

Evangeline seemed to take it all in before heading toward the wagon. She climbed up without assistance. In taking a few extra moments to remember what this place had been, he'd missed the opportunity to help her. But the sad feeling of visiting this place seemed to vanish when their hands had entwined. Now his hand was empty, vanquishing the peace. As he took the reins, his headache once again took a more prominent place in his thoughts.

CHAPTER 9

Evangeline's stomach churned as the wagon stopped in front of the house. A thin girl with black pigtails ran from the house, her legs too long for her dress. Keeping pace with her was a large, mixed-breed dog.

"Uncle Jake! Uncle Jake!" Juliet climbed up onto the wagon to give him a big hug. "I thought you'd never get here." Her greeting was almost drowned by excited barks.

"Hush, Dog!" Jake's tone silenced the mutt.

With a radiant smile, Juliet crawled over her uncle to give her new aunt a hug so full of longing it took Evangeline's breath away. Her heart melted. For this child alone, she was glad she had made the decision to come. "It's nice to meet you, Juliet."

"Come on and let me introduce you around."

She scampered across Evangeline to climb off the wagon. The girl caught her dress on the wagon seat but with a tug, released herself. She signaled the dog to sit before he became the first to greet her. An older man stepped forward to help Evangeline from the wagon.

With a formal voice, Juliet made introductions. "This is Franklin Slade, but everyone calls him Cookie."

The man had a noticeable limp, but Evangeline resisted the urge to inquire.

"Over there is Selena Hernandez and her son Manuel, but we call him Manny." Juliet pointed, appearing to enjoy her self-appointed role as hostess. "She's our housekeeper."

"Happy to meet you, *Señora* Marcum." Selena wiped her fingers on her apron and gave a formal curtsy. Like her son, her eyes focused on the ground.

Manny removed his hat and bowed. "*Señora.*"

"Please, call me Evangeline."

"And that man over there is Artie Weaver."

Evangeline observed the man's reluctance to move forward as Juliet drew him into the circle. "Artie Weaver, it is nice to meet you. Your name sounds so familiar to me. There was an Artie Weaver who was a patient in an army hospital. I wrote letters for him to his family. But he would be much older than you."

Artie's face paled at her words. "Lots of men got my name." He tipped his hat and left.

Evangeline wondered at his reaction, but her mind was too overwhelmed with all the new sights and sounds to think on it further.

"Please, *Señora*, I have a meal prepared. Come and freshen up. I will draw a bath for you after supper." Selena motioned her toward the house.

"You are very thoughtful. A bath sounds divine. May I help you with anything?"

"No … I mean … it is my pleasure to serve you, *Señora* Marcum." Selena offered a nervous smile and held the door open as she and Juliet—who stopped long enough to shoo Dog away—stepped inside.

***

Jake helped Cookie loosen the ropes from the wagon's contents, waiting for the comments and questions sure to come.

"She's quite a looker, Jake. How was the ride back?"

"Fine. Reckon it was a little long for her, though." He removed his hat.

"What in tarnation happened to your head?"

"Hit it on the soddie rafters." Jake tried to sound casual.

Cookie grabbed Jake's head to get a closer look. "Them's fine stitches. Lucky for you she's a nurse."

Jake had shared portions of his letters with Cookie, but correcting the error would break the promise he'd made to Evangeline.

"Are you done examinin' my injury?" Jake asked.

Cookie gave his head a playful pat before releasing it.

Jake emitted a fake groan and swatted at his friend's hand. "Can I put my hat back on now?" Jake replaced his hat, grateful Cookie hadn't asked for the particulars. "Get a few of the men to bring these trunks and boxes into the house."

Cookie worked the ropes off the load. "Man, oh man. She brung a lot of stuff."

"She mentioned she could have her sister send her *other* things."

"Reckon she plans on stayin' then." Cookie smacked him playfully on the back.

"Yep."

"Do you like her? Is she nice? Do you get along?" Cookie's eyebrows raised with the last question.

Jake rolled his eyes and felt his brow tighten. There was no way he was telling even Cookie the details of their honeymoon trip. A honeymoon was something he'd never experienced, even with Mary. Her illness kept them more like friends than spouses. Now, another marriage of convenience for Juliet's sake.

"We best be gettin' inside. Selena won't like it if we're late to the table."

* * *

Selena seated Evangeline at the end of the table she designated for the mistress of the house. The meal's generous portions were more than Evangeline could eat, and the unfamiliar seasoning caused a protest from her stomach. But she did her best, not wanting to offend her new family. "I am so full, I may fall asleep in my chair from sheer contentment."

"Please, don't fall asleep yet," Juliet begged.

"Now, Juliet," Jake playfully scolded. "Your aunt is tuckered from her long trip. She had two days on the train besides the wagon ride."

"Let me get your bath ready right away. It will refresh you." Selena began to clear the table.

"I'll do the dishes," Cookie offered.

"Don't put yourself out for me. I can help with the dishes or draw my own bath," Evangeline protested.

"No, no, you sit. We will do this." Selena escorted her to the parlor and directed her to one of the floral chairs. Evangeline held her protests as Selena placed her feet on a matching footstool. The housekeeper stood and gave her a nod of satisfaction before heading toward the kitchen.

Jake sat opposite her with Juliet perched on the arm of his chair. "You might as well learn right now, Selena considers her job sacred. Unless she gives permission, you won't be workin' in her kitchen any time soon."

"I assume Cookie has permission."

"As far as the kitchen goes, yes. But there's not another chore in this house he's allowed to help with." Jake chuckled as he gave Juliet's braid a playful tug.

The two shared an embrace before Jake signaled for Juliet to occupy a different chair. Evangeline's heart warmed to the sweet way they interacted. Juliet's trust in and affection toward this man surprised her. Her own uncle had not been as trustworthy. Evangeline forced the comparison from her mind.

"Selena seems determined to impress me. As you know, cooking is not among my finest accomplishments. I'm more than happy to relinquish the job. To be frank, I have no idea how to run a house. Looks like Selena does a wonderful job." Evangeline looked around at the spotless, albeit sparse, home.

"I thought all women were born knowin' how to keep house."

"I was the youngest girl and spoiled by my father and grandfather. I spent hours reading and playing with Charley while my sisters did the chores." She searched her fatigued mind for some domestic skill. "I did learn to sew and do fancy work." She hoped those skills gave her an appearance of usefulness.

"Yes, the letters mentioned you liked to sew. "You know you can change anythin' in the house you want to—like the curtains."

Selena approached, a towel over her arm. "*Señora* Marcum, your bath is ready."

"Thank you, Selena. And please, call me Evangeline."

"I am your housekeeper. It would not be proper." Selena crossed her arms and lifted her chin. "Come, let me help you." She opened the bathing room door.

"I would actually prefer to do it myself. Thank you for offering, but you have done more than enough for me today." Evangeline slipped the towel from Selena's arm before she closed the door.

The long soak in the fresh, clean water was like heaven. Evangeline was surprised to find clean clothes on the chair beside her. It appeared Selena had also emptied one of her trunks. She hoped Selena would soon get to the place where she no longer felt the need to wait on her hand and foot. As the warm water washed away the grime, she felt safe from the stares of strangers.

The ranch was not what she had imagined. The home was far more spacious, with lots of potential. Cookie's eyes reminded her of her father's, so kind and welcoming. Precocious Juliet's eagerness brought a smile to her face as she rubbed the coarse soap into the washcloth. The lye soap served its purpose but left her skin feeling rough. She was grateful for the dozen bars of lavender soap tucked away in her things. Maybe Juliet would enjoy using one. Perhaps she could woo friendship from Selena if she offered her some of the scented treasure.

As she began washing her hair, she almost regretted turning down Selena's offer. Her long hair was hard to rinse in the confines of the small tub. She wondered if Jake bathed in this same tub. The thought brought a fearful flutter in her heart and the desire to dress with haste.

***

Juliet paced outside the bathing room door while Jake resisted the urge to do the same thing.

"She will be out soon enough." Selena guided her away. "You need not tell her everything you know in one day."

Juliet sat in a chair but kept her eyes fastened on the door.

Jake stood and reached for his hat. "I'll be close by. Got to go check on things."

"I'll tell her, Uncle Jake. Can I show her my pony?"

"If she wants to see it, honey, but don't be pushy. Your aunt is very tired. Don't keep buzzin' around her." Jake's curt tone brought a nod of consent from Juliet.

"I will keep Juliet from talking the *Señora's* ears off," Selena offered.

Juliet glowered. "I don't talk *that* much. I'm excited is all. A lady from Missouri is my new aunt. I intend to learn all I can from her and copy her ways exactly." She sat up straight and proper, obviously trying her best to imitate Evangeline.

Selena and Jake both turned away to stifle their laughter.

CHAPTER 10

Evangeline woke to the rooster's crow more refreshed than she had been in days. All the details of Juliet's grand tour still danced in her head. She had been introduced to everyone on the ranch but had yet to sort them all out, except for Bart. Him she would remember. All the others had greeted her with a polite tip of the hat, except for Pete who just grinned, then ducked his head. Bart walked away, seeming uncomfortable in her presence, almost angry.

Jake was still asleep on the floor pallet. She sent a *thank you* heavenward for his determination to keep his promise. She sensed the sleeping arrangements were a matter of male ego. He didn't want his men to know they weren't sharing a bed.

Evangeline studied his easy breathing as she thought about the gift he had presented to her. Pride had reflected in his eyes as he stroked the gentle mare he'd chosen. Sage, her soft gray coat lustrous from brushing, had tried to nuzzle Evangeline when Juliet insisted she step closer. Jake's assurances gave no comfort. Her screech at the horse's nearness brought laughter from her new family.

Jake moved his arm as he slept, causing her stomach to lurch. *I wonder how long you will be patient, my husband.*

As if Jake heard her thoughts, he rolled over and smiled.

"Good morning, pretty lady. Did you sleep well?"

"Yes, thank you." Her voice was a whisper, and her chest tightened with a wave of panic. Leaning back on the bed and focusing on the ceiling offered little relief. Being in his bed with him so near caused every muscle in her body to react. The smell of lye soap met her nostrils as she covered her shoulders with the sheet. An unsteady response found its way through her lips. "I slept better than I thought I would. I imagine it will take me a few days to get rested."

"No doubt. I'll go see if Selena has some coffee on."

Evangeline stayed focused on the ceiling. She could hear Jake moving about, pulling on clothes, picking up his boots, and padding out of the room, leaving her to dress in private. She let her breath out in a slow, steady movement, allowing her body to relax. Again, Fiona's favorite verse passed through her mind.

I can do all things through Christ who strengthens me.

Yes, she told herself ... *I can do this.*

Never one to care about appearance, she couldn't explain her need to take extra time. The more she fidgeted with her hair, the more nervous she became. She closed her eyes and waited until a peace settled over her. She redid her hair, and this time her fingers cooperated. Oh, how she wished she would have paid more attention when Katie explained how she did all those hairdos. Gazing at herself in the mirror, she shrugged and managed a half-smile.

This will have to do.

By the time Evangeline came to the table, Selena already had food laid out. The housekeeper's face was unreadable as she brought in the coffee pot. Jake, seated at the head of the table, smiled warmly at her. Once again, her muscles tightened.

Juliet was already at the table. After her initial greeting, the girl remained quiet. Evangeline suspected her new niece had been strongly encouraged to be still. The silence that shrouded the table at that moment could have used some childish chatter.

Breakfast consisted of biscuits, eggs, and a very large steak. "If I keep eating so much of your delicious cooking, I shall become as big as the barn, Selena." Evangeline focused on being cheerful, fighting the nausea her stomach insisted on producing.

"*Señora* Marcum, you are too skinny. You need more meat on your bones. You finish your food. I will pour your coffee."

"Could I trouble you for some tea instead?"

"I have no tea, *Señora*."

Evangeline picked up the cup and waved off the request. "I'll take coffee for now. I brought five pounds of tea with me. After breakfast I will unpack."

"I would be happy to help you unpack the boxes." Selena's stilted smile was not at all encouraging.

"Can I help too?" Juliet asked, her mouth full of biscuit.

"Do not be rude, *mija*. Close your mouth when you are eating." Selena handed a napkin to Juliet, who wiped her mouth and swallowed her food before speaking again.

Evangeline observed how well Selena mothered this child. *What is my role here? Juliet has Selena. What was Jake thinking?* Panic tried to raise its ugly head.

"Please, can I help you unpack your boxes?"

"Of course you may." Evangeline's smile turned genuine at Juliet's wiggles of joy, which abruptly stopped under Selena's disapproving gaze. Evangeline felt a kinship with the child. Her own childhood memories brought an overwhelming need in her heart to protect Juliet.

"Sounds like you got your mornin' occupied. Think I'll get back to work." Jake rose from the table. "Good breakfast, Selena."

"Thank you, *Señor*."

"When will you be back?" Evangeline surprised herself with the question.

"The ranch is busy this time of year. We got the cattle drive comin' up. I'll try not to be gone longer than necessary."

"I'll see you later then." She tried to sound nonchalant while heat found its way into her cheeks. How she hated her inability to keep her face from turning various shades of pink at his words. Her sisters had pestered her about that for years. Evangeline chose to ignore Selena and Juliet smiling at one another as she tried to enjoy her not-too-satisfying coffee.

***

The morning sped by. Juliet's joyous squeals announced every new item removed from the boxes. Under Katie's direction, Evangeline had brought material, ribbons, notions, yarn, thread, and pattern books. As the parlor floor filled with these and more household items, she wondered if she'd overdone it. Wrapped in the material, Katie had carefully packed her silver tea set as well as what she called the everyday teapot. It had a blue floral pattern with matching creamer and sugar bowl. To Evangeline's surprise and Juliet's delight, there were more dishes to match.

"Sweet Katie. No wonder this box was so heavy. My sisters have given me all of Grandmother O'Malley's fine china." Evangeline's fingers traced the large platter's design. "I remember when it arrived from Ireland. Momma cried as she removed each piece. It took hours to unpack because she would tell stories from her childhood with each plate and serving bowl."

The memory made her sad. Another part of her past she could never reclaim. Her mother's words echoed in her mind. *Smile when you don't want to, and your face will have to obey*. Taking a deep breath, she forced a smile and continued unpacking. When she removed the last of the china, she had a genuine smile for the girl.

"Juliet, my sister Kathryn helped me pick out this dress for you." She held up a pink jumper, trimmed in pink bows with puffy sleeves. "If it doesn't fit, I can alter it."

Juliet stared at the dress for a long time before her hand reached to draw it close.

Evangeline enjoyed her expression of surprise. "Here are some hair ribbons to match. Do you like them?"

"Oh, my … yes." Juliet's eyes widened, and her hug took Evangeline's breath away. "No one has ever given me anything so beautiful. Thank you. Thank you so very much. Can I go try it on right now?"

"Wait until we put things away. Besides, I want you to see what I have brought for Selena."

"Me? *Señora*, no, it is not right."

"I will accept no complaining from you. You must take my gift, or you will offend me."

Selena remained silent.

Evangeline pulled out a beautiful red satin dress with lace trim and a velvet bodice. Katie had insisted she take the dress even though the color was all wrong. Now she knew what God had planned for it. The moment she saw Selena, she knew her coal black hair and bronzed complexion would draw out the beauty of the dress. She placed it in the housekeeper's hands.

Selena's eyes filled with tears. "You should keep this dress for yourself. You are the lady of the house."

"That's right, Selena, I am the lady of the house, and I *insist*."

"But it is too beautiful to wear. *Muchas gracias, Señora* Marcum. No one has been so kind to me." Her voice caught.

"I'm quite sure you will find an occasion to wear this dress."

"No matter, I will enjoy knowing I have such a beautiful garment."

Juliet gave the dress a feather-light touch. "Selena, let's have a party today. We can both wear our new dresses."

"This dress is much too fine to serve dinner in. As the *Señora* says, some day. But you may wear your dress to show your uncle tonight."

Juliet's attention turned back to the unpacking. "Is this box empty? Can we start on the other one? Is there anything in the other box for me?"

"*Mija*, too many questions." Selena hid a smile beneath her scowl.

"Let's get started, and we will see," Evangeline said. The last box contained books, framed pictures, other personal items, and the bars of lavender soap. Juliet caressed a bar, breathing in its lavender scent.

"Can I use this here soap?"

"You may have a bar of this soap," Evangeline corrected.

"The *Señora*, she likes to smell sweet." Selena breathed in the sweet fragrance.

"You may have a bar too, if you like. It's my favorite, and I know it cannot be purchased out here. There is a store back home where the proprietress makes it."

"Thank you, *Señora*, this is very special."

"It reminds me of my mother." Odd how so many things in this new place reminded her of home. Evangeline emptied the box.

"What are these?" Juliet held a couple of journals in her hand.

Evangeline snatched them from her. "These, child, are not for you to read without permission. These journals contain my personal family history. I started writing my thoughts and descriptions of things when I was about your age."

Evangeline caressed the covers of each one, arranging them chronologically. There were three new ones. *Thank you, Katie.* "I see she still managed to send along a copy of her favorite cookbook." She handed the last of the books to Juliet—*David Copperfield, Oliver Twist*, and a world history book. "Your uncle said in his letter you had finished the third level in *McGuffey*. You should be ready for these." Reaching into the box again, she produced an advanced mathematics book and a grammar book. There were tablets of paper, a drawing pad, and colored pencils. "These are all for you."

Juliet frowned slightly but managed a polite thank you. Evangeline wasn't surprised this little tomboy found schoolwork less than exciting.

"Your uncle expressed concern you might be behind when school starts up again. We can work through these books a little each day. I promise not to make it too painful."

"When the new term starts, I won't be goin' to school much. Town's too far. Uncle Jake says I'm too young to board at school." Juliet's face showed her obvious pleasure at the fact.

"How far is Charleton from here?"

"About a one-hour ride. Little longer by wagon in good weather. But the boardin' school is in Hardyville."

"Well then, the next thing I have for you will come in handy."

"What?" Juliet's face brightened.

"I want you to have one of these new journals."

"Why?"

"So you can write your history in it."

"What history?" The girl's frown deepened. "'Sides, I don't like writin' much."

"But you like talking about history. You showed me all over the ranch and told me about everything. If you never write it down, it will be lost to future generations. Writing your family history leaves something for your descendants." Evangeline saw comprehension dawn on her face.

"You mean instead of talkin' 'bout stuff I know, I could write it in this book?"

"Precisely. Your children, grandchildren, and great-grandchildren could read about what life was like on this ranch."

"Hmm … could be interestin'. You say you write every day?" Juliet crinkled her nose while flipping through the blank pages.

"No, but I try to fill at least one journal every year."

"Can I read your journals someday?" Juliet closed the book. "It might help me know what to write."

"How about I read some of my entries to you once in a while?" Evangeline offered.

"How 'bout today?" Juliet pleaded.

"Not today, but on a bad-weather day when we are forced to stay inside, I will read to you about my childhood." She hoped her answer would satisfy.

"Can I try on my dress now?" Juliet stood, dancing with the dress.

"You may. I want to see how you look. Both of you. I will finish putting things away."

"*Señora*, let me do that." Selena picked up some plates.

Evangeline removed them from her hands. "Try on your dress first. Afterward, we will decide together what to do with this china."

Evangeline looked around the room, deciding where to place her things. The fine china's delicate beauty drew a stark contrast to the furniture. The chairs needed new covers. The table had no cloth. The sideboard seemed bare. The windows could use new curtains as well. Scanning the large room, her eyes lit on the upright piano in the corner. She wondered who played.

There was a nail in the wall above the piano where something had once hung. The family portrait her father had commissioned would be perfect. Her mother had been so pleased with it. The artist had pre-painted the bodies on the canvas. Only their faces were later added. Her six-year-old face placed over a red dress looked less than flattering. Now, however, she loved the portrait.

Next, she placed the framed photograph Katie had insisted they have made last Christmas, on the piano. Maggie, now a married woman, looked so young. She remembered the frame Jake bought her in Hardyville and decided to place it on the sideboard once the wedding photo arrived. She arranged the silver tea service, leaving room for the picture. Evangeline knew she had enough tatting thread to make a sizeable doily to dress up the sideboard.

"Aunt Evangeline, look." Juliet pranced into the room and whirled around. Her new dress was a little big, so she would be able to wear it a while.

Selena shyly entered the room, her trembling hands lifting the long hem off the floor. "Selena, you are stunning."

The housekeeper's hand went to her face. "I cannot believe this." Selena pranced around the room, swishing the skirt as she walked. "When my cousin Letitia marries in a few months, I shall wear this dress and make every woman there so jealous." Her giggles stopped when she glanced toward the kitchen. "I must change and finish straightening so we can prepare the meal."

Evangeline didn't miss the fact that the woman used the word *we*.

Selena left to change, but Juliet insisted on wearing her new dress for lunch. Evangeline adjusted the ribbons in her hair before the girl ran outside to show off her gift to anyone nearby. Selena soon returned, and they put everything away in short order.

Evangeline could not decide where to hang her painting of the Good Shepherd. Fiona had given her the painting the day she had given her heart to Jesus. *Ye are like that little lamb Jesus is a-carryin' on His shoulder. Ye belong to Him, Lassie; He will always take care of ye.*

Memories of Fiona made her heart ache with loneliness. Shaking herself back into the present, she left the painting propped against the wall atop the chest of drawers in the master bedroom. Later, she would find the right spot.

"*Señor* Marcum ordered the wardrobe and the dresser from the cabinetmaker who lives on a neighboring ranch. The *Señor* thought you would need the room. Before, there was only the bed and washstand. Those hooks were made by Solomon the blacksmith." Selena pointed to hooks secured behind the bedroom door. "He wanted to do something special for you. See how nice your things look." Selena had hung her shawls and robe on the hooks.

"How thoughtful. Solomon is the big, black gentleman?"

"*Sí.*"

"I must be sure to thank him for his gift."

Evangeline was embarrassed to find that after filling the wardrobe and dresser, she had to leave the rest of her things in her trunks along with her journals. "I have taken up all this room with my things. Jacob only has one drawer and a suit in the wardrobe."

"He is a man who had no wife. He does not know he can have more clothes. Do not be concerned. The stores have not many lady things. If a woman wants something, she must order it. If nothing happens, it will come."

"If nothing happens?"

"*Sí* ... no robbers or bad weather to delay the delivery. I am glad you brought the material and thread. No need to go to town." Selena knelt to repack the last of the material.

"You don't like going into town?" Evangeline had caught the

tone in her voice.

"I no like going into the general store." Selena rose from the floor and wiped her hands on her apron. "Mrs. Hanks has no respect for anyone who is not white like her."

"Is there another store in Charleton?"

"*Si*. A China man owns it, and I go there sometimes. He does not have everything, so I still must go to the general store."

"I suppose she does not like this China man either."

"For two reasons—he is not white, and his prices are cheaper."

CHAPTER 11

J ake felt Traveler pick up his pace as they approached the house. Juliet's legs dangled over the fence rail, while Dog lay at her feet. Manny stood nearby holding the egg basket.

Looks like those two are at it again.

His niece often found ways to get Manny to do her chores. It was hard to decide if Manny looked on her as a little sister or something else. Jake dismissed the latter thought as Manny ruffled Juliet's hair. He pulled Traveler to a stop close enough to hear the two. Juliet was being her usual fussy self when it came to the boy.

"Stop that." Juliet scowled and smacked Manny's hand away. "You don't understand anything. I didn't mean to forget my chores. My mind's distracted."

"It is always so." Manny glanced toward Jake and waved.

Juliet scrambled from the fence and tripped over Manny's boot. Her scowl elicited more mirth from the boy.

"Why must you be in such a hurry?" he shouted after her.

With Dog at her heels, Juliet ran to the house and scampered up the porch steps. When the door slammed behind her, Dog found a place on the porch to wait.

Manny took Traveler's reins as Jake dismounted. "Miss Juliet, she is crazy."

Jake pointed to the egg basket. "You gotta stop doin' her chores when she forgets. Take care of Traveler before you take the eggs in to your momma."

"*Si*, I know but—"

"You see things need doin', and you do them." Jake patted his shoulder. "You're a good man, Manny. But Juliet won't learn responsibility if you keep doin' her chores."

Jake entered the house with every intention of rebuking his

niece for her thoughtlessness. Evangeline passed him without so much as a nod as she trekked from the kitchen toward Juliet's room, wiping her hands on a piece of cloth. In a moment they both appeared. When his wife signaled Juliet, she stepped forward, executed a perfect curtsy, and twirled around. Evangeline went back to the kitchen.

Seeing his niece in her new dress melted his resolve. "Who is this house guest we have here? Don't she look like a fine lady?" Jake bowed and kissed her hand as Juliet giggled.

"You like my dress? Ain't ... I mean, *isn't* it lovely?"

"Sure is."

"Aunt Evangeline brung it all the way from Missouri for me. If you'd a come home for lunch, you'd a seen it then. I changed so as not to get it dirty. Look at the table. Them ... I mean those dishes belonged to her grandma. They come all the way from Ireland. Ain't ... aren't they lovely too?"

"They certainly are." Jake glanced around the room, trying to hide a grin at Juliet's attempt to correct her words. "What is your aunt up to?"

"She's helpin' Selena in the kitchen."

"Really?" Jake wondered what could have happened to soften the housekeeper.

"I think Selena likes her now 'cause she brung ... brought her a beautiful, fancy dress too, all the way from Missouri."

"Did she now?"

"*Sí, Señor*, it is the most beautiful dress I have ever seen. The *Señora* is very generous." Selena carried plates of food, and Evangeline followed with more. Selena excused herself as soon as she finished serving. Cookie came in and pulled up a chair at the table.

"I wish Selena would sit with us." Evangeline glanced toward the kitchen. "I've had little experience with servants. Only at my uncle's home." Her eyes flitted to her plate, and her hand went to her chest. She raised her head and straightened her silverware. Jake wondered what kind of experience she'd had with servants to make her so uncomfortable.

"Maybe someday she will," Cookie said.

"You already had one miracle," Jake said as he sat down. "She let you in her kitchen."

"One thing at a time, I suppose." Evangeline placed her napkin in her lap. "Things are just as new for her as they are for me."

Jake glanced at Juliet. "Little lady, would you please say grace?"

"Yes, sir." She bowed her head and folded her hands. "Lord, thank you for all the wonderful things of this day and for bringin' Aunt Evangeline to us ... and 'specially for the beautiful dress. Amen."

* * *

Dinner conversation focused on the workings of the ranch. Evangeline listened, intent on learning all she could about her new home.

With a piece of beef still hanging from his fork, Cookie ticked off the virtues of Double M. "It has the most comfortable bunkhouse and the best workin' conditions of any ranch around. The pay is better, and the food is the best. Selena sees to that."

"I imagine the men value their jobs." Evangeline placed her napkin over her uneaten food. Her stomach refused to enjoy the strange new fare as Mexican spices danced on her taste buds, inviting the nausea to return. Her stomach had behaved all day. Now—along with Jake's presence—it troubled her again. She sipped her tea hoping to ease the discomfort.

"Yes, ma'am. Jake figures you take real good care of the hands, they'll take real good care of the ranch." This was the third time Cookie quoted Jake's philosophy of ranching since her arrival. His admiration for the man was apparent.

It appeared everyone here respected her new husband. But everyone had respected her uncle. He'd treated his employees well.

Uncle Carl was a pillar in the community yet—

"Would you like to take a ride after dinner?"

Jake's words brought her back to the present and—with them—the realization she wasn't ready to face her fears. At least not all of them.

"How about a walk? I want to explore the ranch more thoroughly." She hoped her voice sounded nonchalant.

"That'd be fine."

After the meal, Evangeline went to get a shawl. When she returned, Jake took her hand. She tensed a bit but didn't try to pull away.

"What direction do you want to start?" he asked, moving toward the back door.

Evangeline willed herself to relax. She let out a slow breath. "Shall we look at the garden and work our way to the front path?"

The sun had not yet set. Dusk often brought peace to Evangeline at the end of a day. Today, anxiety distracted her heart. She gazed at Selena's garden. "Everything looks so healthy. I see you irrigate. Have you thought about adding fruit trees?"

"There's fruit trees on the property near my folks' place."

"The homestead? I didn't notice them."

They're kinda grown over. But we still get apples and pears off 'em in season. There's berry bushes around as well. Cookie can tell you where they are."

"I'd like to make some jam for winter. That's another domestic skill I acquired."

"That'd be real nice. I look forward to samplin' it." His thumb lightly stroked her hand as he spoke, sending little flutters up her spine.

Her eyes moved to the small one-room cabin, Selena's home. A colorful flower garden graced the area near the front door. "Jake, I'm very curious about something."

"What's that?"

"I can see Selena loves Juliet very much, and she is such a

wonderful mother to her, not to mention she is extremely beautiful. Why didn't you marry her?"

Jake stopped walking, obviously surprised by the question. "Well, for one thing, Selena's a mite older. Her late husband, Carlos, was like an uncle to me. And in case you haven't noticed, there's someone else who fancies her."

"I *have* noticed." Evangeline recalled how Cookie's face seemed to glow in the housekeeper's presence.

"Selena is more like a sister or aunt." After another pause, he added, "Besides, you're the most beautiful woman I've ever seen."

Evangeline looked away, determined not to let this man rattle her. *When will he stop saying things like this?* After a few moments, they moved on, circling the barn.

"You don't like Sage?" Jake asked, obviously sensing her apprehension.

"She is beautiful."

"But?"

"I'm scared of riding. Horses can pull my wagon, but I prefer not to be on their back."

"Why's that?"

"I have been thrown a few times."

"Pa always said you get back up and try again."

"I received a bad concussion and was laid up for several months with a broken arm. Tell me, how many times have you fallen from a horse?"

"None."

"I find no comfort in the words of a man with no experience." Evangeline attempted to adjust her shawl with her free hand.

"She's broke for haulin' as well as ridin'," Jake offered.

"Good. I can hitch her to the wagon and go into town. I'd like to find some material to reupholster your parlor chairs. I brought nothing suitable." Evangeline waited for his reaction.

"I said you could do whatever you like to make the house your own. We have accounts at the stores. We pay the bills when the cattle drive's over."

"I have my own money. I'd rather not add to your account for frivolous things."

Jake's brows furrowed as he stared at her.

"Are you bothered that I can pay my way?"

"Maybe." His eyes flashed. "It's a man's place to provide for his family."

***

Jake felt tension rise up between them at his declaration. His new wife pulled her hand away as they walked.

"I have been earning my way for years." Stopping mid-stride, she turned to face him. Her green eyes glinted with the sun's fading rays, causing Jake to get lost for a moment in their beauty. "You did say this was *our* ranch. The money I have is also ours. I want to use it to make our house more comfortable."

"I reckon it'd be okay." Jake couldn't argue with her logic, even though it galled his pride. "I don't need your money to take care of our ranch. That's my job. But you can buy whatever suits ya with your money."

Her eyes challenged him. "I suppose I should be grateful you granted me *permission* to spend my own money. You will find, Jake Marcum, that I don't ask permission. I'd rather discuss things. I see the household as a shared responsibility."

Jake found her stormy features endearing. "And you, Evangeline Marcum, will find me a stubborn man when it comes to change. If you give me a chance, you might find my ways are not too disagreeable."

She smoothed her dress and looked at the ground for a moment. When she raised her eyes to his, her countenance had changed. "Shall we continue our walk?"

This woman is a mystery for sure.

They went as far as the trees outside the entrance gate. The grove, a beautiful contrast to the flat prairie and distant hills, framed the lovely spot. Jake indicated the bench at the base of one tree, and they sat to enjoy the sunset.

"This is so beautiful, and the quiet here is wonderful." Evangeline closed her eyes and breathed in the air of the coming darkness.

Before he could stop himself, Jake placed a gentle kiss on her lips.

Her eyes flashed open, reflecting fear.

"Sorry, I—"

"You startled me." She moved away, stiffening her back.

"You looked like you needed to be kissed."

She rose from the bench and dusted imagined dirt from her skirt. "I will tell you when I need to be kissed, Mr. Marcum." Her voice had a wounded edge.

Evangeline fled back to the house. Jake followed, frustrated at her mixed signals and at the same time kicking himself for being such a schoolboy.

One of these days, I'm gonna kiss that independent attitude right outta her. Then she'll probably slap my face.

He slowed his pace as she entered the house. The slamming door echoed on the damp night air.

Lord, I gave my word. Help me keep it.

CHAPTER 12

Artie rushed in, interrupting the family breakfast. He whipped off his battered Confederate hat and glanced at Evangeline before addressing Jake. "Boss, we got a few head of cattle sufferin' from the bloat."

Jake rose from his chair. "Cookie, get Duke and Tony. Pete too if he ain't still busy mending that fence."

Artie bolted out the door without another word.

"What's happening?" Evangeline asked.

"Some of the cattle ate somethin' that didn't agree with 'em." Jake paused at the door. "Could you check on Bo? He broke his foot the other day, and he's tryin' to walk on it too soon."

In the few days since her arrival, she'd seen very little of Jake. He involved himself in every aspect of running the ranch. Her relief at not having much time with him wrestled with her feeling of being an observer on the ranch rather than a part of it. "Which one is Bo?"

"Artie can show you. And if you wanna go to town this morning, he can drive you."

Juliet jumped from her seat, spilling her juice. "Can I go too?"

"It's up to your aunt."

"Of course you may, Juliet, but let me check on Bo first."

"Yes, ma'am. I'll go get ready."

Evangeline peered from the window as Jake and his men prepared to head out toward the ailing cattle, focusing her attention on her husband as he mounted Traveler and struck out to do what needed doing.

I wish I could find my place. Be confident with myself. Jake, Selena, even Cookie—despite his handicap—have found purpose in their lives here.

Could she find purpose and her place in his world? She grabbed her medical bag. Artie waited at the door to take her to the bunkhouse.

"I'm surprised I didn't notice Bo's foot myself," Evangeline remarked more to herself than Artie.

"I ain't. Ever since Bart told him to quit cry-babyin' and be a man, he took off the bandage and shoved his foot in his boot. Ain't been able to get it off since."

"How did he break his foot?"

"He was cryin' 'cause Bart had to shoot his horse. The horse broke his leg trippin' in a rabbit hole. Bo got so upset he started runnin' and caught his leg in the same hole, breakin' his ankle. Bart's been fussin' at him ever since."

"Is Bo afraid of Bart?"

"Nah, he admires him."

Evangeline recalled Bart's angry face. "Frankly, I find him disturbing."

"Most people do." Artie's pants were a few inches too long, causing him to stop every few feet to hike them up. "The war made him a mite touched in the head. Mad all the time. I steer clear, but he won't bother you."

"Why is that?"

"You're the boss's wife."

Evangeline entered the bunkhouse and found a large-framed young man sprawled on one of the narrow beds. "Bo, Mr. Marcum sent me to check on your leg."

"Yes, ma'am, it hurts like fire."

"Artie, please hold Bo down while I remove his boot."

"I shore wish you didn't have to do that." Bo's voice was laced with fear.

"Relax, Bo. Mrs. Marcum can fix ya up."

Artie gripped Bo's shoulders as Evangeline worked the boot off, pressing all his weight into keeping the young man from moving. Bo's shoulder's bucked with the final pull of the boot, propelling the smaller man backward. Artie found the floor with his backside, but rose quickly and resumed his position near Bo's side.

The swollen ankle carried a deep-purple bruise, with a red tinge forming near the toes from lack of circulation in the too-tight boot. The odor of a week-old, sweaty sock caused Evangeline to wrinkle her nose. "It's not broken, which is good, but you have been using it too much. You have to let it heal. I'll wrap it securely." Turning to Artie, she said, "Mr. Weaver, I need something to elevate his foot."

Artie pulled a blanket from a nearby bunk and deftly folded it for the purpose. Once the ankle was bandaged, she rested Bo's leg on the heavy material.

"You must keep your foot propped up. For the next week, you are not going anywhere."

"A *week?*" Bo attempted to rise from his place.

Evangeline pressed him back to a lying position. "Maybe longer. You only made it worse by walking on it."

"But Bart needs my help."

"Whatever Bart is doing, someone else can help him. You are going to stay here and not move. You do, and I'll tell Mr. Marcum to fire you." *I sure hope it doesn't come to that.* Guilt grabbed her as Bo stared at her. Then she wondered if Jake would really fire him on her say-so.

"Yes, ma'am." Bo flopped back on his pillow with a moan. "And thank you."

Once Evangeline heated some water on the stove and made willow bark tea to reduce his fever, she gathered a few more blankets from the unused beds to further elevate Bo's foot. The dirty blanket he was covered with was exchanged for a somewhat fresher one. Washing bedding apparently didn't take top priority in the bunkhouse.

When Bo finished the tea, Evangeline took the cup and mixed a little laudanum with water. "Here is something for the pain. I'll check on you later this afternoon."

"Mr. Weaver, can you get the wagon ready? Juliet and I are

going to town. Jake told me you would be our driver. Bo will sleep away most of the day, which is what he needs. Find someone to check on him while we are gone."

"Yes, ma'am, I'm sure Solomon will do it. And please, ma'am, call me Artie. I don't much care for being called Mr. Weaver." He tipped his hat before heading out.

* * *

Artie put a blanket in the wagon bed for Juliet. "So's your dress don't get dirty, little miss. My, don't you look dandy."

"Thank you, Artie." Juliet smoothed her new dress. "You're a real gentleman."

Evangeline paid close attention to the road ahead, careful to memorize landmarks for future reference. Unlike the city streets she'd traversed in recent years, the trail from the Double M to Charleton had only a few distinguishing characteristics. A chimney, the only remnant of a burned-out cabin, stood to her left. A large boulder caused the otherwise straight road to curve to the right about a mile later, then miles of flat prairie.

The quietness in the wagon surprised Evangeline. "A penny for your thoughts, Juliet."

"I'm thinkin' 'bout how to describe this ride for my journal." Juliet stood and pressed herself between the adults on the buckboard seat. "I brung it to write in while we go along." Resuming her place, she steadied herself as the wagon wheels rocked in and out of a pothole. "Artie, tell Aunt Evangeline 'bout yourself. I can put down you two talked while I was writin'."

Artie and Evangeline glanced at each other, both trying not to laugh. Evangeline's voice was laced with humor when she finally spoke. "Very well, sir, tell me about yourself."

"Ask away." Artie turned his head slightly and yelled over his shoulder. "Juliet, don't write my words in your journal, you hear."

"Don't talk to me, I'm writin'," Juliet responded.

Evangeline began her interview. "Where are you from, Mr. Weaver?"

Artie took his time answering. "Born in Massachusetts, but grew up in Illinois."

"Why do you wear that Confederate hat if you are a Northerner?"

"To rile Duke." Artie's gentle laughter caught Evangeline by surprise. Perhaps he was younger than she supposed.

"I'm only jokin'. I lost my hat and won this one in a poker game. Duke hates it." Artie picked up his narrative as the road smoothed out. "I lost my brother and cousin to the war and my parents to savages. My sister Eleanor and I stayed a spell in both New Madras and Dolton. Them's minin' towns. At least they use to be. I got restless and drifted around till I come to the Double M. Like ranchin' better than minin'."

"What happened to Eleanor?"

Artie hesitated before answering. "She got a job ... in Dolton ... housekeepin'."

Evangeline glanced at Artie, his face expressionless.

* * *

Calling Charleton a town was being polite in Evangeline's estimation. About a dozen homes occupied the two streets paralleling the main street. Charleton General Store, with its colorful signs indicating its additional services of post office and telegraph station, occupied one corner. Sharing the same side of the unpaved street was the livery, undertaker, and a gun shop. Evangeline could make out a blacksmith shop, restaurant, hotel, and a very busy saloon. The edge of town had an Asian influence.

They passed a dilapidated church. "Does it have services?"

"Ever three or four months a circuit rider comes 'round." Artie glanced up. "It's pretty big doin's when he comes. There's a potluck, and if anyone wants to get married or baptized, that's the day to do it. I heard tell the last parson had a run-in with the saloon owner, and he lit out like a cat with his tail afire. That's why we have to settle for a circuit rider."

Evangeline cringed at the thought of a saloon having more influence in a town than the church.

Artie stopped the wagon near the Charleton General Store. "I'll leave you ladies to your shoppin'. I got a few things to pick up for the boss."

Juliet took Evangeline's hand, and they entered the store. A tinkling bell announced their arrival.

"Welcome, ma'am," the storekeeper greeted them. "How can I help you?"

Before Evangeline had a chance to introduce herself, a woman extended her hand. Her bright-yellow dress made Evangeline think of a large canary.

"I'm Cordelia Hanks. This is my husband Angus, and you must be the new Mrs. Marcum. Welcome to our emporium." She looked Evangeline over thoroughly. "I can see by your lovely dress you are a woman of style. And I saw you admiring my new dress."

Admiration is not exactly the word I would use. The color gave the woman a sallow appearance, and the garment clung tightly to her large frame in an unflattering manner.

"I just finished it yesterday. This is made from some of our newest yard goods. You must have a look at the rest of my selection." She drew Evangeline to the back of the store where all the bolts of material were kept.

Mrs. Hanks seemed to suddenly notice Juliet and gave her the same scrutinizing look. "My, oh my, Juliet Marcum, I would never have recognized you." She patted the young girl's head. "I can see a lady's touch has already made a difference over at your place."

As the woman chattered on, Evangeline examined the yard goods. Many bolts of material were similar to Mrs. Hank's dress, which seemed more suitable for tablecloths and window curtains. She found nothing she cared for.

"I'm sure you have lots of work to do there with all those men and that greaser woman."

"Excuse me?" Evangeline's sharp tone was either unnoticed or ignored by Mrs. Hanks. "Let me clear up your misconception. Selena Hernandez is exceptional at everything she does. She has taught Juliet proper manners. I consider derogatory remarks such as *greaser* to be offensive to any woman of good breeding. In the future, you will consider how you speak of anyone in our employ. Now, if you will mail these letters for me, I would appreciate it."

Mrs. Hanks seemed taken aback by Evangeline's forthright words but cleared her throat and made a feeble attempt at a smile. "Of course, I can take care of those right away." She moved to the postal counter, the bustle of her yellow dress swishing back and forth.

"Thank you. I'll give this list to your husband. I have a few more stops to make. We'll return for the items later."

Outside, Juliet put her hands on her hips. "You sure told that old bat what's what."

"Juliet, we do not refer to people as old bats no matter how irritating they are." Evangeline forcefully opened her parasol, releasing some of her irritation for the proprietress.

"Yes, ma'am. Sorry."

"I am not particularly proud of how I behaved. I know the Lord wasn't." Evangeline placed Juliet's hand in the crook of her elbow. "I want to explore the rest of this little town. You shall be my guide."

They headed toward the Chinese section. The building with the dragon on the door contrasted with the general store in its neat and organized appearance. The contents were similar, but many items were distinctively Asian.

An older gentleman dressed in a Chinese robe bowed to Evangeline. He smiled a broad smile and swept his hand around the room to indicate she was welcome.

Evangeline bowed in return, hoping it was the proper response.

A young woman in a simple black dress approached. "May I

help you?"

"Selena Hernandez recommended your store as the superior place to shop. She works for my husband, Jacob Marcum."

The woman turned to the older man. The language between the two had a melodic quality.

"I am Wong Mae, and this is my father, Wong Chow. We hold Miss Selena in high regard. She is kind and brings us much business from the households of white ranchers. If she is your friend, you are ours. My father did not know Mr. Marcum married. He says to give you the best price on anything in the store."

Evangeline smiled her thanks and looked through the material on display. The quality of the fabric was far superior to the general store. Her fingers ran over a thick brocade. "I would like to see some more of this fabric." The texture of the fabric appealed to her seamstress touch, as did the green embroidered with peacocks and delicate vines. She was drawn to a similar pattern in blue with gold threads.

Mae took a few more selections from beneath the counter. Each pattern was delicately woven into the material. Here was something she could do and do very well. Reupholstering and sewing were things she'd enjoyed. Helping Katie in her seamstress shop taught her to sew quickly and with expertise. Excitement beat a pattern in her heart at the prospect of contributing something of value to her new world. "I need about forty yards."

"Forty yards! What you make?"

"I'm going to cover two chairs and a settee, as well as two large windows."

"The blue better. It is heavier and good for cushions."

"I agree," Evangeline said with an enthusiasm she hadn't felt since arriving. "How much?"

Mae spoke to her father. "He says it is wedding gift. Your husband saved his life. When we first come here, some of the cowboys fight him and try to cut off his queue."

"His *queue?*"

"His long braid. He believe in old ways. It is disgrace to cut off. Your husband fight the men for my father. Now father has paid debt."

"Very well. I appreciate your kindness and will be sure to tell my husband." Evangeline did not wish to take advantage of them and explored the rest of the store, determined to make a purchase. "This box is lovely, such fine carving." She picked up the ornate trinket box and found hair ribbons for Juliet. "Do you have any medicines?"

"Yes, over this way please."

Mae took Evangeline to a side room lined with shelves of herbs labeled in Chinese and helped her select what she wanted, even writing out the English translations.

"Why you buy medicine here? Most whites not believe in our cures."

"I believe in them. A friend of mine introduced me to a Dr. Lo. He is a fine doctor whose remedies saved lives the white doctors had given up on."

"You are a healer?"

Evangeline pondered how to respond, not wanting to break her promise to Jake. "With the Lord's help, yes."

***

Evangeline and Juliet returned to the general store just as a young woman wearing a plaid wool skirt, oversized flannel shirt, and a hat with large feathers entered. She stomped toward them. Evangeline liked the woman's infectious smile.

"Howdy, I'm Bertha Eugenia Woods." She extended her hand. "And who might you be?"

"Evangeline O … Marcum." She smiled back and took Bertha's hand.

"You Juliet's new ma? I heard tell she was gettin' one."

"I'm her new aunt. It is very nice to meet you, Bertha."

"Really? Well, wonderful. Would you like to come over for a visit tomorrow?"

"So nice of you to ask. Where do you live?" Evangeline ignored Juliet's tug on her sleeve.

Bertha turned at the tinkle of the doorbell. Artie's appearance caused a crooked grin to form on the young woman's face. "Howdy there, Artie. How are you this fine day?" Bertha flashed her lopsided smile. "Do you know Mrs. Marcum?"

"Yep, I do. I work for her husband."

"Course you do. You work for her husband. You work for Juliet's uncle. Her uncle, Jake Marcum. Yes, you do indeed. Can you bring Missus Evangeline Marcum for a visit tomorrow? Pa and me could use the company."

Artie looked at Evangeline, his eyebrows raised in question.

"I'll see if we can make the time. I'm sure Artie can take me if Mr. Marcum doesn't have something else for him to do. Juliet would love a ride out to your place."

Evangeline disregarded Juliet's open-mouth expression and the stare from Mrs. Hanks. Her heart warmed to the delightful, innocent woman.

Bertha curtsied to everyone. "I gotta go and tell Pa. It's time to go. He's over at the saloon havin' hisself a drink. Gotta go now."

Once Bertha left, Mr. Hanks approached. "Mrs. Marcum, I have everything ready for your order except the laudanum. We're all out, but I can order more."

"Please do. And I'll make a list of a few other medicines I would like for you to keep on hand, if possible."

"Should take about a month to get here. You know, it's hard not to overhear Bertha when she's conversin'. Since you're new to the community, let me offer a piece of friendly advice. If I was you, I would ignore her invitation."

"She is the first neighbor to invite me for a visit. I look forward to getting to know her."

"But you must see she's not right."

Evangeline found Mr. Hanks as annoying as his wife. "Not right compared to whom?"

Mr. Hanks snorted and twisted his lips in what appeared an effort to recapture his words. "I'll put this order on the bill with everything else."

"If you don't mind, I'd rather pay the bill in full at this time."

"This purchase?" Mr. Hanks inquired, looking a bit confused.

"The whole bill, if you please."

The man's eyes were as round as his belly. "It'll take a minute to add it all up." His chubby finger slid down the row of figures. "Let's see, that's three hundred fifty-two dollars and seventeen cents. Let's round it up to three hundred fifty-three to cover the fee for carryin' the credit."

"That much?"

"Most of the ranchers wait till after the cattle drive to settle their accounts. Jake'll be in to pay it then. So why don't I just add these items to your bill?"

"No, I'll pay now, but I would like to check your figures if you don't mind."

Mr. Hanks turned the ledger book around, looking quite surprised at her request. Evangeline ran her finger down the page and totaled it in her head. "The total is *two* hundred fifty-two dollars and seventeen cents. You appear to have miscalculated."

The man frowned and rechecked the figures. "You're absolutely right. My apologies."

Artie approached the counter with a new Stetson in hand. "How much?"

"Three dollars seems about right."

Evangeline studied the hat before she spoke up. "It can't be worth more than two dollars. At least that is the going rate in Missouri."

Mr. Hanks frowned at her again, then turned his attention to Artie. "Let's split the difference and say two-fifty."

"Sold." Artie handed over the money, placed the new hat on his head, and left Evangeline to finish her business. She withdrew the exact amount for the bill from her purse.

"Ma'am, I don't recommend carryin' large sums of money around these parts. Some unsavory character might try to steal it from you. That's why the menfolk don't let their women come and pay the bill."

"I find credit an unsavory robber. Please, may I have a receipt?"

Evangeline experienced a deep sense of relief as she left the store. Artie, who was waiting beside the wagon, took her purchases and stowed them under the seat. The wagon bed, now loaded with a crate and two bales of barbed wire covered with a tarp, left no room for any further purchases.

"I ain't never seen anybody barter with Mr. Hanks before. I appreciate it, ma'am. How did you know I only had three dollars?" Artie adjusted his new hat.

"I didn't. But he struck me as one who prices things according to his customer."

On the trip home, Juliet shared from her journal and rambled on about what she would write next. The journal was full of misspellings, but her vivid descriptions demonstrated a real talent for writing. Once home, the girl jumped off the wagon. "Hey, Selena, wait till you hear what happened in town."

Jake assisted Evangeline from the wagon, causing her an unwelcome shiver. She glanced toward the house rather than at Jake.

"Looks like Juliet had a nice time," Jake said as his niece rushed into the house. He turned his attention back to the wagon. "Ah, I see you have a crate."

"Me?" Evangeline asked, puzzled.

"When you went in the store, Martin from the livery had me collect it for you," Artie explained.

Juliet came out of the house, bringing Selena with her. "What is it, Uncle Jake?"

"A gift for your aunt. I ordered it when I knew for sure she was comin'."

"More gifts. I'm embarrassed by your generosity. I can't imagine what it is."

"I hope it pleases you. I ordered the newest Singer sewing machine."

Evangeline's hand went to her mouth in happy surprise. "This is truly a blessing. I just bought material to cover the chairs and make curtains. It will go much faster with the machine." When Jake and Cookie had uncrated it and removed it from the wagon, she stroked it with her fingers. "My sister has one, and I'm afraid it spoiled me. Thank you so much." She surprised herself by hugging Jake.

"Glad I ordered it," he whispered, his breath tickling her neck. Stepping back, he tucked her hand into the crook of his arm and escorted her to the house.

CHAPTER 13

Evangeline heard the low hum of conversation as she entered the bunkhouse. Angry words caught her attention.

"Bo, you got to get yourself together. I need your help."

"But, Bart, Mrs. Marcum's gonna have me fired if I move afore she says I can."

"Typical woman. Makin' threats to get you to do things her way. She got no authority over you. Tomorrow you're gonna—"

"Continue to stay *off* that foot."

Bart jumped at Evangeline's voice, and his hand touched his holster as he turned. The fierce look in his eyes caused her to shiver, but she faced him down, determined to resist the intimidation tactics of this man, no matter how nervous he made her. She moved past him and checked Bo's forehead.

"Fever's gone. Excellent. The more you rest, the sooner you can get up. The more you walk on that foot, the worse it will get."

"You shore it ain't broke?"

"I'm sure it is only a bad sprain. I don't know how much damage you did to the muscles of your ankle, but rest is the best cure. Take more laudanum for the pain."

Evangeline was conscious of Bart watching her every move but ignored the prickles forming on her skin. "I will see if Solomon can fashion a crutch for you in a few days. If you insist on working, I'm sure Cookie can find something less strenuous for you to do."

"Thank you, ma'am. Just want to pull my weight 'round here."

"I'll check on you again tonight." She patted his shoulder, picked up her medical bag, and acknowledged Bart with a nod as she left the bunkhouse. With her heart in her throat, Evangeline paused just outside the door to listen.

Bart's snarly voice told her enough. "Women ain't nothin' but trouble."

She wrinkled her nose as she heard the man spit.

"Better do as she says. Don't want to draw no suspicion to us."

***

Bone tired, Jake finished currying his horse by lantern light before heading into the house. It'd been a week of long days with an ever-increasing workload. Fatigue left him too exhausted to think much beyond the next chore. Frustration with his inability to track down the missing cattle or the cattle rustlers added to his sleeplessness.

A soft light from the kitchen window guided his path to the house. His heart warmed at the sight of Evangeline writing at the table. The lamplight reflecting off her hair captured golden flecks dancing around her face.

"Hello, Jake." Her smile lifted his spirit. "Let me get your dinner for you. Selena left it in the oven. You look like you have some worry mixed in with your fatigue."

Jake savored a few bites before answering, his hunger grabbing his full attention now. "Missin' steers." His wife poured coffee and listened as he recounted his suspicions. "Walters and Tony been helpin' me keep an eye on the crew."

"Do you suspect one of your men?"

"Always suspect cattle rustlin' from within first." Jake pointed in the air with his empty fork before snagging the last piece of roast beef.

"Pie?" she asked and started to rise.

"Not tonight. I'm too beat to eat more."

"Come sit in the parlor and let me help you with your boots."

Jake moved toward the parlor with Evangeline on his heels. "Well, ain't this room somethin'?" he said as his eyes widened. "The furniture is too fine to sit on with my dirty clothes." A look of pleasure appeared on his new wife's face as her right hand rested on her chest for a moment. The transformation of the room was amazing. Not only the elegant curtains and chair coverings but all the little touches, including the framed wedding picture. It was obvious his wife knew how to occupy her time.

"Whoever heard of a room no one can sit in?" She pointed to his favorite chair.

He hesitated only a moment before lowering his aching body. Evangeline's hands trembled as she removed his right boot. Did his presence still rattle her? Or was this bold action leading to something more? A tingle of desire formed in Jake, but the sensation faded when Evangeline bolted upright.

"Wait here," she commanded and then scurried toward the kitchen. His curiosity piqued at the noise of clanging pans. Evangeline returned with a basin full of warm water and a towel. "Put your feet in here."

Jake removed his socks and soaked his feet in the floral-scented warm water. The aroma drew out some of the fatigue and released the tension from the week.

"Man, oh man. This is nice. Thank you."

"I'm not finished yet." Placing the towel across her lap, she dried his right foot and began to massage it.

This was a side of her he had not yet experienced. *A fella could get used to this.*

"I thought perhaps this would help you relax. All this cattle rustling business has upset you more than you realize. You have cried out from nightmares every night this week. I'm hoping this might improve your sleep. I also want you to sleep on the bed. I'll take the floor."

Jake's eyes flew open. *So much for thinkin' this was of a romantic nature.* "I can't let you sleep on the floor." He tried being stern, but the massage gave his voice a gentler edge than he intended, and his eyes drifted shut once more.

"I've slept on the floor in many a sick room. I won't break."

"Have my nightmares disturbed your sleep that much?"

"Some. I have taken to napping in the afternoon. I had almost given up on you coming home tonight. I thought perhaps you might sleep in one of the line cabins."

"Thought about it." Jake opened one eye. "But I was hopin' to find you awake. Been busy. We haven't had time to talk about things." The even rhythm of her fingers brought relaxation flowing throughout his whole body. Maybe conversation could wait.

"Jake?" Evangeline's voice invaded his sleep-filled head.

Jake's eyes flickered open. "Yeah?"

"For a minute, I thought you were asleep." He heard teasing in her voice.

"Won't be long. Wish I'd known you were willin' to rub my feet … I'd have come home earlier."

"Better stop now if you want to talk."

"Hmm, maybe I'll have some pie after all." Jake rose from his place, and his bare feet padded to the table. Evangeline placed a glass of milk and a generous slice of apple pie before him. He seated himself and picked up a forkful. "Tell me about your day. I mean, your week."

Evangeline seated herself across from him. "I suppose we haven't had any real conversation since my trip to town. Juliet and Cookie have had your attention at mealtimes."

Her words pierced as a barb he well deserved. He hoped the guilt he felt didn't show. Thankfully, Evangeline didn't seem to notice.

"Let's see, most of my time has been spent figuring out the new sewing machine and making the slipcovers and curtains. Did I mention the material was a wedding gift and a thank-you from Mr. Wong?"

"Very generous of him," Jake said around a mouthful of pie.

"He insisted. Apparently, my husband is a hero."

"A few fellas needed a lesson in good manners is all." Jake shrugged as he gulped the last of the milk. "But if Mr. Wong wanted to give you a gift, I'm glad you didn't refuse."

"He has an interesting array of medicines and herbs. I bought a few."

"Heard you ordered some too."

"Who told you?"

Jake wiped his mouth with a napkin and pushed back from the table. "Juliet's been ridin' out to see me every day."

"I've wondered where she rides off to after chores."

"She tells me all she knows while I work."

"What else has she told you?" Evangeline crossed her arms as she leaned on the table. Her mouth formed a straight line while her eyes flashed. Jake wasn't good at reading women and hoped his timing was right for what he wanted to say.

"She was impressed how you put Cordelia Hanks in her place for insultin' Selena. I'm sure the woman deserved it. But the thing I want to talk about is you payin' off my account." His jaw tightened as he steeled himself for her response.

Evangeline stood and began to pace. "Mr. Hanks gave me the impression it was unseemly for a wife to pay off accounts. He also implied I was an imbecile for carrying around large sums of money."

"He called you an imbecile?" Jake's hands fisted.

Evangeline stopped her pacing. "No, but he implied it."

"So you paid off my bill."

"I'm not known to take those sorts of comments lightly." Her look was unreadable as she took her seat. "If I recall, you said this was *our* ranch, making it *our* account. I have never been in the habit of using credit. The biggest reason I chose to pay off that debt, I must confess, is because owing anything to the likes of those two galled me."

"That makes sense. If there was another mercantile in town, they'd be out of business."

"You mean besides Mr. Wong? I gather the majority of his customers are Asian."

"Yeah, people tend to stick with their own kind." Jake unclenched his fists and flexed his fingers.

"I'm glad to support Juliet's acquaintance with them. They seem quite nice."

"Honest too, not like some folks. Juliet also told me Hanks tried to cheat you."

Evangeline seemed to be measuring her words. "I assume he made a math error. It challenged Juliet to learn how to cipher long rows of numbers in her head."

Jake leaned his chair back on two legs. "I s'pose that's one good thing that come out of it. The Hanks tend to bend the scales in their direction at times. They'll probably try to overcharge us again. Might oughta keep checkin' their ciphers." *Should have thought of that myself.* "In the future, I'd like to discuss payin' off charge accounts together."

Her eyes went from green to gray. "I'm truly sorry if I put you in a bad light with Mr. Hanks."

"I don't much care what Hanks thinks. But I would prefer knowin' your intentions ahead of time." Further thoughts of money left with the sweet smile of assent she gave him.

"Did Juliet tell you we went to visit Bertha Woods and her father yesterday?"

"Juliet said you were goin'. None too happy 'bout it either."

"I assume the whole town ignores Bertha. Let me tell you, they are ignoring a treasure. Bertha really knows how to turn sheep's wool into the most beautiful yarn and fabric I have ever seen. The cabin walls are covered with lovely tapestries. She has her own special dyes. I bought some yarn from her. Mrs. Hanks would do well to stock her store with it. Let me show you." Evangeline went to retrieve the yarn and returned with a variety of colored skeins.

Yarn. Can't believe I'm listenin' to talk about knittin'. But she looks plum beautiful when she explains it, the way her face lights up.

"I find sewing and knitting therapeutic."

What? "Thera ... *what*?" Jake felt foolish asking. He should have just kept quiet.

"Therapeutic. Healing. Relaxing. Something familiar. If I

didn't have any sewing to do right now, I would feel a little lost and lonely for home."

"You miss your kin?" *What a stupid question.*

"Of course. But I'm enjoying my new friends here. Most are more than kind." She rose and turned toward the kitchen. "Would you care for more milk?"

Jake signaled for her to sit back down. "Most?"

"Everyone … except Bart."

"Well, he's just plain ornery. The war really got into his head. You should stay clear. I can let him go if he makes you uncomfortable."

Evangeline's hand went to her chest. "That would be unkind to fire him just for being disagreeable."

Jake wondered at her compassion for Bart while her dislike for the Hanks held a bitter tone. *Another mystery to ponder.*

"Bart seems to have some kind of control over Bo. What is it you have Bart doing that makes Bo so determined to work with an injured foot?"

"Nothin' special. Maybe I'll have a little talk with Bart."

"I don't think he appreciated my meddling. I overheard him tell Bo I had no authority over the men."

"If you can keep the men healthy, that's good for the ranch."

"Speaking of healthy, it's past time to remove your stitches. I'm going to get my bag."

While she was gone, Jake took the dirty dishes to the sink. When he returned to the table, he found her removing things from her bag.

"Amazing. A man who cleans up after himself."

Jake made a silly face and took his seat once again.

Evangeline moved close. "This is going to hurt some. These stitches should have been removed a few days ago. The skin has begun to heal over them."

Her closeness, mixed with her heavenly scent, gave Jake an overwhelming desire to wrap his arms around her. He resisted the urge and tried to sit still while she worked. A sigh of relief passed through his lips when she was finished.

"Most people find the removal of stitches painful," Evangeline remarked as she moved to the kitchen sink. She placed the scissors in a pan and poured in hot water from the kettle.

"They never had a pretty doctor do it." Jake followed her back to the parlor.

"You asked me about my week. I meant to tell you Mrs. Farley sent an invitation to come to dinner. I haven't responded." Evangeline picked up a pillow from the settee and fluffed it.

"Good. I'm too busy right now. 'Sides, Thomas Farley can get under my skin."

"She also extended an invitation to tea tomorrow, and I accepted. I'm sorry, I should have asked you. I just thought …" Again her eyes went gray as her arms crossed her chest.

"No, you go on. I don't really know the missus, but Farley himself thinks he's king out here. Old Man Farley was a fair man, but his son is another story."

"I gather you two are not friends?" She perched on the end of the settee, giving him her full attention.

"Good guess. The man's only been here about five years. He was raised by his ma back East. Attended some fancy college and brags about knowin' important people. He owns quite a bit of Charleton as well."

"I assume Farley senior passed five years ago?"

"More like seven. Junior didn't even come for the funeral." Jake knew his tone reflected disgust.

"What do you know about Mrs. Farley?"

"The missus come here about three years ago. She ain't never give me the time of day. Farley only does because we both have cattle interests. About the same time she come, things got bad around here for everybody. We lost a lot a cattle to a winter of blizzards and a lot of crops to grasshoppers. Lot of folks borrowed money from Farley. Sorry to say, I did too. I barely managed to keep this place. I sold all I could spare, includin' all the fancy furniture

Ben left here. When you go to Farley's, you'll find it there. It's the only thing kept him from takin' some of my land in payment. He wanted the furniture for his wife. Ever since, I've kept my distance. He expanded his kingdom quite a bit that year."

Jake saw sympathy in Evangeline's eyes.

"I have been acquainted with people like Mr. Farley. I'll not go if you prefer."

"It's fine. She probably misses the East and wants to hear any news you may have."

Her pensive demeanor changed as a bright smile formed on her face. "Well, that's settled then. Can Artie take me?"

Her request caused a prickly sensation to go down his spine. "Why Artie?"

"I suppose because he has been my driver thus far, and I'm comfortable with him. And he has not placed me on a pedestal like the rest of your ranch hands."

Jake sensed no deceit in her logical explanation. "I'll arrange it." He carefully studied her expression. Was that a sigh of relief or longing? He pressed down the uneasy feeling plaguing him. *Evangeline ain't Nora.* His thoughts tore at his mind while he did a mental checklist that drew him out of the present. He blinked at his wife, realizing he hadn't heard anything she'd said in the last few minutes.

"I'll go wash up the dishes for Selena." Evangeline headed for the kitchen.

His mind had fixated on Nora too long, stirring emotions that unsettled him. Jake jerked out of his chair, willing the motion to erase the memories. From the doorway, he observed his wife, unnoticed. Her burgundy hair glistening in the lamplight and her slender figure reminded him she was nothing like Nora. "Are you *sure* you want me to sleep on the bed?"

"By all means, please," she replied without looking.

"That's where I'm headed before you change your mind."

"I'm staying up awhile. I want to finish my journal entry."

Jake's thoughts tumbled all over each other as he made his way to the bedroom.

CHAPTER 14

Jake woke later the next morning than he intended. Sleeping in his bed was rejuvenating.

The pallet on the floor was empty, and the sun left a track of light across the bed. A passage from Scripture came to his mind. *The Lord is my light and my salvation, whom shall I fear? The Lord is the strength of my life—of whom shall I be afraid?*

His thoughts turned quickly to prayer. *Father, I need your wisdom. You know where them cattle are. You know who the thieves are. Lord, I been friendly with the Indians round here for a while—surely it ain't them.*

The prayer drew his mind to the idea of visiting his friend Joseph Skywater. Maybe he knew something. He owned a ranch toward the southwest, nearer the mountains. He was half-Cheyenne, and his wife was half-Shawnee. They kept to themselves, but their relatives often visited. Perhaps they would have information.

Jake's thoughts moved to his crew as he analyzed each one. *Lord, give me wisdom. You know I gotta make a handy profit this year.* Wasn't there a Scripture saying to not worry about anything but pray about everything? He'd have to look it up.

His quiet reflection dissolved when a knock sounded on the door.

"Uncle Jake, are you awake?"

"Just a minute." He rose and pulled on his trousers before opening the door to see a forlorn look on his niece's face. "What's wrong?"

"Dog's missin'. I called him for breakfast, but he didn't come. I looked all over, and he ain't here." Juliet's eyes filled with tears. Dog had been her comfort since the death of her parents. Jake never worried when Juliet went riding, with the large hound following close.

"Don't worry, honey. Dog knows his way home." Jake lifted her chin. "Probably got the scent of some animal. Remember the skunk?" He hoped the memory would bring a smile.

It didn't.

Juliet's lip quivered. "You think he's okay?"

"Sure 'nough." Jake stroked her cheek, his voice gentle. "Dog'll be fine."

"Aunt Evangeline sent me to fetch you for breakfast." Juliet's voice cracked. She wasn't to be comforted.

Cookie sat holding his coffee mug, the remains of breakfast on his plate. He greeted Jake with a nod, then looked at Juliet. "Child, don't worry. Dog probably got hisself a lady friend and went a courtin'." Cookie's chuckle was cut short by Juliet's piercing look.

Evangeline followed Selena out of the kitchen. Jake admired the way the floral green dress complemented his wife's figure. He'd had no nightmares last night, only dreams of her.

Selena held a cookbook close to her chest. "I will try the stew recipe you like. We can have it tonight for dinner. Perhaps you can help me to be sure it is just the way you like it."

Jake was impressed. He had never seen Selena try a new recipe.

"I should be back from the Farley's place in plenty of time. However, I'm not sure how helpful my cooking skills will be. Would you mind showing me how you make your biscuits?"

"Sure, it is easy." Selena smiled, her white teeth a stark contrast to her brown skin. "I will teach you."

Jake was enjoying the easy exchange between the two women. "Looks like you ladies have big plans, and I can't wait to eat the results."

Evangeline brought Jake's breakfast and poured his coffee. She offered a brief smile and sat down at the other end of the table. How Jake wished she and Juliet would change places. His mind filled with the delicious feeling of holding her hand.

"Selena is going to try some new recipes from the cookbook

my sister sent. Juliet, would you like to help?"

Juliet shot her a piercing glance, and Jake caught the look. "Juliet, answer your aunt."

"Sorry. Maybe after Dog comes home, I might help. Right now, I'm too worried to care 'bout much else." She began to cry again.

Evangeline stood and took Juliet in her arms, stroking her hair and cooing to her. In a few minutes, the girl calmed and turned to Jake.

"Sorry I'm so sour. I'll go do my chores now. Maybe Dog will be back before I get done." Juliet wiped tears with her sleeve as she headed out the back door.

"You shore do know how to get that young'un outta her sour mood." Cookie's remark echoed Jake's thoughts, but he remained quiet and continued eating.

"I see you slept well." Evangeline's eyes lingered on him a little longer than usual.

"Yeah, I did, and I took time givin' all my worries to the Lord."

"No wonder you look rested." Evangeline poured him more coffee. "When your spirit is at peace, it makes all the difference."

"Miss Evangeline, did I hear you say you was goin' to the Farley's today?" Cookie asked.

"Yes. Jake arranged for Artie to take me. Once I learn the way, I can take myself."

"Not in these parts, missy." Cookie's voice was paternal. "We don't like our womenfolk goin' nowhere alone."

"*Sí*, there are banditos and Indians who could bring you harm or kidnap you," Selena added. "A white woman could bring a good price."

"I had no idea." Evangeline's hand trembled as she removed Cookie's plate.

"Cookie could take you," Jake offered. "I have to go out again and see if I can find those strays."

"I thought we agreed Artie could take me—unless you have something more important for him to do."

Evangeline's insistence bothered Jake. How much time was she spending with that kid anyway? "How 'bout I send Manuel along with Artie?"

Evangeline crossed her arms and studied him. "If you think I need both of them—fine."

"Boss, I thought you wanted Manny to fix the broken door on the chicken coop?"

Cookie's mouth puckered, causing the upper lip to press against his nose—a sign the man was confused by Jake's comments.

"That won't take long. Artie's a little puny, and if an Indian sees two men, he won't bother to come near." Cookie's eye widened at Jake's words. The possibility of Indians bothering his family was slim, but Jake couldn't help the jealous feelings starting to surface.

"I'll tell Artie and Manny before I leave." He tried to sound matter-of-fact, wrestling with the idea of escorting her himself.

* * *

Evangeline, Manny, and Artie arrived at the Farley home about one in the afternoon. Juliet had declined to go. Her gloomy mood had returned when Dog did not.

Evangeline's breath caught at the castle-like structure before her. The place felt more like a fortress than a home. Where the Farleys got the wood for the three-story mansion, she could only begin to speculate.

A large woman, one of several household servants, greeted the visitors. In Spanish, Maria exchanged what Evangeline could only assume were pleasantries with both Manny and Artie.

Artie Weaver speaks Spanish? Surprising.

"Mrs. Marcum, me and Manny will stay out here while you visit." Artie sat on the steps.

Maria escorted Evangeline into the sitting room.

She guessed Mrs. Farley to be in her early twenties. Although her smile appeared genuine, her dull blue eyes were set in a sallow complexion surrounded by mousy brown hair. Her beige dress, although the latest fashion, did nothing for her appearance. She indicated the seat next to her.

Evangeline ran her hand over the luxuriant fabric of the chair. The gold threads running through the white roses were superior quality to the fine fabric she had purchased earlier.

Maria brought a silver tray with a tea service and plate of small cakes. Mrs. Farley dismissed her with her hand. "One lump or two?"

"A dear friend of mine once said a good cup of tea stands on its own." Evangeline raised the cup to her lips. This tea, much too strong, needed cream. Now she was forced to drink the bitter brew or risk insulting her hostess.

"Tell me all about yourself. Where do you come from? And please, call me Violet," her hostess said as she perched on the edge of her chair.

No sooner had Evangeline answered one question when Violet shot out another.

"Whatever possessed you to come out here?"

"Marriage."

"Were there no eligible bachelors in Missouri?"

"None I cared to marry." Evangeline squirmed in her seat, searching to turn the attention toward her hostess. "How did you come to live here?"

"Mr. Farley—Thomas—came to a party my cousin hosted back in Boston. He was quite the charmer."

Violet's accent sounded nothing like her school friends from Boston. *I wonder how long she actually lived there.*

The question remained unspoken as Violet went on. "One might say Thomas swept me off my feet. But there are days I would say he tripped me." There was no laughter, only silence as Violet picked up her teacup. "Thomas is quite the successful businessman. He holds interests in several companies back East."

Her hostess rambled on about her husband, their ranch, and

whatever else came to her mind. Evangeline had given up trying to actually respond to this stream of one-sided babble. The woman jumped from her schooling to who she knew in Boston to being the second Mrs. Farley. The first had died while birthing their baby.

"Lily has recently returned from boarding school."

"Where is she now?" Evangeline asked.

"I think I hear her on the veranda. But I don't know who she's talking to."

"Artie and Manny, I suppose. They brought me here."

"Common ranch hands?" Violet's face said it all. She went to the window and shouted, "Lily Farley, come in at once." She returned to Evangeline. "You must meet Lily. She is at the top of her class."

A young lady of about fifteen years, with curly brown hair and deep brown eyes, entered the room. Her royal blue riding frock accentuated her voluptuous figure.

"Yes, Mother." Lily glared at Violet.

"I want you to meet Mrs. Evangeline Marcum."

Lily gave a practiced curtsy. "It is nice to meet you, Mrs. Marcum."

"Come and have some tea, dear."

The girl began to whine. "Please, Mother, may I attend to my horse? Father would be so upset if I left him saddled on such a warm day. You know how particular he is about the horses." Turning to Evangeline, she spoke in a much friendlier tone. "Father purchased a thoroughbred for me and insists he be cared for properly."

Violet frowned at the girl. "Very well, then."

"Mrs. Marcum, would you mind instructing Artie to help me? No one is in the stable at the moment." Lily's syrupy pretense nauseated Evangeline.

"Why not go and ask him yourself?"

After Lily left, Violet's words turned sharp. "Go and ask him? Evangeline, dear, servants do not get a choice. You must be careful. If you do not take charge, they will take advantage of you at every turn."

Why do people insist on telling me how to behave? First the Hanks, now Violet.

"My husband warned me when I first came here. But I was too kind. Learn from the voice of experience. If you give them choices, they will choose to do nothing but lay about." Violet patted Evangeline's hand like a mother instructing a toddler.

Evangeline ignored the unpleasant tea and looked about the room. "My, what a lovely painting." On closer inspection, she found the painting rather uninspired, but the new focus brought back Violet's more pleasant side.

Soon, her hostess had Evangeline's arm tucked into the crook of her own and was showing off the house. Violet mentioned the paintings and furnishings had all been imported from a mansion in England. Evangeline assumed this was the very furniture Jake had spoken of. She could only glance at it before Violet dragged her over to the china cabinet, pointing out the new platters Thomas had bought for her on his last business trip. When they returned to the parlor, Evangeline heard Lily's voice on the porch and assumed Artie was there as well.

"This time has been delightful, but I really must be going." Evangeline extricated her arm from Violet's grip.

"Yes, of course." Violet sounded disappointed. "We must do this again soon."

"Certainly. Perhaps you should come to my home next." Evangeline tried to say her good-byes, but Violet kept talking. Even after the wagon pulled away, she could hear her voice.

"That woman must not get much company," Artie said.

"Ay, *mamacita*, that is certain. And her daughter is the same," Manny added. "You should have seen how she look at Artie. The girl, she bat her eyes." Manny batted his eyes at Artie and put on his best female voice. "Sir, would you help me with my horse? I am too helpless. You are so big and strong."

Artie grabbed his hat firmly and flayed it at Manny, who

skillfully dodged the blow. The boy laughed and ducked as Artie tried to strike again. The hat landed squarely in Evangeline's face. She grinned in amusement as their expressions turned to stone. When laughter bubbled up inside her, it quickly spread to the men.

"So what did you think of Lily?" Evangeline asked.

"I didn't think nothin'." Artie kept his face forward.

"She *did* seem to like you," Evangeline added while winking at Manny.

Manny closed his lips tight and made a smooching sound.

"Next time, *you* help her with her horse," Artie shot back.

Peals of laughter erupted from the trio as they made their way back to the ranch.

CHAPTER 15

Jake took his time heading back from Joseph Skywater's spread. During their lunch, he learned Thomas Farley had taken it upon himself to interrogate all the local ranchers while his men checked brands.

Who does that skunk think he is, anyway? He has no right actin' like the law.

Smoldering anger pervaded the rest of his journey. Later, he found Manny in the corral grooming the black stallion he had recently unhitched from the wagon. "How was your trip to the Farleys'?"

"I think Mrs. Marcum was glad to leave."

"How do you mean?"

"When we left, that Farley woman was still talking. We could hear her up the road. The *Señora,* she laughed about her tired ears."

"What did you and Artie do while the ladies visited?"

"We waited outside. Maria, she brought us some food, and after that, the *Señorita* Lily, she flirted with Artie. He had to go help her with her horse. She did not need no help." Manny grinned, looking so much like his mother. "Your wife, she is funny."

"How is she funny?" Jake had never seen that side of her.

"She teased Artie about *Señorita* Lily, and they kept saying funny things to each other. I have never met a white woman as friendly as *Señora* Marcum."

Jake's mind went down a dark path. What kind of relationship was growing between his wife and Artie? Jealousy churned in his stomach, bringing reminders of Nora's attentions toward Robert when she was promised to him.

Juliet's screams interrupted his thoughts. Gunfire split the air. Angry shouts spurred Jake to action. He raced from the stable toward the melee, Manny at his heels.

Juliet's fists pummeled Bart's chest as Evangeline tried to pull the girl away. Juliet grabbed Bart's shirt. "I hate you. I hate you." Tears streamed down her face as Bart pulled her hands off his shirt. His pocket ripped with the effort. Evangeline gripped Juliet's arms as she disengaged from her prey. Evangeline hugged her close and half-dragged her toward the porch.

"How dare you upset this child with such a heartless deed," she shot back over her shoulder.

"What's happening here?" Dog's right front leg was mangled. Jake squatted down to get a better look, and Dog growled. Muscles and tendons were severed, blood trickling everywhere.

Bo broke the silence. "Bart was gonna put Dog outta his misery like they done for my horse. He didn't mean to upset the little missy." Bo's words were childlike and pleading.

Bart turned his head away and spit a stream of tobacco.

"I told Bart to hold off," Walters added, irritation filling his voice. "We all knew how upset Miss Juliet would be about killing her dog."

"He was just tryin' to help," Bo whined.

Bart flashed a look that was surely meant to silence him. Bo pulled his hat from his head and stared at his feet.

Walters shot a fierce look at the two men. "Juliet went at Bart like some wild thing, and the gun went off in the air. Then Mrs. Marcum lit out after her. Well, you heard all that."

As Jake rose to his feet, he looked at each man individually, not only to establish his authority but to contemplate his next move. He fixed his gaze on Bart. He could see anger and humiliation in the man's eyes. "I know you weren't tryin' to upset Juliet. Lord knows she upsets easy. But this was not your decision."

Bart walked away swearing under his breath with Bo limping after him.

Jake turned his attention back to Dog. He found himself torn between shooting Dog or shooting Bart for being so stupid.

Evangeline reappeared with Juliet as Tony said, "Shall I take Dog somewhere?"

"We are *not* shooting Dog, and that is the end of it." Evangeline knelt to get a better look at the leg. The mongrel showed his teeth, and a low growl pierced the air. "Let me take care of him." Her voice softened as she turned to Jake. "I agree … it's bad. Let me try amputating. He may make a full recovery."

"Who ever heard of a three-legged dog?" Manny scoffed, his remark causing more tears to pool in Juliet's eyes.

"Aren't you the smart one? If she can save his life, Dog will figure out how to walk on three legs."

Jake's heart melted at the girl's face. Against his better judgment, he gave his consent.

Evangeline went into action. "Jake, fashion a muzzle. Take Dog into the house and lay him on the table. Selena, cover the table with some old bedding, and get my black bag. Cookie, start boiling water for my instruments. I'll get things set up."

***

"Hold still." Jake forced a makeshift muzzle on Dog's growling mouth as the animal writhed.

"I cannot hold him much longer," Manny said.

Dog howled when Jake hoisted him up off the ground. He struggled as he rose with the wiggling mutt. *I'm gonna drop this fool animal.* "Boy, you're gonna be fine."

Loud whines replaced the growls.

Juliet touched her pet. "Be brave. It'll be okay." Dog whimpered, his eyes fixed on Juliet.

Once inside, the animal tried to wiggle free.

"Now, now," Juliet cooed. Dog calmed at her voice.

Jake, Manny, and Cookie held the animal on the table as he growled and whined. Jake turned to Manny. "Take Juliet outside."

"No, I want to help," the girl protested.

"Let her stay." Evangeline's hands held the girl's shoulders.

"She's a child," Jake snapped.

"It's her dog." Evangeline matched his tone. Her next words were softer. "I think Dog needs her. He trusts her."

"It's gonna be fine. Don't worry." Juliet stroked the mutt's massive head, and his growls reduced to whimpers.

Once Dog was positioned securely on the table, Evangeline poured chloroform on a rag.

"Juliet, take this cloth and place it on Dog's nose."

Juliet lovingly rubbed the animal's fur as the medication took effect. After a few sniffs, he stilled and the men released their grip.

"Is he dead?" Manny asked.

"Course not," Juliet snapped, turning to Evangeline. "Right? He ain't dead."

"No, the chloroform put him to sleep." She paid close attention to the animal's breathing. "I suggest everyone pray."

Cookie took her cue. "Father, we commit this here surgery into your hands. And this fine dog as well. We trust you to make things go well. We ask this in Jesus' name." A chorus of *amens* ended the prayer.

"I have never operated on an animal before, and I have no idea if I gave him the correct amount of chloroform." Evangeline ran her hands down her apron. "Juliet, I want you to keep an eye on him. If he looks like he's waking up, give him more chloroform."

Juliet's face was etched with determination. "Yes, ma'am."

"Selena, are the instruments sterilized?"

"*Sí.*" Selena handed the pan to her and slipped out of the room.

Jake's stomach lurched as he waited for instructions. The chloroform reminded him of field hospitals.

Evangeline used tongs to arrange all the instruments on the table. "Cookie, you hand me the instruments when I signal you. They are laid out in the order I will need them."

Cookie agreed, his face a little ashen.

Evangeline handed a blanket to Manny. "Hold this up between

Juliet and me." Manny went around to the other side of the table out of Evangeline's way but close to Dog's head.

"Jake, talk to Juliet. Ask her about our visit to Miss Woods."

One look at Juliet confirmed to Jake the wisdom in Evangeline's words. She looked so tiny and helpless petting Dog's nose. She needed her focus away from the surgery. He hoped he could keep her talking. He'd rather be anywhere else at this moment himself. He exhaled and tried to give his best smile to his niece.

"Darlin', tell me about Bertha Woods. Your aunt told me she had great cookies."

"Yes, sir." Her voice was weak.

"Heard you had six."

"Did not." Juliet looked up at her uncle, defiance in her tone. "I only had three. It would be piggy to have six."

"She a good cook?"

"Yes, sir." She stopped talking and stared at Dog.

"Tell me more."

"What do you wanna know?" Juliet's voice was barely audible.

Jake looked at Evangeline for help.

"Tell him about her house and the story she told you." Evangeline motioned for Cookie to hand her the saw.

Jake wished he could remain as calm as Cookie. Sweat formed on his back as his eyes fell on Manny's youthful face. The boy was obviously mesmerized by Evangeline's actions as his white knuckles gripped the blanket.

Jake turned his attention back to Juliet and touched her cheek. "Tell me about her home."

Juliet described the house just as Evangeline had the night before. She had not mentioned, however, the ram's head over the mantle. Jake wondered if Evangeline left out that detail just to give Juliet the joy of sharing it. He only wished it were under more pleasant circumstances.

"Did Mr. Woods shoot the ram?" Jake realized his poor choice of words, but it was too late to take them back. Fortunately, Juliet didn't make the connection.

"Oh, no, Mr. Ram was a pet." Juliet gave him her full attention.

"A pet?" Jake could hear the saw. His muscles tensed.

Juliet's voice quickened at the sound. "Yes, Bertha told me. She said to call her Bertha, so I did. That was okay, wasn't it? Should I have called her Miss Woods?"

"That's fine, honey." Jake again touched her cheek.

Juliet rambled even faster. "She said when she was a child that Mr. Ram was her only friend. Her pa had raised him from a baby 'cause his momma didn't want him. Her pa gave him into her care. Mr. Ram didn't like nobody but her." Juliet grew quiet as she stared at her unconscious pet. As the blanket fluttered near her head, she turned from it and continued her story, stroking Dog with more vigor.

"She told me somethin' funny 'bout how he used to butt people who came too close to her. I don't remember it right now, but it sure was funny." A tear trickled down her cheek. "He was the papa to most of their flock. When Mr. Ram died, Bertha's pa had his head stuffed and hung over the mantle."

"What did you think of that?" Jake asked. He had to keep his mind on Juliet's words. The smell of chloroform and blood made his stomach queasy, bringing back unwanted battlefield memories. He reached for her still hand. Together, they stroked Dog's head. He tried his best to encourage the frightened girl while battling his rumbling stomach.

Juliet broke the momentary silence. "I thought it a bit peculiar, but Bertha's pretty peculiar herself. She repeats herself a lot. But she's real smart." The girl took a cleansing breath and fixed her eyes on him. "Uncle Jake, she can tell you what the weather was like on any day. She asked me when I was born. When I told her, she said it be a Tuesday and the day rainy and cold. Then she said the moon be full that night. Seems pretty smart, don't you think?"

"Yes, I do."

"And we are done." Evangeline's words drew a collective cheer from the group.

Juliet kissed Dog's nose. The large animal's upper torso was bandaged.

"*Señor* Dog's bed is ready." Selena pointed toward the hall.

Cookie and Jake lifted Dog from the table and took him to a pallet on the floor in Juliet's room. His niece arranged the blankets around him.

Jake hugged her tight. "You're such a brave young lady. I'm so proud of you."

"I'm gonna sit right here and be his nurse," Juliet said from her place on the floor.

Jake ruffled her hair and left the room. He found his wife putting her instruments in boiling water. "Thank you."

"Don't thank me too soon. He could still die. I took the whole leg off to be sure there was clean flesh. Otherwise, there is a chance of gangrene. I have no idea what to give a dog for pain."

"I'm sure you'll figure it out."

"Your confidence is appreciated. But I'm not an animal doctor. I'm afraid if Dog dies, I am only delaying her sorrow." Evangeline scrubbed the table thoroughly with carbolic acid. "This table wasn't the best place to perform surgery. If I had been thinking, we could have set up something in the barn. I need to scrub it a few more times."

"If you say so. Thanks again for what you done for Juliet."

"You're welcome." Evangeline kept her eyes on the task at hand. "You did a great job yourself. I couldn't have done it alone."

"I think you could do anything you set your mind to."

As he turned to leave, Evangeline spoke. "Thank you."

"For what?"

Evangeline laid down her rag and pushed stray hairs out of her face. "For not arguing with me. For having confidence in me."

Jake shrugged. "One look at Juliet, I couldn't say no."

Besides, he was finding it hard to say no to Evangeline about anything.

CHAPTER 16

B art was not in the stable, so Jake headed toward the back door of the bunkhouse. He needed to explain a few things to the man. Warn him to rein in his surliness. Jake's mind filled with visions of what might have happened if Bart hadn't been stopped. Through the open window, he saw Bart sitting at the table working his way through a whiskey bottle. Pete sat quietly in the corner whittling on a piece of wood.

"Dumbest thing I ever saw—savin' a dog. Shoulda shot 'em."

"Bart, shhh. Not so loud. You're in enough trouble," Bo whispered from across the table.

Bart raised his head and took another swig. "Who cares who hears me? Looks like that woman wears the pants 'round here now."

Jake's muscles twitched as the interaction unfolded before him. Alcohol was contraband on the Double M. He fisted his irritation and remained silent.

"You need to stop now!" Bo knocked his chair over as he stood and lunged for the bottle. Bart slapped his hand away, and Pete shot out the door.

Leaning closer, Bo flayed his hand toward the bottle until his fingertips touched it. Bart jerked it away and rose up, punching Bo in the face.

The front door opened just as Bo's head bounced off the wall. Duke and Artie rushed in with Pete on their heels. Artie knelt beside his friend. "Bo, what happened?"

Bart glared at him. "Come any closer, and you'll get the same."

Artie was trembling but returned the glare before turning back to the injured man. "Your lip's split open. How's your head?"

"I feel a mite faint."

"Here, let me help you to your bunk." Artie and Pete lifted Bo as he whimpered in pain.

"Quit your cry-babyin'. You ain't hurt that bad," Bart snarled through slurred speech.

Duke stepped forward, fists clenched. "Shut your mouth and put the bottle away."

Bart drank the rest of the whiskey and turned the bottle upside down. "None for you."

Artie spoke up as Duke moved toward the drunk. "Hey, Duke, he ain't worth losin' your job over. He can't get no drunker. Leave him be."

Jake moved from the shadows. The voices grew louder as he headed toward the door.

"Yeah, this cow pie ain't worth losin' my job over." Duke smirked as he straightened his stance and turned his back.

Bart growled.

"Watch out!" Artie screeched.

Jake stepped in the back door just as Bart smashed the empty bottle on Duke's head. One of the shards caught Artie on the cheek. Bart stormed out the front door without giving Jake a second glance. The sound of Artie's high-pitched wails filled the room.

*** ***

Before Jake could take any action, Manny, Tony, and Solomon appeared.

Duke sat in a pool of blood. Solomon grabbed a sheet off the nearest bunk and applied pressure to Duke's head. Tony led Artie to a chair. Pete stood in the corner and remained silent.

Artie drew himself up to his full height. "I'm gonna kill Bart."

"Hold on there, *gringo*." Tony grabbed his arm.

Jake's boots crunched broken glass as he offered Duke a hand and helped him to a chair.

Evangeline appeared in the doorway with her medical bag.

"What happened?"

"Bart slammed Bo against the wall." Artie's voice trembled.

"I got me a split lip," Bo said. "Bart didn't mean nothin'. It was the whiskey done it."

Artie glowered at Bo. "The whiskey didn't bust a bottle over Duke's head and almost kill him. Bart done it on purpose."

"Hey, kid, your face is bleedin'," Jake said as he pointed toward Artie.

Artie touched his face. He tried to stand but turned white as his legs wobbled.

Jake helped him sit back in the chair. "Evangeline can see to it."

Walters rushed in. "Bart lit out on his horse. You want me to go after him, Boss?"

"We'll deal with him if he bothers to show his face 'round here again." Jake wondered if anything else would happen before the sun went down. "Boys, clean up the mess in here."

Evangeline picked glass shards out of Duke's head. He moaned, his eyes closed and his hands gripping the chair.

"How can I help?" Jake asked.

"You could clean Bo's and Artie's cuts. I can stitch them after I'm done here."

"I'd rather you do it, Miss Evangeline," Artie said.

Jake disliked the familiar way Artie addressed his wife. He scowled as he cleaned Bo's split lip. Bo winced from the sting.

Still scowling, Jake moved on to Artie. The young man lowered his eyes, avoiding Jake's scrutiny. Jake grabbed his jaw, causing Artie to grimace and jerk away.

"Sit still." Jake's tone was harsh as tears glistened in the kid's eyes. "Buck up, boy."

"Jake needs to see if there is any glass in your face," Evangeline said.

Artie let Jake clean his wound. Jake saw no glass but derived a measure of satisfaction from dabbing the man's cheek one more time. Artie grimaced from the sting of the antiseptic.

Evangeline wrapped Duke's head in a bandage, reminding Jake of his first night with her. A smile replaced his frown as she deftly stitched Bo's lip.

"Two should do it. Don't suck on your lip, and it will heal nicely."

Next, she moved to Artie. She touched his face tenderly, running her finger down his cheek. Jake's scowl returned.

"Will it leave a scar?" Artie asked.

"Maybe a little one. I'll try sewing it so there is little scarring when it's healed." Her voice was gentle as she spoke. "We can pray for the Lord to heal it nicely so your face is handsome for Miss Lily."

Artie tried not to laugh while being stitched.

"Stay still." Evangeline touched the tip of his nose.

"Stop sayin' things to make me laugh."

Jake wadded the damp disinfectant cloth tightly in his hand as he saw the look that passed between them.

"Sorry." Evangeline giggled as she moved in closer again.

Jake slammed the door on his way out.

***

Jake turned the dirty straw over and over with the pitchfork before depositing it onto a pile. His mind was filled with thoughts of Nora and Robert. Seeing them together after she had implied Jake was her choice. Drinking to chase away the pain. Memories long since buried, yet oh-so-fresh now. His heartache rekindled. *I should never have sent for Evangeline.* Jake stabbed the soiled straw with a vengeance. *How stupid I am.*

He turned toward the stable door as it creaked open.

"There you are." Evangeline looked flushed, a tendril of burgundy hair falling down her cheek. "You left so suddenly I was afraid there might have been another fight."

Jake kept his back to her.

"What's wrong?"

The thick silence lingered as he filled another pitchfork and emptied it. "How long you been carryin' on with Artie?"

"What?" Evangeline's voice trembled.

He felt bile rise in his throat. "I ain't blind. I saw you flirtin' with him in there."

"With Artie? Please, Jake, I—"

"Don't play games with me. I know flirtin' when I see it." Jake looked her full in the face. The tight muscles in his neck began to throb.

"Jake, you don't understand."

"Oh, I understand. There was your flirty smile, and the laughin' all close-like." Jake waited for the familiar. He steeled himself. This was when Nora would laugh at his jealousy. Her coquettish smile would wrap itself around his heart, and he would believe anything she said. *Not this time. I'll not play the fool twice.*

Evangeline walked away a few steps before turning back. Her eyes were sorrowful. "Please believe me when I say I have had no experience with flirting." A single tear trickled down her cheek. The quiet that followed, unnerved Jake as she looked at him.

He turned away, confused by this unexpected response. *Can I trust her?*

She came closer and took the pitchfork out of his hand, leaning it up against the wall. Her words came out slowly. "Jacob Marcum, I am married to you. I made a commitment before God to be your wife." Her fingers caressed his face.

Her touch stirred him. Jake saw the sincerity in her eyes. As relief replaced anger, he drew her to him, encircling her with his arms. She looked up at him—tears still pooled in her eyes. No words came. Instead, his lips covered hers, and she relaxed in his arms.

After a moment, Jake released her.

Evangeline seemed to be searching for words before speaking. "Artie is like ... like a sister to me."

"A *sister*?"

"Did I say sister? I meant brother. You make me say the strangest things." She backed away. "Sometimes, Mr. Marcum, you don't see the truth when it's standing right in front of you."

CHAPTER 17

Before daybreak, with her hair in a long braid and still dressed in her nightgown and robe, Evangeline puttered around the kitchen. Her dreams had turned to nightmares, caused by the excitement of the previous day. Her subconscious had transformed the wounded animal into a dying man. Stitches became bloody battlefield injuries, and jealous words brought back her own hurt feelings from an unfaithful fiancé. Throughout the nightmares, memories of a soft kiss and firm caress kept her from entering into deeper despair. Perhaps Fiona's vision *was* from the Lord, and shame could be replaced with love.

Evangeline's mind struggled to find a place to bury the past. Comforting Scripture lay dormant somewhere in her fatigued brain.

The dawn brought Jake, rumpled and unshaven, to the kitchen. In his presence, Evangeline felt peace flow through her. She was becoming accustomed to his admiring gaze.

"I need to check on Dog," she said.

"I'll go with you."

He followed her to Juliet's room and opened the door. They found the girl snuggled close to Dog on her bedroom floor. The mongrel raised his head without a sound.

"Looks like he made it through," Jake whispered.

Evangeline leaned wearily against the doorframe. "At least I didn't kill him with the surgery or the chloroform. As long as he's quiet, I'll not disturb him. Once Juliet is awake, I'll look closer."

Jake followed her back to the kitchen. "In case I haven't said so, you were somethin' else yesterday."

She brought his coffee to the table and sat across from him. "I told you I was good at sewing," she said playfully.

"You got a lot of practice yesterday." He picked up the mug. "I owe you an apology."

Evangeline looked away from his penetrating gaze. "For the misunderstanding about Artie? That's forgotten."

"Jealousy makes a man act like a fool."

Evangeline's heart fluttered at the thought of him being jealous. It was an unfamiliar feeling she pushed aside.

"I don't care to play the fool." He set his mug down and flexed his fingers. "What I'm apologizin' for is another foolish action—my pride. Keepin' your doctorin' a secret is wrong."

"I'm glad no one knows." Evangeline fidgeted with the spoon in the sugar bowl.

"Why?"

"People here need to get to know me. I want them to like me for me. Violet already expects me to be something special because I'm a white woman married to a successful rancher. What kind of expectation will people have when they find out I'm a doctor?"

"We don't have a doc within fifty miles," Jake argued.

"Do you realize how much time I would spend away from home if word got out?"

"But I see how gifted you are. If you need my permission, I'll gladly give it."

"You do realize I'm not seeking your permission." Evangeline's clipped words shamed her. She resumed stirring the sugar, clinking the edges of the bowl as the spoon circled the white crystals, the sound magnified by the silence between them.

"While I practiced medicine with my brother-in-law, people had expectations of me. Mostly that I would fail in my duties. The men seemed to need to take me down a few pegs, and some of the women thought it unseemly for me to do a man's job. Some became jealous if I treated their husbands. Right now, I have no desire to be more of an oddity than a mail-order bride."

"I think everyone will accept you over time." Jake's confident assurance fought against her experience. His respect for her abilities warmed her, but if she threw herself back into her career, it would no doubt end badly for both of them.

She searched for the right words. "I read in the Bible where a soldier who married was exhorted to spend a year with his wife before going off to war again. So I'm taking time off from my medical practice to spend with you. It's obvious we still don't know each other."

"You're a wise woman, Evangeline Marcum." His deep voice spoke her new name in a way that caused a sweet tremor down her spine. "I wish I could follow that furlough advice." A playful growl accompanied his words.

"You could start by going to town with me this morning." She smiled sweetly as she went to pour hot water from the kettle into her teapot.

"You sure go into town a lot. If I get there once a month, that's somethin'. What you have a mind to buy now?"

"Nothing. I promised Bertha I would meet her there today."

"You've gotten pretty friendly with Miss Woods, I see."

"There is something else I learned from my visit to the Woods' home." Evangeline wrapped a rag around the teakettle handle and poured water through the strainer placed atop the teapot opening. "The Hanks won't extend any more credit to them until their bill is paid."

"You figure on payin' their bill too," Jake groused. "You plan on payin' off everyone's bill?"

Evangeline matched his frown as she carried the coffee and tea on a tray back to the table. Jake refilled his mug before Evangeline had the opportunity.

His aggravation obvious, she changed her tactics. Lifting her cup to her lips, she gave him a saucy smile. "If you are going to make false accusations, I'll not tell you what I'm doing, and I'll ask Artie to take me. He doesn't question what I do." She feigned a pout.

Jake's eye brightened at the teasing. "He's not married to you either."

"Aren't we both glad of that?"

He chuckled, and she raised her cup, blocking his view.

"Tell me your plan. Then I'll decide if I'll take you."

"I showed you the beautiful yarn Bertha makes and the fine cloth she weaves."

"You figure they could sell it to the store and settle their bill."

"More than settle it. They could get cash for other things as well. I promised to go along and help her negotiate a good price."

"I'd like to see you wrangle with that Hanks outfit. Cordelia's known to buy from the locals as cheap as she can." Jake leaned his chair back on two legs. "What time?"

"I promised to meet her at ten o'clock. We can't be late or Bertha will worry."

"Think Dog'll be alright while we're gone?"

"He'll have to be. Bertha is too excited to delay the trip. I hope I'm not taking you away from more pressing matters."

"They'll be here when I get back. Besides, my crew's able to handle the ranch while I'm gone. Escortin' my beautiful wife 'round town seems like the most important business I have goin' today."

"I guess I should check all my patients before I leave," she said.

"Good idea. Wonder if Bart came back to the bunkhouse. I doubt he'll show his face unless it's to get paid."

"Are you going to fire him?"

"Got no choice. Drinkin' ain't allowed on my ranch. I knew he was drinkin'. Shoulda fired him months ago. But up till yesterday, he did his work and minded his own business."

"Won't you be shorthanded?"

"I can manage till the cattle drive. I'll hire more men then."

Evangeline placed her cup on its saucer. "Can I ask you something personal? Something I've been curious about for a while now."

"Sure thing."

"Who is Johnny? You mention him in your sleep."

Jake's coffee splashed as he set it back on the table. He retrieved a cloth and, without looking at his wife, wiped up the spill. "I guess you should know. I ain't never talked about it."

"I'm a good listener."

He returned the cloth to the hook near the sink, tarrying longer than necessary before lowering himself back into his chair. "Johnny was a young kid who should never have gone to battle. He claimed he was fourteen but looked more like ten. He joined up the last year of the war. Stuck to me like a tick on a dog. I kept tellin' him not to follow me so close. When a cannonball exploded a few feet from us, it killed him. I came out with a wound on my face, and that was all. I'll never forget Johnny layin' there covered in blood." Jake fingered the top of the table. "Before I got to him, the sergeant grabbed my arm and made me keep goin'."

"So you dream of the explosion?"

Jake remained silent for several heartbeats. "No, I dream I'm searchin' for him."

"Do you know his last name?"

"It was Holt. Why?"

"Clara Barton had a list of soldiers missing in action. She has been successful in reuniting families with their kin. I realize it has been a few years, but I imagine she still has the list. I could write and see if she knows about him. All I would need is the regiment, his name, and age."

"You know Clara Barton?"

"I know of her. She secured permission for medical teams to go directly to the field and collect the wounded. She opened the door for Shamus and me to do the same."

"I told you he's dead."

"Do you know that for sure?"

Jake picked up his coffee. "Sure seems impossible he'd still be alive. Maybe when things settle down around here, we can write to Miss Barton and see if she can help."

***

Selena hurried in past Jake and put on her apron. "*Señor*, I am so sorry to be late."

"Nothin' to be sorry about, Selena. Me and Evangeline beat the rooster out of bed is all."

"Is something wrong? Is it Dog?" The housekeeper wrung her hands.

"No, everything is fine." Evangeline gave her a reassuring smile.

"I will have the breakfast pronto."

"And I will get dressed in the meantime." Evangeline rose as Cookie's familiar whistle signaled he was headed toward the house.

Jake remained seated, savoring his coffee. *What if Johnny is alive?*

"Hey, Boss, what you up so early for? Dog okay?" Cookie's face showed fatigue.

"Yeah, he's doin' fine. Can't a body get up early to greet the day without everybody assumin' somethin's wrong?" Jake scolded.

"How's Miss Juliet?"

"Sleepin' soundly on the floor next to Dog."

Juliet entered the room just then. "I'm up." She yawned and gave Jake a big hug.

"How's Dog?" Jake hugged her back, kissing the top of her head.

"He woke up cryin' so I laid down next to him. I think he's gonna be fine. But he probably needs to go out."

"Cookie, call Manny to help me."

Manny joined Jake in the bedroom a few minutes later. Together, they managed to get the big dog outside. It took a few tries, but Dog finally maneuvered around on three legs. He was slow and wobbly, but he took care of business—after which he collapsed on the ground and gave Manny a mournful stare.

Manny rubbed his chin. "I think he wants to go back to bed now."

Juliet had brought the bedding out to the porch, so Jake and Manny laid Dog on it.

"*Señor*, are we going to stay here and move the dog every time he needs to sniff a tree?"

"Maybe Solomon can make a cart to push him around in so Juliet can tend to him."

Evangeline appeared, holding a pan of fresh water. Clean bandages were tucked under her arm. She showed Juliet how to change the animal's bandages and pulled something from her apron pocket. "If he starts crying a lot, you can give him this tablet. If you can get him to swallow it, he'll feel better."

Manny knelt beside Juliet. "If Dog will let me touch him, I can get him to take it. My pa taught me how to get horses to swallow medicine." But when Manny tried to pet the animal, a growl rose from the canine. Manny jerked his hand back. "Or I can show Juliet."

Jake covered a chuckle with a cough.

Evangeline looked away before speaking. "Cookie, can you have my other three patients stop by the house after breakfast so I can look at their wounds?"

* * *

Evangeline gave Duke some powder for his headache, but there wasn't anything she could do for his disposition.

"Next time I see Bart, I'm gonna pound his no-account hide into the dirt." Duke pressed his right fist into his left hand for emphasis.

"Let it go, Duke," Artie remarked from the kitchen chair while Evangeline looked at his wound. "He's probably long gone by now."

Duke seemed to shake it off, and Artie said no more.

"Well, young man, your stitches look clean. In a few days, if all goes well, I can take them out." Evangeline gathered up the soiled bandages. "I have a cream that helps reduce scarring. Do you want some?"

"Sure thing." Artie smiled his thanks.

"Ha! You afraid the ladies won't like you so much with a scar? Not that they like you so much now." Duke punched Artie's arm as he rose from his place at the table.

Artie ignored him.

"You got too purty a face for a man anyway. A mark would make you look manlier like me," Duke said.

"You're gonna have wounds on the top of your head. Maybe you should shave your head so the ladies can see those scars?"

Duke strutted about the kitchen. "Maybe you should shave your head to make the ladies think you're older."

Artie rolled his eyes, and Duke slapped him on the back. "Now don't get all mad, kid. You know I was joshin'."

Artie placed his hat on his head. "Yeah, well, ain't my fault God made me so good lookin'." He slapped Duke's back in return.

Evangeline couldn't help but laugh at their tomfoolery. "Where is Bo?"

"He won't leave his bed." Duke placed his hat gingerly on his bandaged head. "Been cryin' 'bout Bart may be lost and somebody ought to go find him."

"Bo is awful attached to Bart. Can't figure out why," Artie said as the two men headed out the door.

***

Evangeline knocked on the bunkhouse door before entering. She found Bo huddled under his blanket, rocking back and forth. She placed her black bag on the table.

"How are you feeling today?"

Bo turned to face her, his lip swollen to twice its size.

"Let me see." She placed her hand on his jaw and rotated his head to get a closer look. "If you chew on your lip, it's not going to heal. I might need to add some more stitches. I'm going to give you something to help you sleep. When you wake up, your lip should be normal size."

Bo's large hand grabbed her arm as she turned toward her bag. "No thank you, ma'am, I don't intend to sleep. I need to go find Bart."

"I think …" Evangeline saw the determination in his puffy eyes. She removed his hand from her arm. Staring into the young man's eyes, she knew there was no way to stop him. *Lord, I need your wisdom.*

"If you promise to stop bothering your lip, I'll tell Mr. Walters you are well enough to work, and you can ask him about finding Bart."

"I promise."

"May I ask why you have such affection for the man?" She hoped her repulsion didn't show.

Bo lowered his voice. "Don't tell Bart, but he reminds me of my pa."

"How?"

"Pa went to the war too. He was nice when he wasn't drinkin'. Then he come home from the war, and he weren't nice no more, even when he was sober."

"How is your pa now?"

"Don't know. He up and left one day when I was twelve. Ma never would tell me why he left. But I know why."

"I'm listening."

He looked at the floor. "I told him I hated the mean pa, and I wished the nice pa would come back." Bo rose from his seat. "Excuse me, ma'am, I got to go find Bart."

Evangeline's heart broke as he walked away. *A child's guilt is a powerful thing.*

CHAPTER 18

Jake turned at the sound of the wagon, a protective arm around his wife. Bertha waved with childlike enthusiasm from her perch.

"Miss Evangeline, lookee here. I brung what you asked." Her voice rose above the creak of the old wagon.

Jedidiah's restraining hand kept his daughter from leaping out of the wagon before it stopped. As soon as he helped her down, she hugged Evangeline.

Jed shook Jake's hand. "I hope your wife's plan works." The older man took off his hat and wiped the sweat from his brow with his shirtsleeve. "Since the blizzard two years past wiped out most of our sheep and the drought ruined our crops, it's been hard." He put the hat back on. "Never thought of sellin' Bertha's weavin' to the general store."

"Evangeline'll be sure Mrs. Hanks does right by Bertha," Jake said with confidence.

"Hope so. Ain't seen Bertha this excited in a long time. Your wife's a fine woman."

"Yes, she is." Jake listened as Evangeline gave instructions to Bertha.

"Don't forget, my friend, to wait here. Count to one hundred before you come in."

"I will, *friend*." Bertha beamed. "I will count to one hundred. Pa will help me."

Jake took his wife's arm and led her toward the mercantile. Out of the corner of his eye, he saw Thomas Farley coming out of the saloon next door, dressed like a gambler except for the knee-high riding boots. He stopped to grab a cigar from inside his jacket pocket when he looked up and locked eyes with Jake. "Marcum, I'd like a word with you."

Under other circumstance, Jake wouldn't have given the man the time of day. But Evangeline and the Woods didn't need the man in their business.

Farley led Jake around the corner of the livery and looked around as if to ensure no one could overhear. "Are you aware there's been a considerable amount of cattle rustling?"

Jake's fist flexed involuntarily, expecting some insult to follow.

"I have been doing some investigating," Farley said.

"So I heard." Jake's fist tightened.

"Then you may have also heard not every ranch has been hit." Farley pointed his finger at Jake's chest. Jake stepped back, but Farley adjusted his stance to close the gap. "You and I need to get together and discuss this. Come up with a plan for catching the thieves."

"My guess is you already have a plan." Jake stared at the man without flinching.

Farley kept a poker face. "Perhaps you might ... help me perfect it."

"Who do you suspect?"

Farley bit off the end of his cigar and searched for a match before answering. "I prefer not to share my suspicions here." He lit his cigar and puffed on it methodically. Smoke rings filled the momentary silence. "Mrs. Farley would like to extend a dinner invitation to you and your wife for tomorrow night. We could discuss it then."

Farley's voice took on a superior tone which irked Jake. Sarcastic words formed on his lips, but the wiser notion of finding out what his neighbor was up to stopped him. "I'm sure Evangeline would enjoy an evenin' out. Why not ask some of the other ranchers so we can all discuss it?"

"The two of us have the largest investments and should come up with a plan first before informing the others."

Jake frowned at the man. "I don't see it that way."

"We will discuss a few ideas first, which gives us a starting place," Farley insisted.

"Fine." *Might as well give in.* "What time do you want us?"

"Seven would be excellent. I have heard wonderful things about your wife from Violet. She can't stop talking about her. Says she is a woman of refinement, comes from a fine family."

There it was—the reason Farley was getting so friendly all of a sudden. Jake suppressed a smile as he pictured all of them together. "I'm sure she'll find you very interestin'." Jake shook hands with Farley and walked back to the wagon.

Farley's in for a surprise when he meets my gal.

***

Cordelia Hanks greeted Evangeline before she stepped through the door. "Why, Mrs. Marcum, it is so good to see you again. How can I help you this fine day?"

"I remembered the dress you were wearing the first day we met and thought I'd like to buy a few yards of that material."

"Of course. Right this way." Cordelia maneuvered between the aisles back to the yard goods table. "Are you going to make a dress for yourself? The yellow is an excellent choice."

"Actually, my plan is to make curtains for Juliet's room."

Mrs. Hanks's eye twitched and a disgusted look enveloped her face as the doorbell chimed. "What is *she* doing here?"

"I told her to meet me here." Evangeline waved to Bertha, who clomped toward her, arms full of yarn and material.

"I brung you what you said." Bertha's face beamed with happiness.

"Look at this, Mrs. Hanks. You are in for a treat." Evangeline took the goods from Bertha's arms and laid them deliberately on top of the yellow material. "I have never seen broadcloth as finely woven as this." She held it up for the woman to examine.

The proprietress fingered the material. "Yes, it is very fine."

"You like it then, Mrs. Hanks? You like it fine?" Bertha's smile broadened.

"I had Bertha meet me here because I plan to send some of this fine broadcloth to my sister. She can make a suit for her husband. He's a *doctor*." Cordelia's brows flew upward, and Evangeline was glad the emphasis was not lost on the crass woman. "Notice the superior quality of the yarn, not to mention the brilliant colors."

Cordelia picked up a skein of yarn and examined it carefully. "Yes, this is finely spun."

"Do you like the colors? I can make any color you want. I can do green and red and brown and yellow and lots more. Do you like the colors?" Bertha stared at Cordelia in anticipation.

"Yes, they are lovely." Cordelia ran a strand through her fingers but kept her eyes on Evangeline. "Are you sending this to your sister as well?"

"Absolutely. And I'm confident she will want to purchase more yarn in the future." Evangeline turned to Bertha. "I did mention I wanted you to knit a scarf and hat to go with the sweater you are making for Juliet?"

"The sweater's done already." Bertha extracted the garment from under the broadcloth.

"Bertha, your talent is amazing," Evangeline exclaimed.

Cordelia's eyes squinted, relaxed, and sparked as she glanced sideways at Bertha.

Evangeline reached into her bag. "Bertha, let me pay you for all this, and Mrs. Hanks can help me wrap it securely for mailing." She deliberately counted out the money. "Twenty-three dollars. That's right, isn't it?"

"Yes, ma'am, it shore is." Bertha looked slyly at Mrs. Hanks. "I should have enough here to pay our bill."

"Let's go look, shall we?" Cordelia moved toward the front counter and tripped over a fifty-pound sack of flour in her excitement. After smoothing the front of her dress and patting her hair back in place, she stepped behind the counter and opened the ledger. "Let me see. You owe thirty dollars and fifteen cents."

Bertha turned to Evangeline. "Would you check them numbers? I'm not clever in numbers."

"May I?" Evangeline pointed to the ledger, and Cordelia turned it toward her.

"Mrs. Hanks, there appears to be a mistake. I see by my calculations, the Woods only owe twenty dollars and fifteen cents."

Cordelia shrugged her apology. "My husband tends to get in a hurry. Now, Bertha, I have a proposition for you. I want to stock your yarn and broadcloth in my store."

Bertha looked surprised, then placed her yarn and material on the counter. "Sure thing, Mrs. Hanks, but if you don't mind, I'd like Miss Evangeline to help figure out a fair price 'cause I'm not good at numbers. You can pay me, and then I can pay you for things we need."

"I was thinking of store credit."

"No, ma'am. I'll take cash."

"Very well. How is twenty-five cents a yard?"

"How about fifty cents a yard and twenty-five cents for each skein of yarn," Evangeline countered. "At that price you can add thirty percent, make a profit, and still keep the price fair. Bertha has another pattern that is suitable for lady's wool dresses and coats."

Cordelia extended her hand to Bertha to seal the agreement. "I must thank you, Mrs. Marcum, for bringing Miss Woods' talent to my attention. How clever you are." A knowing smile formed on her lips as she fingered the fine broadcloth.

Bertha ran outside to her father, who helped her carry the yarn and cloth from the wagon into the store. A few minutes later, Evangeline came out with a parcel and greeted Jake.

"I see you done good for Bertha." He looked quite pleased.

"I'm happy for the Woods. They are fine people. I wish others saw it." Her friends returned to the wagon for another load.

"I'm right proud of you." Jake looked long at his wife, and it made her neck tingle. He helped her into the wagon, his hands lingering longer than necessary. "By the way, Farley invited us to dinner tomorrow night, and I accepted."

"I'm surprised you agreed." Evangeline took the parasol from under the seat.

"He wants to discuss the rustlin' problem. I think he's made up his mind who done it and how to solve it. He wants my backin' before he goes through with his plan." Jake squinted against the bright morning sun.

"Backing? I thought—"

"Violet apparently thinks you're a *woman of refinement*, improvin' my station. Almost makes us equals."

"Almost?"

"There can only be one king." Jake laughed as he flicked the reins.

"How should I behave under the circumstances?"

"Shoot, I don't care none about impressin' his royal highness." Jake flicked the reins once more, causing the horses to quicken their pace and his wife to grip his arm tightly. "Be yourself, darlin'. Just be yourself."

She surprised herself with the silly giggle that filled the space between them. "You may live to regret that statement."

CHAPTER 19

Evangeline hurried to the wagon and took Jake's hand as he helped her in. After a long, full day, Jake wished he hadn't agreed to the dinner meeting. He barely got home in time to clean up and change into his new suit before they left.

"My, you look dashing." Evangeline's admiration warmed him.

"I can't escort my beautiful wife in my work clothes."

"Well, your new suit fits nicely." She reached over and straightened his collar. "Bertha's material makes this suit the finest I've ever made."

"I could never have afforded a suit this nice." Jake smoothed the front of the jacket. The gray cloth still had a new sheen to it. "When do you find the time?"

"Other than helping Selena at mealtime, I do little else. Sewing is my way of contributing to the household. Katie and I ran a seamstress shop before the war. I learned to produce a garment very quickly."

"My wife's a woman of many talents, I see."

Evangeline tugged on her gloves and patted her hair. "I hope this dress is appropriate. I didn't take the time to press a party frock. But if you are trying to impress the Farleys, maybe I should have."

"If you wore a feed sack, you'd impress the Farleys." Jake shot an admiring glance her way and enjoyed the look of pleasure that appeared on her face. "That blue dress is somethin'. Did you make it too?"

"No, Katie did. I won't be sewing anything for myself for quite a while. She has me well supplied."

"I thought you bought that yellow material to make a dress."

"And compete with Mrs. Hanks? Hardly. I made curtains for

Juliet's room."

Jake shifted the reins from one hand to the other. "I can't figure why you bothered with curtains. Not like we have neighbors close by."

"Juliet's growing up. And someday the men around here will notice and …"

"Of course, you're right. I don't like to think about her growin' up." Jake took her hand and squeezed it gently. "Thank you for carin'."

"You are very welcome." She returned his squeeze. "I love her so much."

"I can see that." He warmed to her confession. Jake placed both hands back on the reins, flipping them to encourage the horses to go faster. "Better not be late."

* * *

Jake sat in silent observation after Violet greeted them. She seemed anxious to make an impression. Her green party dress with silver accents was much better suited for a grand ball. He understood Manny's reference about the woman's need to talk. She carried the conversation from the weather to her new furniture to the latest fashion.

Throughout the meal, Thomas corrected her. "No, dear, it rained Thursday, not Tuesday." His voice was syrupy, and it made Jake want to go outside and hurl.

"I am so sorry, you are right." Violet seemed flustered and twisted her napkin. "My sister writes that satin slippers are the latest fashion."

"When you read her letter to me the other night it was silk, not satin." This time, her husband's voice was harsh.

"Perhaps you are right." Violet laughed nervously. "I am sure you are right."

Jake flinched at the way Farley spoke to his wife but held his tongue.

Once the last dish was removed from the table, Thomas loudly cleared his throat. Violet stopped mid-sentence and ducked her head. Farley patted his lips with his napkin and placed it on the table.

The man had to be at least ten years his wife's senior, his medium build neither handsome nor plain. His mannerisms and posture were those of a man full of conceit. He wore tall riding boots more suited to a fox hunt than a ranch. Jake felt a bit of pride when he compared his new suit to the one his host wore. Evangeline had done herself proud. He wished he could wipe the smug, kingly expression off his host's face.

Once Thomas had everyone's attention, he turned to Jake. "Women tend to have interest in such petty, unimportant things. Their little minds can't understand the weightier matters."

Jake knew trouble was brewing when Evangeline's eyes flashed. "I wouldn't say *all* women."

"The only intelligent ones I've had the misfortune to meet were ugly as dirt." Farley laughed, and the sound sickened Jake.

Violet intervened. "Let's have dessert in the parlor. I'll instruct Maria to serve us there."

Jake helped Evangeline from her chair, and Thomas extended his elbow to escort her to the parlor. Jake did the same for Violet. Maria followed with a tray of cake and coffee.

Evangeline smiled at Maria. "*Su pastel se ve delicioso, muchas gracias.*"

"I see you have picked up Spanish," Thomas remarked, obviously impressed. "That is a good way to keep these people on their toes. But there is no need to thank Maria. She is only doing what she is paid to do."

Evangeline's nostrils flared slightly, and Jake bit his lip to keep from grinning. "I find thanking the servants and being kind to them makes them better employees."

"On the contrary, my dear. One must show authority at all

times. Having a strong upper hand is important. Otherwise, they will try to steal from you. Mrs. Marcum, I am surprised you are not more aware, being from a fine New York family."

Jake saw a startled expression flash across his wife's face. She hesitated before answering. "I was born in New York State, but I am most recently from Missouri."

"Your maiden name is Olson. I've heard you are related to Carl Olson of Olson and Grayston." Farley leaned back in his chair, appearing to enjoy his interrogation.

Jake saw Evangeline's face pale.

"Yes, he was my uncle. He passed away last year."

Jake caught the slight tremble in her fingers as she set her coffee cup back on its saucer.

"I believe I heard of his passing the last time I visited New York." Thomas paused, obviously to allow his words to sink in, then shifted the conversation. "I am quite surprised you do not handle servants better. Violet tells me you consider your housekeeper a friend. I must advise you, that is a mistake."

"We all have our own ways of handlin' the help. Evangeline seems to do well," Jake said, jumping to his wife's defense.

"Jake, *you* were once the hired help, so you naturally feel that way. But trust me, if you want to have what I have, you must be of sterner stuff."

"More dessert anyone?" Violet picked up the cake knife.

Jake ignored the man's barb. "I'll have another slice. This is right fine cake, Mrs. Farley."

Violet looked at Thomas, who waved her off, preparing to light a cigar. Next, she turned to Evangeline.

"No, thank you. I'm so full I might burst. Your meal was delicious from start to finish."

Violet beamed at the compliment.

"Do you cook, Mrs. Marcum?" Thomas leaned back, drawing deeply from his cigar.

"Yes, on occasion."

"How interesting. Violet doesn't bother with cooking. She tells me you sew as well."

"I enjoy sewing."

"Perhaps you could teach Violet. She expresses to me often enough how bored she is. With servants doing all the work, she needs a diversion." He reached over and patted his wife's hand, a patronizing smile on his face.

"If she wants to learn, I will be happy to teach her." Evangeline turned to Violet. "I admire how well-read you are, Violet. Your collection of books is extensive."

Thomas smirked at her words. "Violet doesn't read those books. They are much too heady for her."

Jake searched his mind for a subject change. He was finding it difficult to do while holding his temper in check.

Evangeline defended her friend. "Violet graduated at the top of her class. How could they be too heady for her?"

"The top of her class at *finishing* school," Farley corrected. "She is well-versed in art and all manner of ladylike things. My library is too advanced for her. Her brain cannot comprehend the nuances of such writing."

"Apparently, you don't think much of intelligent women." Evangeline's voice no longer held the edge in check.

Ignoring her as if they had never spoken, he turned to Jake. "Shall we retire to the library to discuss our cattle?"

Jake reluctantly followed him. His mouth ached from biting his tongue. Once the door closed, he looked around the room. His eyes took in the shelves lined with books, the fine leather chairs, and the gun collection displayed tastefully in a mahogany cabinet. He walked over to the case to get a closer look. Every moment he remained silent calmed his anger. He perused the collection of weapons and admired a Whitworth Sniper rifle among them. He dismissed the thought of using it on his host.

"I'll thank you to be careful how you speak to my wife," Jake said as the man busied himself at a liquor cabinet in the corner.

Farley, cool and obviously undisturbed by Jake's words, extended a glass. "Brandy?"

Jake waved off the proffered drink. Thomas tasted the brandy as he indicated one of his overstuffed leather chairs. "I asked you here to talk about a plan to catch the cattle thieves."

"Go on."

"My plan is simple. We confiscate the cattle of Skywater and Abernathy."

"That's who you suspect—an Indian and a newcomer?" Jake frowned in disgust.

"We confiscate their cattle as a warning."

"A warnin' to who?"

"Many of these ranchers owe me money, and they need to give me a certain amount of respect." Farley finished his brandy and went to the cabinet to pour another.

Jake stretched his hands across the arms of the leather chair as his anger rose. "You think they should just let you come on their place and check brands."

"You have a better idea?" Farley placed his glass on the end table and drew out another cigar. "I don't suppose you smoke either."

"Not anymore."

"Your loss." He lit his cigar. "I gather by your silence you have no plan."

"I have a plan. We all keep watch and compare information. We only have two weeks before the cattle drive. Surely the thieves will make a move soon."

"And if they don't?" Thomas blew more of his irritating smoke rings.

"They will. Cattle thieves always show their hand. I been ranchin' long enough to know."

Farley sneered at Jake's comment. "In the meantime, we just let them keep stealing?"

"You can afford to lose a few head."

"Come now, Marcum, you married your wife so you, too, can

be secure from loss."

"What are you talkin' about?"

"Apparently, your wife has been keeping secrets from you. I received a newspaper from back East several months ago. It contained an article regarding Carl Olson's estate. When your wife's uncle died, he left half his fortune to her, although I am curious as to why. After all, he had two daughters of his own. But men have their reasons."

Jake found this new information hard to swallow.

"If you want to benefit from her good fortune, I suggest you take a more active role in teaching her how to be an obedient wife." Thomas's last barb hit its mark.

"For your information, my wife is a strong, independent, and intelligent woman. Those are the qualities a woman needs to survive out here. I didn't marry her for her fortune, *Mr. Farley.*"

"Please don't tell me you married for love. And don't think for one minute I accept that story of a mail-order bride. I suspect some kind of business arrangement."

Jake rose from his chair. "We're done here."

Farley rose at the same time. "Jake, you will learn soon enough. Intelligent women are a bane to a man's existence. You must put them in their place."

By now, Jake was seething. "Farley, not one more word about my wife, or I promise you'll regret it."

***

Evangeline's conversation with Violet was interrupted by the slam of the library door.

Jake's face was colored with anger when he entered the room. "We're leaving—now!" He turned to their hostess, his voice a little softer. "Thank you for the dinner, ma'am." He took Evangeline's arm and grabbed his hat from the hook as they left. She had the feeling if she hadn't walked quickly, he would have dragged her out.

Evangeline felt the pressure on her arm relax as their feet hit the porch. Once they were in the wagon, she dared to speak. "Jake, I want to apologize for the way I spoke to Mr. Farley. I'm sure it did not help your cause."

"No need to apologize. I should have spoken up sooner. He was baitin' you, and like an idiot ... I let him. I'm sorry he spoke to you like that. It'll never happen again."

Jake whipped up the horses, and Evangeline had to hang on a little tighter. They didn't speak again until they raced by the men guarding the gate.

"While discussin' his plan for catchin' the rustlers, that sidewinder kept makin' remarks 'bout you. Said I need to put you in your place." Jake's eyes flashed with an intensity she hadn't seen before. "If he wants to criticize his wife in front of God and everybody, that's his business. I warned him."

"What happened?"

"He couldn't resist sayin' one more thing about you. And I couldn't resist punchin' him in the mouth."

"Oh, Jake, you didn't ... What did he say?"

"Smart women are more likely to go insane."

"Is that so?"

Jake relaxed his grip on the reins. "I s'pose those are the kinds of things you hear from ignorant men."

"I have never heard intelligent women were ugly as dirt, though." She had a hard time stifling her laughter. "I suppose this evening ruined your chances of being Mr. Farley's equal."

"I don't care whether he admires me or not. I don't trust that snake, and gettin' on his good side wouldn't improve my opinion." Jake's frown darkened his face. "His plan to solve the cattle rustlin' problem is plain stupid. He wants to take the cattle from two of the ranchers he suspects, as an example."

"Example of what?"

"Don't mess with King Farley, I guess." Jake spat out the

words, then sat silent for several minutes. "I got this feelin' Bart has somethin' to do with it. But I can't prove it. Gotta wait for him to show his hand."

"Did you tell Mr. Farley your suspicions?"

"My suspicions are not his business. I wouldn't be surprised if he knows all about it. He has little to lose from what he got stolen. It's the rest of us who can't afford the loss."

"It's sad how Bo lets Bart lead him around by the nose." Evangeline wrapped her arms around her shoulders against the cooling breeze.

Jake placed the reins in one hand and maneuvered his jacket off with his free hand. He offered it to his wife. "Can't figure that kid out."

She pulled on the jacket. "I asked Bo why he liked Bart so much. It appears he reminds Bo of his father."

"Poor kid, that could get him fired. Worse, he may get hanged along with Bart if he's involved and we catch him."

"Hanged?"

"Afraid so. Around here, cattle rustlin's akin to killin' a man."

"I'll be praying for Bo. It would be tragic for that child to hang because of Bart's influence."

CHAPTER 20

Wrapped in her blanket, Evangeline sat in the parlor's semi-darkness. The nightmare had returned and invaded her sleep. Old fears caused her heart to race. The guilty burden she thought she'd wrestled into submission clung to her afresh. At the mention of Uncle Carl, it came back from some hidden recess of her mind to torment her. The smell of Farley's tobacco and whiskey reminded her of being trapped. The oppressive pain and humiliation engulfed her. Every graphic detail resurfaced, causing her body to shake.

How does Thomas Farley know of my uncle? How well he knew him was another question. *Does he know ...*

Evangeline willed her mind not to go there. *Though I walk through the valley of the shadow of death, I will fear no evil.* She meditated on the Twenty-third Psalm and other Scriptures that spoke of peace and comfort. Her uncle's business acquaintance, Prentiss Davis, was no longer a threat to her physically. Yet her self-worth teetered on that one horrible night.

"Evangeline, you alright?"

She jumped at his voice, and her trembling increased as he stretched his hand toward her.

"Don't touch me!" Evangeline hissed, raising her hands in defense.

Jake recoiled at her words. "What's wrong?"

"Noth ... nothing." She knew her quivering voice betrayed her.

"I have a hard time believin' it's nothin'."

Evangeline took in a few short breaths before answering. "You don't like to be awakened from a nightmare. I don't like to be touched after one."

"Want to tell me about it?" His invitation was both comforting and terrifying. When she didn't answer, he offered to make tea.

"Yes, please." She turned away.

Jake lit a lamp before going to the kitchen.

Evangeline was embarrassed and ashamed. She rose to check on Juliet, concerned their voices might have awakened her. She found her sleeping on the bedroom floor with Dog. *Thank you, Lord, she can enjoy her childhood.* She stood close by, watching the child sleep for a few moments before returning to the parlor where Jake had the tea ready.

"Must have been some nightmare."

"I guess. I don't really remember it," she lied. "I just remember the way it made me feel when I woke."

"Sorry I scared you."

"At least I didn't hit my head on anything."

"Yeah, I don't sew too good."

"You sew? How charming." She hoped the light conversation would lead him away from further questions, even though his concern made her feel secure.

"Now that I have an expert, I won't need to sew."

"Could you pour another, please?" Evangeline raised her cup.

"Sure thing." He took the cup from her trembling hands and placed it back on the saucer before refilling it.

She tried to still her hands as she raised the cup to her lips.

"Can I do anything for you?" he asked.

She felt like the patient instead of the doctor as he observed her. "Talk to me, Jake."

"About what?"

"Anything. I need to put something fresh in my mind."

He ran his fingers through his disheveled hair, then scrubbed the stubble on his face. Filling her mind with his movements helped push aside her fears. For a fleeting moment her mind pictured him holding her close. A shudder caused her to pull the blanket closer.

"You sittin' there wrapped up in a blanket reminds me of my mother."

"Tell me about her."

"One cold winter night durin' a blizzard, Pa went out to get more firewood. We children were afraid he wasn't comin' back. That winter, a neighbor had died just ten feet from the barn 'cause he couldn't see in the storm. We gathered 'round the stove wearin' every stitch of clothes we had and wrapped in every blanket and quilt in the house. Mamma told a story 'bout the hot days of summer. Then she would stop, and we young'uns would add to the story. Soon, we were laughin' so hard we forgot all about Pa. We near jumped outta our skin when he blew in the door with a gust of wind. He'd been gone over an hour, and if he hadn't bumped into the house, he'd never of found his way. We all took off our blankets and wrapped up Pa. Clevis and I took charge of puttin' more wood on the fire, and Robert sat in Pa's lap rubbin' his cold cheeks and tellin' him all 'bout the story we made up together."

She relaxed as the scene played out in her mind. "How wonderful."

Jake's eyes caressed her. "Can we go back to bed now?"

"Yes." Evangeline rose and headed back to their room. Pausing at the doorway, she turned to see Jake clearing the dishes. "Thank you."

"My pleasure. Why not sleep on the bed tonight? I'll take the floor."

"You'll get no argument from me."

* * *

Jake took the teapot and cups into the kitchen, then stepped outside to look at the stars. He wondered if that snake Farley didn't have something to do with her bad dream. What was the man trying to prove by his accusations? Viewing the vast sky, he determined whatever Farley thought he knew, he would protect Evangeline from it. Jake knew he loved her, but times like tonight he wondered if she would ever come to love him. She pushed him away when he wanted to comfort her, and yet just now her smile seemed to draw him in.

Lord, you sure know how to pick 'em. Show me how to love her best.

As he gazed at the stars, God's peace descended on him. He went back into the house, back to his room—their room. He could hear her gentle breathing as he lay down on the pallet. The smell of her scent on the pillow filled his senses as he drifted off to sleep.

* * *

Thud! The noise woke Jake from a foggy sleep. He opened one eye and turned toward the sound. Evangeline, in her nightgown, was bent over one of her trunks. Piles of books were stacked at her feet. He rose on one elbow as his wife methodically flipped through each book before setting it aside.

The nightgown, although modest, showed off her womanly form. Jake studied her with an appreciative grin for several minutes before speaking. "Whatcha doin'?"

Evangeline let out a squeal and pulled one of the books tightly to her chest. "Shhh! You'll wake up Juliet."

"Me? You're the one that screamed. Whatcha lookin' for?"

"Here it is." Evangeline went to sit next to Jake. Her nearness sent all manner of amorous thoughts through his mind. He corralled them as she spoke.

"I woke up this morning with an epiphany."

"A what?"

"An epiphany—a revelation. I know what happened to your friend Johnny."

"How?" Jake moved a little closer to see the book she had.

She flipped through her handwritten journal. "During the war, Shamus and I were often on the battlefield in the aftermath tending the wounded. We'd take those we could back to the field hospital. We took Johnny there."

"But I saw him covered in blood. He wasn't movin'."

"Yes, but he didn't die." Evangeline held her finger on the page. "During the war, I kept journals on all the wounded we treated. I found the journal where I recorded the entries regarding Jonathan Holt." Pointing to the entry, she showed him the page. His eyes widened as he read.

Jonathan Holt, age twelve, Confederate soldier. Came in unconscious and covered with blood. Thank God it was not his. He regained consciousness after reaching the hospital. Private Holt suffers from a concussion. Prominent symptoms: severe headache and hearing loss.

Evangeline flipped a few more pages and showed him an entry two weeks later.

Private Holt's hearing has returned. His headache is gone. I wrote his family in Brokenridge, Kentucky, on his behalf. Although his parents cannot read, Johnny assures me Mr. Wright at the general store will read the letter to them.

"Johnny is alive?" The revelation stunned Jake. His shoulders felt lighter. The burden of guilt lifted.

"The Union officer in charge of the hospital took pity on him and sent him home if he promised not to take up arms again."

Jake rose, rummaged through a drawer, and retrieved a postcard-sized photograph. "Johnny wanted me to send this to his parents, along with a letter, if anythin' should happen to him. I lost the letter when someone stole my coat, but I still have his picture. I guess I hoped to give it to his folks someday."

Evangeline joined him as he gazed at the tintype. "That's him, that's Johnny Holt. I can only assume you are his guardian angel."

"I'd forgotten. Johnny used to tell me his momma asked God to send a guardian angel to protect him." Jake heard the strangeness of his own voice and willed the tears to stop forming. "He'd follow in my shadow everywhere."

"Obviously, God sent him to you."

Jake saw the joy in her face as she spoke.

Evangeline took the picture from his hand and stroked it with her finger. "He was such a sweet boy. How glad I was when he was allowed to go home rather than prison camp."

"Thank you." Jake reached out and drew her to him. Fond recollections of the lad replaced his sorrow. He shuddered, and the movement drew Evangeline's arms around him in comfort. He hugged her close before releasing her. "Such a load is off my mind now. You know, I thought it strange you keepin' all these journals. Now I'm glad." Jake picked up the book and reread the entries.

"My father kept journals too. He is the one who got me started." She began repacking the books.

Jake buttoned his shirt. "How many of those are about the wounded you cared for?"

"Three, perhaps four. You can thank Katie. She's the one who packed them all."

"How many journals you got?" Jake was silent as she unbraided and brushed her long, burgundy hair. How he wanted to touch it, bury his face in it.

"Twenty."

He picked up his boots and sat next to her on the bed to pull them on.

"As a child, I kept a journal on birds and drew pictures. You saw one of my patient journals. I have a few full of lecture notes and articles on anything new in the medical field I heard. Around Juliet's age, I kept one on interesting people I met or read about."

"When did you have time to write it all down—let alone remember it?"

"I broke my arm twice, so I wrote to pass the time."

Jake frowned at her. "How do you write with a broken arm?"

"You write with the other one, of course." She set the brush on the dresser.

Jake delighted in her relaxed air. He was mesmerized by how deftly Evangeline braided her hair as she spoke. He dared not draw attention to it, fearing she'd become embarrassed and the intimacy of the moment would be broken.

Her eyes looked toward the ceiling as her face took on a thoughtful expression. "While I sat near a sick bed for days at a time, I wrote. Even on the train coming here, I wrote."

She looked through the wardrobe, then turned with a pensive look. "While I wait up at night for you to come home, I write."

A knock at the bedroom door kept him from responding.

"Uncle Jake, you awake?"

Jake opened the door to Juliet. She was dressed in trousers and boots, her hair in pigtails, but she wore a new ruffled blouse—another of Evangeline's creations. The child seemed to be divided between wanting to be a cowboy and a lady. Evangeline had been right about the curtains. "Mornin', sunshine."

"Mornin'." Juliet gave him a quick hug and a peck on the cheek. "You gotta come and help Dog."

"Surely by now he can take himself outside."

The child shrugged and smiled sweetly at him.

Jake tweaked Juliet's cheek. "I'll do it, but tonight he sleeps outside."

***

Breakfast was nearly over when Dog began to bark frantically from his new wagon on the porch.

Cookie rose to look out the window. "It's Farley, Boss."

Jake's breakfast turned sour in his stomach. "You all stay put. I'll see to this."

Farley dismounted his black stallion as Jake approached. "Marcum, I've come to apologize for being such a cad the other night. I deserved the bloody lip, and I'm a big enough man to admit it." He extended his hand.

Jake crossed his arms. "In all the years I've known you, I've never heard you apologize to *anybody* for *anything*."

"I have rarely felt the need."

"What do you really want, Farley?"

Thomas reached into his pocket for a cigar, bit off the end, lit it, and puffed. "I want to work with you to find the cattle rustlers. That's not possible if we are at odds with each other."

"That I can believe."

"Marcum, you're a smart man." The man's smile was condescending. "Maybe as smart as your wife."

"I'll take that as a compliment."

Jake's remark evoked a guffaw from the egotistical rancher.

"I got coffee in the house. You're welcome to some."

"I'll take you up on your hospitality." Farley took a long draw from his cigar and flipped his ashes on the porch.

As they entered the house, Jake noticed how Evangeline's back stiffened. Farley removed his hat and stepped toward her.

"My dear Mrs. Marcum, I am here to apologize for my rude behavior the other night. Can you ever forgive me?"

Selena snorted as she removed the last of the dishes to the kitchen. Cookie leaned against the kitchen door.

Evangeline vigorously wiped the table. Jake could see her calming herself with every stroke of the cloth until at last she turned and looked the man full in the face. "Mr. Farley, I have had similar conversations with men of your ilk. I find them monotonous and boorish. You are forgiven. I only hope in the future you will take the time to get to know me before you cast your wide net of aspersions." She smoothed her apron and shook his extended hand.

Jake couldn't have been prouder.

"I will indeed, ma'am." Farley's voice sounded surprisingly sincere to Jake.

"If you will excuse me, I have things to attend to. It's time for Juliet's lessons. Selena will serve your coffee in the parlor."

Farley joined Jake in the parlor as Selena brought in a tray. Jake poured the coffee and waited for the rancher to speak first.

"I'm sure Juliet will become a fine scholar under your wife's tutelage."

"No doubt." Jake was not in the mood for small talk. "What's your plan?"

"I thought we might ride out together today. I have been going over in my mind where a man, or men, could hide cattle."

"What makes you think they aren't long gone by now? Already sold?"

"I think these rustlers are local. Think about it. If they were merely passing through, we wouldn't still be losing cattle."

Jake despised the smug look on the man's face. "The last two weeks I haven't had any more stolen."

"Apparently, neither has anyone else."

"That's my point. They're long gone."

Farley leaned forward and lowered his voice as if letting Jake in on a secret. "I think not. I suspect they are hiding somewhere close by, and once we leave on the cattle drive, they will move their cattle at the same time."

"Interestin' theory."

"I propose we take a ride west toward Abernathy's place."

"You still suspect him?" Jake's hackles went up at what Farley was suggesting, but he was committed to hearing the man out.

"Perhaps. I say we ride up the hills back behind his place."

"You figure the cattle are hidden in one of those canyons?"

"I realize it would take a very clever man to drive the cattle up in there."

"Well, the thought crossed my mind, but I dismissed it. There's limited grazin' up there," Jake said, hoping the man was blowing as much smoke as the rings from his expensive cigars.

Farley's arrogant tone softened for a moment, and his words turned pensive. "I recall my father talking about a grotto when I was a boy."

"If there is one, it'd be worth findin'." At this point, Jake was willing to take a look.

"That is the challenge. As a youth, I had little interest in the ranch and didn't pay attention to the location."

"If what you're sayin' is true, Cookie or Walters might've heard of it."

"Let's get as many of our men as we can spare and meet near Abernathy's place in two hours." Farley rose from his chair with a self-satisfied look on his face. He retrieved his hat, headed out the door, and rode off.

Jake was glad this little meeting was over. "Cookie?"

"Yeah, Boss?"

"You ever hear of a grotto in the hills behind Abernathy's place?"

Cookie scratched his chin for several seconds. "I believe Ben mighta mentioned it once."

"Do you recall where it is?"

"No, but I remember him sayin' there be a narrow passage into the grotto, and once you're in there, you be an open target for anyone up on the hills."

"A box canyon would be a good place to hide stolen livestock," Jake said. "Funny how Farley *sorta* remembered that."

Cookie's eyes narrowed. "Yeah, funny."

His neighbor's convenient revelation left a feeling of dread in Jake's chest. "Gather the men." Jake took his hat from the peg. "Then get your gear. I want you to come with me."

***

An anxious sensation passed over Evangeline as the men rode away. "We need to prepare and pray," she told Juliet and Selena.

"Prepare what, Aunt Evangeline?"

"An infirmary."

"You think there will be injuries, *Señora?*"

"I'm sure of it. Thomas Farley is up to something." Evangeline bobbed her head up and down. "Yes, we need a place for surgery."

"What about the bathing room?" Selena crossed the dining room and opened the door.

"Perfect. We can lean the tub against the wall. Put in a table and a bed."

"I asked Solomon to make you a table. I think maybe you might do surgery again. I think about germs." Selena shuddered and nervously wiped her hands down her apron.

Evangeline appreciated her friend's foresight. "Is the table finished?"

"I will go ask," Selena said as she hurried toward the door.

"You could take one of the empty beds from the bunkhouse. Uncle Jake won't mind," Juliet offered.

"Is anyone still here to help move things?"

"Just Solomon and Manny. Manny's momma wouldn't let him go. I'll go fetch 'em."

Is this how I resume my medical practice? Her mind checked off all she needed to do. *Please, God, keep them safe. If there are injuries, let them be minor. Keep my Jake from harm.*

She knew it was true—he was *her* Jake. If anything happened to him today, she would never forgive herself for not being a better wife. Why was it so hard?

She forced those thoughts away. Right now she had a job to do.

CHAPTER 21

Jake sat astride Traveler like a sentinel taking in the scene before him. The majority of the group consisted of Farley's men with Jake's crew and a few other ranchers in the mix. Cookie had extra rifles and ammunition in the wagon. Jake recalled battlefield wagons serving as either an ambulance or hearse. A cold shiver sprinted down his back. The craggy hills revealed no entrance into this mysterious canyon.

Cookie pulled the wagon up beside Jake as the sun climbed over the hilltop, causing both men to squint. "Boss, I don't see nothin'."

"Me neither." Jake turned to Farley. "So, where is this canyon your father told you about?"

"About a mile beyond that first bluff, east of here." Farley pointed, then signaled for his men to head out.

Farley and his men seemed relaxed in the saddle. Jake's crew and the other ranchers appeared anxious, some with hands on their holsters. He saw Cookie's pinched expression. "You feel it too?"

"Yeah, too convenient Farley rememberin' the exact location after all this time."

"Keep the wagon close at hand."

Cookie released the brake. "My thinkin' exactly."

Jake checked his crew. Walters and Tony rode in front of the wagon. Pete and a few others moved to ride behind it. Jake had sent Bo into town for supplies. If Bart was involved, he wanted the boy to have an alibi. Duke and Artie were still fixing fences and hadn't made it back. He could have used the extra guns to even things out a bit more.

* * *

Jake followed his gut by taking the lead with his crew. An overwhelming feeling of dread pushed his desire to get to this hidden canyon before Farley. His instincts had never failed him in the past, and he was counting on them now.

Gunfire rang out. The sound ricocheted off the surrounding hills. Artie's horse stood grazing up ahead. Jake's heart tightened when he saw the pony, wondering why Artie would be anywhere near this canyon. *Please, Lord, don't let it be so.*

"Look, there's the entrance." Tony pointed toward a spot near the mare.

The narrow passage, shaded from the morning sun and overgrown with sagebrush, would have been impossible to find if not for Artie's horse. Tony dismounted and examined the hoof prints, his firm nod an unspoken confirmation. They'd found the stolen cattle. Tony remounted and, along with the others, followed Jake. The men passed through the entrance single file, led by the sound of muffled voices. A single shot echoed ahead.

Spurring their horses forward, Jake and his crew entered the box canyon. Bart was on his knees, wrapping a bandana around his bloody hand. Duke held his rifle on the man. His horse stood near two men on the ground—Jose De Fuentes, Tony's cousin, with a bullet between his eyes, and Artie. Jake and the rest of the Double M ranch hands quickly surrounded them. The rest of the search party swarmed in behind them.

"Caught me some cattle rustlers." Bart held his injured hand against his chest.

Jake kept his gun drawn. "Not what I see."

"That's exactly what I see." Thomas Farley turned to his men, and they all agreed.

"See, Farley, I got 'em for you just like I promised."

"You hired this lying snake?" Jake's fury threatened to overtake him. A growl escaped his lips. "Men, help this *hero* to his feet, and take all three back to the ranch."

"We can take care of our own, thank you," Farley said.

"Suit yourself." Jake stared at Bart for several seconds before putting his gun away. "My wife could take a look at your hand."

"I don't need your *wife* to help me. It ain't much of a wound 'cause the kid ain't much of a shot." Bart pushed two of Farley's men away as they tried to help him to his horse.

***

"Artie's still breathin', Boss." Duke ripped off his shirt and pressed it against the blood flowing from the kid. "He saved my life." Duke stared daggers at Bart. "That skunk was about to shoot me when Artie raised up and shot the gun out of his hand."

Jake instructed Duke and Tony to lower Artie into the wagon along with De Fuentes's body. As soon as Duke climbed aboard, Cookie headed out. Jake stopped Farley before he remounted.

"What's this all about? You take me for a fool?" Anger pushed the fence of calm surrounding it.

"Look around you. This is the rustlers' hideout. Here is the corral, and the two men responsible are laid out in the wagon." Farley's eyes challenged Jake to push the matter.

"Bart is a drunken liar." Tony spat out the words.

Farley kept his tone and his stare steady. "He works for me. He caught them, killed them, and saved the territory a trial. You should be pleased to get your cattle back."

Jake stepped closer. "Not at the expense of innocent men."

"Innocent? Ha! That Mexican is a known cattle rustler. You can ask his cousin about his character." Farley pointed toward Tony. "As for the kid, some of my men heard him talking in town about needing a sizeable amount of money. He's sweet on some whore." A sadistic smile formed briefly on his face. "Wonder how many more of your men were in on it."

"Seems you got it all figured out." Jake felt fire burn in his gut. It took all his willpower not to punch the arrogant dandy in the face. But a fight would only end in more bloodshed.

"I usually figure things out quite well." Farley mounted and signaled his men to head out. His crew made quick work of separating the cattle, leaving the Double M hands to herd their cattle through the narrow opening.

Tony stayed to help Jake investigate. Nothing about it looked right. Jake had no doubt the fresh hay had come from Farley's ranch.

"Boss, my cousin would not let himself be shot so easily. Jose was always watchful. He had many enemies." Tony pointed to the bedroll and other items ready to be put on his cousin's mount. "Jose was a thief, this we all know. But I think he was set up."

"Lots of things are shady here. Artie must have found this place about the time Bart shot your cousin." Jake gazed up at the high ridge. "A man would be an idiot to believe Bart's story."

"Then why did we let him go? Let's get the men together and hang the hombre." Tony's angry words choked out through clenched teeth. He knelt to gather up his cousin's things.

"Nothin' I'd like better. But we got to prove it. Otherwise, we could start a range war, which would suit Farley. Let's head back and talk to Duke. There has to be a way to prove Bart and Farley were in on this together." Jake grabbed the reins of Jose's and Duke's horses before mounting Traveler.

"You thinking Farley got Bart to rustle cattle for him?" Tony took one more look around before turning his horse toward the opening.

"Probably." Jake pressed Traveler forward. "Kings always need others to do their dirty work."

CHAPTER 22

Evangeline heard the creak and rattle of the wagon, but Selena rushed to the door ahead of her. The two women stood in the doorway as Cookie pulled hard on the reins. The horses rose on their hind legs before everything came to a halt.

"Help me!" Duke's pleas sent Solomon, Manny, and Selena racing to lift Artie from the wagon.

"Bring him this way." Evangeline's heart raced as she led the way to the new infirmary. "Put him on the table."

Duke held pressure on the wound as he helped Solomon position his friend on the table. He began to shake.

Evangeline had never seen this tough cowboy so upset. "Duke, you can leave now."

"I want to stay." His face was pale and perspiring.

"No, Selena will help me." Evangeline's voice was authoritative as she turned to Cookie and Solomon. "Help Duke before he passes out. Manny, grab the smelling salts out of my bag."

"What do you need?" Cookie asked over his shoulder as he held Duke up.

"Start boiling more water. I already brought some in. The buckets are by the door. Knock when you're ready. Selena will take it from you."

"Yes, ma'am."

"One more thing."

"Ma'am?"

"Pray like you have never prayed before."

Selena closed the door behind them.

***

Evangeline went to work on her patient as muffled prayers and sobs filtered through the closed door. She placed a mesh mask on Artie's mouth and administered a mixture of morphine and chloroform.

"This is very bad, *Señora*."

"I'm hoping it looks worse than it is." Evangeline began to cut away Artie's shirt. To her great relief, there were several layers of padding and corset stays.

Selena helped her remove all the layers. *"Ay, Dios mio, el ′ es una mujer!"*

"Yes, *he* is a woman. Which is why I kept the men out."

"How did you know?"

"I treated a few women during the war who disguised themselves as soldiers."

"Why would a woman do such a thing?"

"Men are paid more for any job they do." Evangeline wiped away the blood. "A woman I met in an army hospital told me she dressed as a man to help support her family. She worked as an orderly."

"I understand about money but not fighting." Selena clicked her tongue as she gathered up the bloody material.

The two worked in silence. Evangeline probed inside the wound for the bullet and deposited the slug in a nearby bowl.

As the last stitch took shape, Selena spoke. "Why would he … I mean she, do this?"

"You can ask her when she wakes up."

"She will not die then?"

"I feel sure she will recover. The thick padding saved her. I need to watch for infection the next couple of days. She lost a lot of blood, so she'll need time to recover."

"What do we do now?"

"We let her rest. We need to find her some kind of nightshirt and move her to the bed. And, Selena … we can't let anyone know Artie is a she."

"Si, Señora, I understand."

"I brung more water." Cookie's voice preceded him into the room. Evangeline covered Artie with a clean sheet.

Selena stood in the doorway blocking his view of the surgical table. "*Grácias*, Cookie. Ask Manny to bring one of his father's nightshirts."

"Yes, ma'am." Cookie strained to see around Selena, but she shut the door before he could.

* * *

Jake studied Duke's face, watching the color return as he sat at the table, gripping a coffee mug.

"Why don't you go to the bunkhouse and clean up? The women will let us know how things are in due time."

"I will, but I'm comin' right back, Boss."

"Sure thing."

Jake hoped Duke would be ready to talk when he returned. The prayer seemed to help, along with a few cups of strong coffee. Duke's reaction seemed out of character, and it worried Jake. He'd seen perfectly sane men come back from the war then fall all to pieces over less traumatic encounters. What had caused Duke to react this way? Up until a few weeks ago, these two men weren't on friendly terms. And what would happen if Artie died?

Manny returned with the nightshirt and knocked on the infirmary door. Selena grabbed the garment and disappeared before Manny could peek inside.

"You reckon the nightshirt is a good sign?" Cookie asked as he poured coffee.

"I hope so," Jake replied. "Warm up my cup, would ya?"

Cookie hobbled over and topped off Jake's cup before returning the pot to the stove.

They sat in silence until Duke returned. He had cleaned the blood off his hands and wore a clean shirt. His jeans still carried splatters of blood.

"Want some coffee?" Cookie asked.

"Nah. I've had enough. Sorry I broke down like that, Boss. It's my fault Artie got shot. I was teasin' him."

"About what?"

"You know how Artie always tries to find a tree or bush far away from everyone when he has to relieve himself. We were gettin' a late start back to the ranch as it was."

"Is that how he found the entrance?"

"I guess. We had words and he stormed off. The next thing I heard was gunfire."

"How'd you manage to find where he went?"

"His horse follows him like a dog. The animal was standin' right near the entrance."

Cookie chuckled. "Tony trained Artie's horse to do that as a joke. Good thing he did."

"I couldn't get there fast enough to save him from gettin' shot. But Artie raised up and shot Bart before he could draw on me. Never seen shootin' like that before. He saved my life."

"You two had been at the line cabin all night?"

Duke looked uncomfortable and shifted in his chair. "Artie, he uh … left for a while."

"What for?"

"He leaves at night to go spend time with his sister."

"His sister?" This was the first Jake had heard of any family members.

"She ain't here, but he promised her he'd spend some time every night prayin' with her. He goes off by hisself with the family picture and prays. He told me not to tell the other fellas."

"How long was he gone?"

"A while. I don't know. I was asleep when he come back." Duke slammed his fist on the table. "There's no way he's a cattle thief."

"No one believes that for a minute." Jake leaned over and placed his hand on Duke's shoulder. "But we got to prove Artie's innocent. His bein' gone last night looks bad."

"We know that no-account Bart is to blame," added Cookie.

Jake looked from one man to the other. "Let's keep Artie's story to ourselves for now. No need jumpin' to conclusions till we can actually talk to him." He turned as the door opened. Evangeline appeared, strands of hair trailing down her neck. She wiped perspiration from her forehead and closed the door behind her. All conversation ceased as the bloody mess in her arms captured the men's attention.

"The wound wasn't as bad as it looked."

Duke's face relaxed. "Artie's gonna be okay?"

"As long as there is no infection, yes."

"Praise the Lord!" Cookie exclaimed with a broad smile.

Jake expelled a breath he didn't realize he'd been holding. "Told you, Duke, God answers prayer."

Duke's relief was evident. "Can I see 'em?"

"Not right now. He needs rest. Maybe in a few days."

"A few days?" Duke looked confused. "You said he was gonna be fine."

"I also said as long as there is no infection. Too much company could spread germs."

Duke's eyes widened. "Germs?"

"You don't want to know," Manny said.

Jake stood and put an arm around Evangeline's shoulders. "Duke, I trust my wife. If she says we got to wait a few days to see Artie, then that's what we'll do. Understood?"

"But, Boss, I need to thank him for savin' my life."

"There'll be plenty of time for that," Jake assured him.

"All you men, out of the kitchen … now." Selena strode across the room toward the kitchen sink, shooing them with her hands. "*Ahora vallense de mì cosina*. I must prepare dinner."

Evangeline readjusted the bloody clothing in her arms. "Jake, can you bring a shovel. I want to bury this mess."

Jake tried to read his wife's face. "What about Artie?"

"The patient will be fine while we take care of this. No one disturb him while I'm gone." Evangeline looked around the room, focusing on Duke. "No one. Is that clear?"

"Yes, ma'am," the men responded in unison.

"While I help bury this stuff, you all get back to work." Jake waited for them to leave before turning his attention back to his wife. The flush on her cheeks warmed his heart. The top two buttons of her blouse had disengaged from their holes, revealing her soft, white neck. How he wished this time together had a different purpose. He led her to the shed and grabbed a shovel.

"We need to talk," she whispered.

Jake moved to an open area behind the corral. "Is this a good spot?"

"I'm not as concerned about where we bury this as being overheard."

Jake looked around and began digging. "Start talkin'."

"Artie didn't die, because Artie is a *she*."

Jake's shovel stopped in midair. *"What?"*

"Artie is a woman. She had some kind of binding fashioned from corset wire and very thick padding. That kept the bullet from going deeper. It nicked a rib and lodged in the muscle. She lost a lot of blood, but the bullet missed any vital organs. God truly intervened."

"Artie's a woman," Jake said more to himself than his wife. "How did I not see that?"

"Because she dressed and talked like a young man and did her best to respond like a man would to any situation. You saw what you expected to see."

Jake wagged his finger at her. "You knew all along."

"Suspected as much."

"What made you suspicious?"

"Men have Adam's apples and women don't. Her hands are small and her face too smooth."

Jake felt foolish for his jealous thoughts. "No wonder you were so friendly with Artie."

"I told you I don't care for any man but you."

Jake laughed with embarrassment as he dug the hole. "Why didn't you tell me before?"

"I was frightened." Evangeline kept her head down. "Besides, revealing her secret would have accomplished nothing."

"I'm sorry. I should have trusted you."

"It's in the past." Evangeline pushed a stray hair behind her ear. "We need to learn to trust each other."

Jake dug in silence. Trusting women had never been his strong suit. But their marriage would never get beyond the convenience stage if he didn't put more effort into it.

Evangeline placed her hand on his shoulder. "Now, what do we do with her secret?"

Jake removed his Stetson. Staring at nothing, he mulled over the problem. Replacing his hat, he turned and caught the trusting look in her eyes. Oh, how he wished he had an answer to earn that trust. "Not much we can do at present."

"Is it still possible Artie might be hanged as a cattle thief? Does being female change things?"

"If she'd been known as a woman all along, it might make a difference. But because she played the part of a man, it might make things worse." Jake finished the hole. "I've heard of a few women being hanged as cattle thieves in other parts. For now, we keep everyone out of the room, and we pray—a lot." He took the bloody things from Evangeline and buried them. After the last shovelful of dirt was in place, he stomped it down as flat as he could. "Why didn't we burn this?"

"Because corset stays and wires don't burn."

Jake picked up the shovel and took her hand as they walked back to the house. "You're somethin' else, Mrs. Marcum." Jake lifted her hand and gave it a feathery kiss. "You had everythin' ready like you knew somethin' was gonna happen."

Evangeline looked straight ahead. "I was afraid you'd get killed before I had a chance to be a good wife to you."

"Lucky for me you still got time."

Evangeline's smile filled her face.

Jake returned the shovel to the shed as Evangeline went back to the house. His mind was distracted as he approached the porch. Manny had joined Juliet next to Dog. Jake saw that Juliet had a book in her hand, something she rarely did.

Manny grabbed the book from her. "I said, did you hear Artie is going to be okay?"

"Yes, now give that back." Juliet tried to grab it. Manny raised it far above her head. Just as Juliet stretched to retrieve it, Jake snatched it away.

"What is this?" Jake asked as he skimmed the pages. "Juliet Elizabeth Marcum, did you have permission to read this?"

Juliet's downcast eyes focused on Dog. "No, sir."

Jake signaled for her to follow him. She rose without looking at Manny.

"I'll keep an eye on Dog," Manny called to her.

Jake took Juliet into her room and closed the door. "Why?"

"'Cause I wanted to know."

"Don't you think if she'd a mind for you to read her journal she woulda told ya?"

"I'm sorry. I couldn't help myself." Juliet began to cry, and the words came in a rush. "I thought I'd peek at one of her journals— you know, to see how she done one. I found her childhood so fascinatin' I had to keep readin'. Then I had to read another one."

"How many did you read?" Jake's nerves tightened as the girl squirmed.

"Three. I know it was wrong, but I been cooped up in this room watchin' over Dog. Then you two went off visitin', and then Artie got shot, and with everyone lookin' to their own business, I just kept readin'."

Jake sat on the bed and wrapped her in his arms. "You know you gotta tell her. Apologize and take whatever punishment she gives you. I'm mighty disappointed in you, princess. You know better."

Juliet cried as if he had thrashed her with a switch.

"Juliet, what's wrong?" Evangeline called from the other side of the door.

Jake opened the door, and Juliet held out the book. His niece cried even harder when her aunt's face paled. Evangeline took the book and walked out of the room without a word.

"Go and plead with her for me. Tell her how sorry I am." Juliet clung to him.

"I don't think that'll do any good."

"Uncle Jake, will she ever speak to me again?"

"I imagine she will. But if I was you, I'd keep quiet and wait for her to speak first."

CHAPTER 23

For two days, Evangeline kept vigil over her patient. Each time she emerged from the room, exhaustion claimed her body, but her mind was fresh with a plan that needed executing.

"Selena, have Cookie take you to town. I'm hoping my order for more laudanum has arrived." Fatigue added brusqueness to Evangeline's tone. She pulled off her apron and smoothed her wrinkled skirt.

"I can go this afternoon, *Señora*."

"No, I want you to leave now!" Her voice was sharp. "Once you're ready, come with Cookie to see me. I'll have instructions for you."

"*Sí*." Selena went to the door and shouted, "Manny, tell Cookie the *Señora* needs him to come right now, and you hitch the wagon!" Selena grabbed her shawl as Cookie rushed in and let the door close behind him.

"What's all the fuss? Artie worse?"

"The *Señora* will tell us."

Evangeline sat at the kitchen table with a cup of tea. "Forgive me for snapping at you, Selena. Fatigue makes me contrary, but that is no excuse."

"I understand," Selena said as she sat next to her. "What is it you need from us?"

Evangeline reached over and gave her friend a hug. Her response ministered comfort to Evangeline's heart. "I need you to check at the mercantile to see if the medicine I ordered weeks ago has come in. I'm almost out of laudanum. There is probably another package waiting for me as well. Please collect it. I have a few letters to be mailed. I need you to do all those things. but ..." She patted Selena's hand before continuing.

"Cookie, I need you to send a telegram. It is imperative Mrs. Hanks does *not* see it. Give it only to Horatio, and make sure he returns the message to you after he has sent it." She handed the note to Cookie. "Tell him to bring the answer out to the ranch when he gets it—only him."

Cookie put the note in his vest pocket. "How you gonna keep that nosey woman outta your business?"

"Offer Horatio twenty dollars to keep it quiet and to deliver it personally. Remind him I'll know if anyone else has found out the contents. Once he delivers the response to me, he will be paid, and not a moment sooner."

"Smart thinkin'."

"Here is more than enough money to pay for what I ordered and the telegram." Evangeline handed Cookie some folded bills, then looked at Selena. "If the medicine has not come, go to Mr. Wong. See what he has that might work."

"*Sí, Señora.*"

"Selena, I think it's time you let Cookie in on Artie's plight." She caught the confused look on Cookie's face at Selena's solemn nod.

"There will be much time to tell on the way to town," Selena assured him as they rose from their places.

Their departure left Evangeline alone and longing for an uninterrupted nap. She enjoyed the flavor of her tea, which reminded her she would soon be out. "I should have asked them to add tea to their list." Evangeline spoke the words out loud, thinking she was alone.

"Want me to catch up with the wagon and tell them to get you some?" Juliet's question startled her.

"No, that's not necessary."

"I don't mind. It don't take long to saddle my horse. I could catch up with Cookie in no time. He drives slow."

"I said *no.*" Her voice was shrill.

Juliet's eyes were brimming with tears as she turned away, and guilt tapped on Evangeline's shoulder.

Forgive me, Lord.

* * *

Juliet raced from the house to the stable. By the look on her face, Jake could tell she was upset again. Every little thing turned into a drama with his niece.

He knew Manny was still working in the stable. *Poor kid is going to have to endure her foolish chatter.* Nora used to pour her sorrows to Robert often enough as they were growing up. Should have seen the signs. *Maybe Manny is Juliet's Robert.* Jake put away the ridiculous thought. *Maybe I'd better relieve Manny of his burden.* Jake realized how much he avoided Juliet's woeful lamenting. What kind of a man didn't listen to his kin?

"Hey, sunshine," Jake called, making his presence known as he entered the stable.

Juliet wiped her tears with the back of her hand. "Oh, Uncle Jake." Tears still glistened in her eyes as he drew her into a hug. "How can I help her to be happy again?"

Manny touched her shoulder. "When she has made Artie well, she will be ready to talk."

"You think so?"

Manny returned to brushing Sage. "Yes, I do." His words seemed to bring her comfort.

"Do you think I should write her a note?" Juliet sought out her friend's counsel even with Jake standing near. A new sort of jealousy danced in his mind.

Manny glanced at Jake before he answered. "Maybe, but don't ask me. I am not the one she is mad at. Ask your uncle. She is his wife. He would know if a note would be good."

The sound of thundering hooves broke up the discussion. The three gathered at the stable door as Thomas Farley and two of his men came into the yard. Jake regretted not wearing his holster.

This can't be good. He strode out to meet Farley, careful to keep his face expressionless. The youngster followed close behind.

"Marcum, we came to collect the prisoner." Farley's voice filled the space between the house and the stable.

"No need," Jake replied coolly.

"He works for you. I don't think you can be trusted to turn him over to the law."

"Right now, I ain't even sure he'll live to be turned over."

"I'll just send my men to check, if you don't mind."

"I do mind." Jake stepped forward, every muscles on high alert.

"And I most certainly mind." The voice came from the porch where Evangeline held Cookie's shotgun.

"Surely you are not serious." Farley laughed as he pulled out a cigar.

"Deadly serious." Evangeline pulled back both triggers.

Jake heard Juliet gasp behind him. Fear for those he loved constricted his heart.

"A lady of your refinement wouldn't shoot anyone," Farley responded while trying to light his cigar. A menacing smile appeared on his face. "You do realize three guns are pointed at your husband."

"You do realize this shotgun is pointed at that fine thoroughbred horse of yours. I assume you paid quite a fortune for it—good bloodlines and excellent markings. But I must say, Mr. Farley, it makes no difference to me. It's a horse, and I dislike horses." Her voice was venomous.

"You would shoot my horse, madam, and risk your husband's life?" His voice had a tinge of doubt in it.

Jake's answer was cold as steel. "That shotgun kicks up a hair when you fire it. Best keep that in mind, Evangeline, or you'll kill Farley instead." He touched his non-existent holster then placed his fisted hands at his side, feigning a relaxed stance. He saw Solomon sneak around the north side of the house.

"Let me propose a compromise, Mr. Farley." Evangeline's

command was unwavering.

Manny nudged Jake and pointed toward Farley's flinching horse. The animal appeared to be sensing his master's fear.

Farley puffed on his cigar as Evangeline spoke.

"Give me one week. Either Artie will die, or he will be well enough to stand trial. Either way, you can come and get him. I don't like to let a patient out of my care until he is either recovered or dead."

"Why should I trust you, madam?" Farley's words were laced with fear.

"'Cause I got my rifle beaded on you, Mr. Farley," Solomon bellowed. "This here buffalo rifle will blow your head clean off. If she don't git you, I will."

"I must say, Marcum, your wife certainly has grit." He held his cigar up to his lips with a wavering hand. "If that cattle thief isn't dead in the next week, I will be here with many more men and the territorial marshal to see he stands trial." Farley signaled to his men and rode out.

As the group left, anger rose up in Jake at the thought of what might have happened. He stomped toward Evangeline and jerked the shotgun from her hand.

"Never, *ever* do that again."

"I will do whatever needs to be done and no one, including you, will tell me different." She turned on her heels and slammed the door.

***

Jake was seething as he stormed into the house. "Evangeline!" The temper he kept so closely guarded erupted. Knowing she had willfully put his life at risk unsettled him. He flung the bedroom door hard against the wall. The sound of smacking wood reverberated, releasing more of his irritation.

Her strangled sobs reached him as she lay shivering on the bed, face buried in the pillow. Jake stared at the helpless scene, and his anger drained away. He perched on the edge of the bed, not daring to touch her.

She turned her tear-streaked face to him. "Forgive me, Jake, I didn't mean anything. I'm so afraid. What are we going to do?" By now she was shivering uncontrollably.

He pulled the quilt over her. When she didn't recoil, he lay down next to her and stroked her cheek, curving his body to match hers. It felt so right, so natural to comfort her this way.

After a time, she relaxed. Sniffling, she spoke again. "What are we going to do?"

"We wait and see how Artie does."

Evangeline rose from the bed. "She's recovering. I keep her sedated so no one knows. In a week, I'm sure that horrible man will hang her before the marshal ever comes."

Jake stood and pulled her close. "We could sneak her out."

"We need to think of something to save her."

"Might I suggest we kill me?" Artie stood against the open door in the oversized nightshirt, sweat pooled on her pale brow.

"What are you doing up?" Evangeline led her back to her bed as Jake followed.

"I must say, things have certainly gotten lively around here since I've been convalescing," she replied in a voice Jake did not recognize. As she reached her bed, she looked at him. "We have not been properly introduced. I am Isabel Hawthorne Weaver."

Jake stifled a grin. "And where do you hail from, Miss Weaver?"

"From London, actually."

"London?"

"The Hawthornes are a well-known theatrical family. We brought our acting troupe to the colonies. We performed predominately in New York and Massachusetts."

Evangeline covered her with the blankets. "How did you end up out here?"

"I fell in love with an American. Arthur Weaver was a minister, which shocked my family. We were only married a short time before the war broke out. He served as a hospital chaplain. Diphtheria took him from me." Her brief biography was delivered as if she were the narrator of a play.

"I'm so sorry, Isabel," Evangeline said.

"After that, I attached myself to his family and came west with them. They loved the Lord, and I wanted to follow the faith I had come to know."

"Why dress like a man?" Jake asked, still trying to deal with the reality of the situation.

"The Weavers' homestead did not do well. Savages murdered my in-laws. My sister-in-law made the acquaintance of an unsavory character who loaned us money to get back on our feet. Amelia was smitten with him. He promised to establish her in business if she came with him to Charleton." Isabel laid her head back, looking exhausted.

"You really should rest." Evangeline finished tucking her in.

"I will, but let me finish my soliloquy." Isabel gave a little smile as she took in a deep breath. "I stayed behind to settle our accounts, Amelia came to Charleton, and, of course, that scoundrel had lied. He told her she needed to repay the money he loaned us and forced her to work at Madame Rose's establishment. When I didn't hear from her, I came to investigate but had to disguise myself to get close."

"You came as a man so this evil person would not know you?" Evangeline asked.

"I needed a disguise that gave me access. I donned a red wig and mustache and posed as a peddler. Once I found Amelia, it was hard to persuade her to let me help. Her shame kept her from seeing me at first. She believes God will not forgive her, and she is doomed to hell."

"You mentioned you could make more money working as a ranch hand," Evangeline recalled.

Jake's head was spinning, but things were beginning to make

sense. "So you took on another disguise and came to work for me." It was a statement more than a question.

"I am dreadfully sorry for the deception, Mr. Marcum." Isabel shivered as she pulled the blanket up to her chin.

"Well, considerin' the situation, I see why you done it."

"I often go to visit her, usually as the peddler, but on occasion as Artie."

"Is that where you were the night before you found the cattle rustlers?" Evangeline asked.

"Yes. Amelia needs to see me at least once a week. I hadn't been there in two. I took a risk and got back about midnight. I'm the only one who can protect her."

"It's understandable why you didn't go to the law," Jake added.

"I suppose you are going to tell me the owner of Rose's Place owns the law here, as well." Evangeline's expressive eyes and deep furrowed brow reminded Jake his wife was a woman of action.

"Let's just say places like Rose's have a lot of support out here. The sheriff isn't going to stir up trouble over one woman's complaint."

Evangeline's shoulders sagged. "Then what do we do?"

"You can kill me," Isabel said without flinching.

"I swear, all women must be insane by nature." Jake began pacing.

"Perhaps she has the right idea." Evangeline's declaration broke through Jake's musings.

"I assume you gals don't actually mean killin'-killin'. More like play-actin'." Jake feared these women, in their desire to find a solution, had lost all touch with reality.

"I propose we play the Juliet death scene." Isabel's smile was weak.

"What are you talkin' about?" Jake was more confused than ever.

Isabel raised up on her elbows as a spark of excitement danced in her eyes. "From *Romeo and Juliet*. I assumed your niece was named after the character from Shakespeare's play." A dramatic sigh escaped her lips. "Juliet arranges with the priest to take poison that gives her the appearance of death so she can revive and run off with her lover. The only flaw in her plan was no one had told Romeo. It was all rather messy."

"What you're sayin' is Evangeline gives you some kinda poison, and after everyone sees you dead, you revive."

"Yes. I reappear as myself and rescue dear Amelia."

"This is crazy." The women stared at him as he took his second lap around the small room. "But I can't think of nothin' better." What was it about Evangeline's deep green eyes and Isabel's confident smile that sucked the common sense right out of him?

Evangeline had an odd look on her face. "I am familiar with belladonna, hemlock, and a few others. I doubt a small dose would do the trick, and I don't care to take a chance. Opium, laudanum, even chloroform have distinctive odors. I am not comfortable with experimenting with your life."

Isabel looked first at Evangeline then Jake, tears pooled in her eyes. "Mr. Marcum, I truly am sorry for all the trouble I have caused."

"Don't you worry 'bout it none, Mrs. Weaver. You rest now."

As he and Evangeline left the room, Jake closed the door behind them and sent up a silent, urgent prayer.

Father, we need wisdom.

* * *

Jake stood by, feeling helpless as Evangeline sat on the floor of their room perusing her medical books and lecture notes, all to no avail. His inability to make things right was hard to swallow. He reached a hand to help his wife to her feet.

"Now what?"

"Prayer, something we should have been doing all along."

As they prayed together and committed the situation to the

Lord, a sense of God's intervention settled over him. Handing the last medical journals to Evangeline, he caught a glance out the window and saw a cloud of dust headed toward the ranch. "Looks like Cookie and Selena will be here soon."

"I'll take that." She held out her hand.

He fingered the leather cover before handing it to her. "When you gonna forgive Juliet for readin' your journals?"

"I already have."

"It'd be good to tell her. She's been miserable the last two days."

"Well, I must admit I hoped she would be. I'll speak to her this evening."

"She thinks she's committed the unforgivable sin."

"If I hadn't been such a nosey girl myself growing up, I might have considered it unforgivable." A mischievous smile formed on his wife's face.

"I can't imagine you bein' a nosey girl."

"Someday I'll let you read the journal I wrote when I was twelve."

Jake headed to the door with Evangeline on his heels. Cookie and Selena entered the house, along with the Wongs.

Mae bowed. "Mrs. Marcum, your house is beautiful. You are truly an artist."

"Thank you. But I know you did not come to admire my drapes."

"No, my father has come to care for Mrs. Weaver."

Jake's eyes followed Evangeline's as she glanced at Selena and Cookie.

"Many women come from China dressed as men to meet their husbands. It is illegal for Chinese women to immigrate here."

"How long have you known?" Evangeline asked.

"Since the first day she came into town. We provided her with the men's clothes and the padding. I told her about you, Mr. Marcum. I knew a job with you would be safe. You are a good man, and everyone praises the Double M as an honorable place to work."

"Well, that explains a lot," Jake remarked.

"My father admires Mrs. Weaver's courage and wants to offer assistance."

This was getting crazier by the minute, and Jake wondered how many others knew Artie's true identity.

***

"Is she dying?" Mae inquired as Evangeline directed them to her makeshift infirmary.

"Quite the opposite. I fear the hangman's noose for her."

The others remained outside as Evangeline and the Wongs entered the small room. Evangeline gently touched Isabel's shoulder. "You have company." She turned to Mae. "As you can see, she is far from well."

Mae and her father approached the bed. "Mrs. Weaver, how are you?"

"Doing nicely, considering the state of affairs. So good of you to come."

Mr. Wong spoke in Chinese as he checked her wound. "My father says you will be well very soon. He has something to help your blood restore."

"Tell your father he must give me something to kill me for a few days."

Mae's confused expression wasn't lost in translation. Mr. Wong smiled as he pulled a bottle from his box. "This very special," Mr. Wong instructed in English. "This very good for two-day dead."

"My dear friend, you are full of surprises. I feel like I am in a melodrama."

"Are you sure this is safe?" Evangeline examined the tiny amber bottle. "What is it?" *Father, is this an answer to our prayers?*

"Something my grandfather created to save a friend from an evil warlord. Do not worry, Dr. Marcum. Tell her it is safe, Father."

The old man nodded vigorously. "Only if you do as I say. Two drops on the tongue. One you sleep a little. Three, you may die. Four or more, you dead."

"How will she look?" Evangeline's stomach knotted as the plan came together.

"Sleep of death," Mr. Wong answered simply.

"How long before the drug takes effect?"

"A little time. You get very sleepy first." Mr. Wong picked up his box. "We go back to store now."

"Are you sure you can't stay for tea?"

Mae bowed again. "No, my father rarely leaves the store. He fears robbers."

"Cookie will take you home." As soon as the Wongs left the room, Evangeline turned to her friend. "When do you want to die, Artie Weaver?"

"Not just yet. I need to say good-bye to my friends."

CHAPTER 24

Evangeline took Juliet aside before dinner. The girl's remorseful look tugged at her heart. "I want you to know, young lady, I am not mad at you."

Juliet's face lit up as she reached to hug her aunt, but Evangeline held up her hand. Juliet placed her hands in her lap and stared at them, waiting.

"I understand how tempting it was for you. But I must say, I am terribly disappointed. I do not appreciate your taking my things without asking."

Tears formed in Juliet's eyes. "I am so sorry. You do forgive me, don't you?"

"Of course, and you do promise to stay out of my private things?"

"Yes, ma'am, I promise to never read them journals ever again ... unless you tell me to." Juliet ended her declaration with a bear hug.

Evangeline rocked her niece as the hug came to a close. "I'm sorry we didn't have this talk sooner. Now, let's go have dinner." Juliet took her hand as they walked to the dining room. She kissed Juliet's head, savoring the child's new happiness but knowing it would be short-lived. Guilt tugged at her heart.

* * *

Jake and Cookie joined the family at the table. "We're gonna need more help before the cattle drive. I'll go into town tomorrow and put out the word. We should get a few extra hands by week's end." Jake turned to Juliet. "Would you like to come with me?" He was anxious to have her away when Artie *died*.

"Really? Can I? Can Manny come too?"

"If he wants to."

Jake worried about crushing Juliet's joy. The child seemed oblivious to the silence around the table. She carried the conversation about Dog and her day's activity with little more than an occasional comment to spur her on to her next topic. Everyone appeared to be waiting for someone else to interrupt Juliet to set the stage for tomorrow.

Cookie began the ruse. "How's Artie doin'?"

"Artie has requested to see his friends to say good-bye." Evangeline's tone was sad.

Juliet stopped her fork midway to her mouth and looked from one adult to another.

"So Artie's end is near?" Cookie's voice had just the right amount of sorrow.

The sound of Juliet's fork hitting her plate caused Evangeline to jump. Jake had to press his lips together to keep from smiling. This was going better than he thought it would.

"I shall miss him," Selena added as she brought in the dessert.

"I don't know how you all can eat pie at a time like this," Juliet cried as she ran outside and sat on the porch with Dog.

"Let's move to the other room so little ears do not hear," Selena suggested.

The group took their dessert and coffee to the parlor before Jake doubled back to check on Juliet. "She's headed to the barn," he said as he settled into his favorite chair. "So the plan is to do this tomorrow for sure?"

"I suppose so. Tomorrow gives us time to have a funeral before the cattle drive." Evangeline placed her plate with her untouched pie on the small table.

Jake did the same. "It would. Reckon we should invite the Farleys to the funeral?"

Evangeline gave a slight shiver. "Do you think they will come?"

"By the gossip in town, everyone plans on comin'." Cookie

frowned as he stirred his coffee. "This is quite the sideshow for the town folk."

"Everyone wants to see the bandito." Selena muttered something in Spanish under her breath. "It must be done or there will be suspicion."

The room fell silent as the extent of their charade hit them.

"Speaking of town, Cookie, did you get my telegram sent?" Evangeline asked.

"Yes, ma'am. It was a trial with Mrs. Hanks there, but Selena asked to look at a few expensive lamps. You know Cordelia Hanks can't resist money. It gave Horatio time to send it, and I took the telegram and receipt from him. He promised to bring out the reply as soon as it comes."

"You did make it clear there is no money if the contents are revealed."

"You betcha. He wants that twenty dollars." Cookie cackled as he took a bite of pie.

"What telegram cost twenty dollars?" Jake almost dreaded the answer.

"I promised Horatio twenty dollars if he could bring me the answer to my telegram and not let his mother know about it."

"You really think she will not find out, *Señora*?"

"I'm hoping so." Evangeline started stacking cups.

"What's the big secret?" Jake tried to keep his tone even.

"I sent a telegram to my Cousin Ida. Mr. Farley remarked he knew my Uncle Carl. I want to know what she knows about him or if he is merely name dropping." Evangeline's usual confidence seemed strained.

"Good idea, I guess." Jake made a mental note to ask his wife about her Uncle Carl later. Farley was becoming way too involved in his business.

"Did the package arrive?" Evangeline asked Selena.

"Yes, I will get it now."

"I hope you will not be upset over this purchase, Jake,"

Evangeline remarked as Selena brought the brown paper package to her. "Please, go try these on."

Jake knew his face must have registered surprise, but without comment, he took the package and disappeared. Viewing himself in the bedroom mirror a few minutes later, he felt both shame and appreciation. He'd sacrificed buying the needed chaps, work pants, and boots in order to purchase the sewing machine for his new bride. It shamed him that she'd paid his bill, thus paying off her gift. And now this.

"Well, Jake," he spoke to his reflection, "you can be ornery or you can be thankful."

Admiring the fine new duds, he decided there were more important things to worry over. Taking a few minutes to change into one of the new shirts, he gave his reflection one more look before exiting the room.

"Oh my, you do look dashing. That new shirt fits nicely." Evangeline stroked the sleeve and smoothed down his collar, prickling the hair on his neck.

Seeing the pleasure on her face, he wondered why he had wasted so much energy fuming about the shirts she'd made for him. His thick skull was finally grasping the notion his wife loved doing special things for those she cared about. He hoped there was more than just care for him in his future.

"Do the boots fit comfortably?" She pressed the toe of the boot.

"Yes, indeed they do. I got some time to break 'em in before the cattle drive. How'd you know what to buy?"

"Artie—I mean Isabel—helped me order a few weeks ago. Mr. Hanks recommended the boots."

Jake strutted around the room. "I never had such fine boots before."

"You aren't going to scold me for buying them?"

"Just don't buy such expensive boots in the future." *Even if it is your own money.* "They're just gonna get covered with trail dust and stable muck."

"You need a pair of Tony's silver spurs for them fancy boots." Cookie laughed at his own remark.

"That's one thing I won't be needin'." Jake pointed to Evangeline as he sat back down. After a few minutes of light-hearted banter about his boots, his voice took on a more serious tone. "How we gonna play out Artie's death?"

"I got an idea, Boss." Isabel appeared, once again addressing them in her Artie-voice.

"Why do you insist on getting out of bed?" Evangeline scolded. "Juliet might see you."

"I know exactly how Artie will die." She took the chair Cookie offered her. "I promise to go back to my sick bed and be your obedient patient after I tell you the parts you shall all play in my little drama."

***

As the sun rose, Evangeline entered the infirmary. She wanted to visit with her friend before the household awoke and the charade was set into motion.

Isabel sat with her theatrical makeup case in her lap and a mirror in her hand. Her face was transformed. The careful application of gray coloring gave a ghostly appearance. "For dramatic effect is all," she said.

"Looking at you now, I would say you died last week." Evangeline helped Isabel change into a clean nightshirt. Tucking her back into bed, she looked closely.

"What?" Isabel squirmed under her gaze." Is something amiss?"

"No. It's amazing. You look—very dead."

Isabel's eyes appeared sad. "Remember, you must bring Juliet first."

"Is that really necessary?"

"Her genuine sorrow upon seeing me dead will help with the pretense."

Evangeline dreaded upsetting the child. "I wish there was another way."

"Wishes are like fairy dust. They do nothing for our real lives. My friend, I truly believe everything will be fine."

Evangeline went to join the others at the table.

"How is *Señor* Artie?" Selena's somber expression spread to the others.

"It won't be long, I'm afraid," Evangeline said.

"May I go see him?" Juliet played right into the drama. "I'm not hungry."

"Go ahead, but don't stay long." Jake's voice gave nothing away.

"I'll go with her." Evangeline hugged Juliet to her as they walked into the room together. The girl stared at her friend who was covered up to her neck in blankets with her eyes closed. Juliet started to step toward the bed, but Isabel's appearance drove her from the room.

Evangeline closed the door and followed Juliet through the dining room into the kitchen. Selena, her arms elbow deep in dishwater, turned at the sound of Juliet's sobs. The housekeeper wrapped her soapy arms around the girl. Juliet seemed to take little notice of the wet embrace as her tears dampened Selena's shoulder.

"*Mi pequeño, por favor no llores. Dios está en control de todo,*" Selena cooed.

"If God is in control, why is Artie dying?" Juliet pushed away and ran out the door.

Evangeline's heart ached at the deception.

Selena looked her way as the screen door creaked, and Manny came in. "I hear Artie is bad." His eyes were full of tears. "*Me Puedo despede mi amigo?*"

"Say your good-byes, *mijo*, then go back to work. Work is the best thing for sadness."

Manny went to see Artie and in a short time, came out wiping his tears, not looking at his mother as he left the house.

Around mid-morning, Isabel was in pain. Evangeline had

refused to give her any laudanum, not knowing how it would interact with the strange drug she would be taking.

"The pain only makes my death more believable, I suppose."

Selena knocked on the door. "*Señor* Duke and *Señor* Tony are here."

"Give me a few minutes before you let them in," Evangeline said.

"I am ready now for the final act. Administer the potion," Isabel said in a brave voice.

"May we pray first?"

"Of course." Isabel led the prayer, and Evangeline added her agreement, drawing courage from her friend.

Taking the bottle from her bag, she placed exactly two small drops on Isabel's tongue. She put the bottle away, then leaned down and kissed her friend on the hand. "Thank you for your help and friendship in this strange place. I will see you soon, Lord willing." She wiped a tear from her face as she let the men in.

Duke and Tony said nothing. Evangeline's tears and Selena's expression must have fueled their heavy hearts. She remained quiet as the men paid their last respects. Isabel's moans drew the men to the bedside. This time, there was no acting—the pain and the strangeness of the drug had captured her body and mind. Her speech labored, she fought hard to sound like Artie. "Hey, glad to see ya."

"Hey, *amigo*, what you go and get shot for?" Tony's lighthearted attempt fell flat.

Duke struggled to find his voice. "I wanted to say ... I wanted ... thanks for saving my life. I owe you one."

"I'll collect someday." As she tried to laugh, pain appeared on her face. "I need you both to promise me somethin'."

"Anything, kid," Duke said.

"First, forgive Farley and Bart."

The men stared at their friend, disbelief etched on their features.

"I can't go before my maker with any unforgiveness in my heart.

I want to see you both in heaven someday. Don't hold nothin' against 'em. God will bring 'em to justice."

Still, the men were silent.

Evangeline could see the request weighing on them. Isabel was wise to exact a promise. Otherwise, these men would go to any lengths to get revenge for their friend.

"And please promise to treat my sister Isabel right when she comes. Evangeline sent her a telegram to say I was dyin'. She ain't gonna make it to say good-bye. Tell her about me. Tell her I ain't no thief."

Duke found his voice. "Sure thing."

Tony leaned against the wall. "Ah, my little friend, you know I am always nice to the *señoritas*."

"You'd better be nicer than that." Isabel tried to smile through the pain.

"*Sí*, I shall be the perfect gentleman." Tony doffed his hat.

"I'll tell Jesus how good you both have been to me." Isabel gasped and became very still. Duke and Tony rushed forward. Evangeline joined them.

"He's dead," Duke said flatly. He stared for several seconds, turned, and left the room.

Tony followed without a word.

* * *

Jake met the Farleys at the gate on his return from town. "What brings you around here?"

"We have come to pay our respects to your cattle thief. A couple of your men came to tell us he died." Farley pointed at one of the men escorting the wagon. "I brought another of his friends."

Jake ignored Bart lest he say something he would regret. He suspected Bart's motives for coming along. Artie's death insured the man's lies stayed hidden. *Lord, I hope you got a plan to bring that hombre to justice.*

"Afternoon, Mrs. Farley." Jake's words were stiff and formal. "Evangeline is in the house. I'll join you shortly." He tipped his hat and maneuvered his horse ahead of the wagon toward the stable.

When Jake got back to the porch, Thomas was helping Violet down from the wagon. She fidgeted with the ribbon on her bonnet, looking like she would rather be anywhere else but here.

***

Evangeline's tone was formal as she opened the door for her guests. "Violet, please come in and have some tea."

"Thank you, I think I shall." Violet looked around, then at the floor. "I really do not wish to view the deceased. I shall leave that to Thomas."

Jake went into the room with Thomas as Bart sat in a kitchen chair.

Evangeline had washed all the theatrical makeup off Isabel. The young woman looked quite deathlike without it. She invited Violet into the parlor.

"Oh my, this room is breathtaking. Where did you get such beautiful fabric?"

"Mr. Wong's store." She saw the uncomfortable expression on Violet's face and was surprised she made no derogatory comment about the Chinese. Instead, she accepted the tea and said little.

"You look pale, Violet, are you well?"

"I am with child."

"Congratulations. I wish you God's blessing with this child."

"You are still my friend after all my husband said about you? Your husband was so upset, he bloodied Thomas's lip." Violet looked frail and vulnerable, her shoulders slouched.

Evangeline smiled tenderly to reassure her. "Yes, you are still my friend. Let's put that behind us, shall we? Your husband is not the first man to inform me of his strong opinions on women. I have learned to take those opinions, as they say, with a grain of salt."

"May I ask you something?" Violet placed her cup and saucer on the small table. "I understand you have stitched up the ranch hands and even tried to save Mr. Weaver. Do you know anything about childbirth?"

"Are you asking me to help when your child comes?"

Violet stammered. "I am ... I am asking you to watch over me from now on, as a doctor would back East. I am afraid I shall lose this child. I have already miscarried twice since coming to this godforsaken place."

"How far along?"

"I calculate four months."

"You wanted to wait to tell anyone until you felt life?"

"Yes. I told Thomas yesterday."

"I am sure he is happy."

Violet's lip quivered. "Actually, he told me not to get my hopes up in case ... you know."

"When the men leave for the cattle drive, we can arrange a check-up."

"That's only a week away. I can wait. Forgive me for my self-centeredness. How are you doing? I know Mr. Weaver was your friend."

"It is difficult, especially since he has been falsely accused."

"I am afraid my husband is of another opinion. But we won't speak of it." Violet took up her tea again.

Farley emerged from the infirmary with Jake. "It is probably for the best your wife could not help him recover. A hanging is not a proper thing for a lady to see. With your permission, Bart would like to pay his respects."

"As long as he leaves his guns outside."

Evangeline bit her lip to keep from saying something she would regret.

"I assure you he won't shoot a corpse. Actually, he may not be able to shoot again. I had Javier try removing the bullet, but he only succeeded in causing further damage to the hand." Farley stepped to the door and signaled. Bart entered, and Farley directed him to the body.

Evangeline stepped into the room with the men and saw an expression of shame briefly pass over Bart's face. He knelt down next to the bed, speaking softly, but she caught remnants of his words. "Hey, kid … sorry … wrong place … nothing personal." Rising from his knees, he took out his handkerchief and mopped his brow.

"Mr. Vickers, let me take a look at your hand."

"It's fine," Bart mumbled.

"It is most certainly not fine. Let Mrs. Marcum look at it. Perhaps she can help." Violet's objection seemed to surprise everyone, including the woman herself.

"Yes, sit in that chair and let her look at it," Farley commanded.

Bart obeyed with a snort.

Evangeline took off the dirty dressing. "You have quite an infection."

Bart said nothing.

"If I remove some of the infected muscle and clean the wound, we may be able to avoid gangrene. If the bullet had been removed properly, you would have been well on the mend by now." Evangeline derived a certain amount of satisfaction scolding him.

Again, Bart kept quiet and stared at his hand.

Evangeline's tone was stern. "Here are your choices. We can use chloroform, and you will be unconscious and feel no pain, or you can have something to bite down on while I work."

Farley spoke for the man. "He'll take the chloroform." He glared at Bart. "Violet is too delicate to hear your screams, as I am sure there would be."

"Go into the infirmary and lie down on the table," Evangeline instructed.

"But there's a dead body in there," Bart protested.

"I've no place to move him until Solomon finishes the coffin."

Evangeline's words left him no choice but to follow her.

* * *

By the time Evangeline had finished, Bart was coming around. The Farleys had already left, leaving Bart on his own. "Is my hand gonna be better?"

"Time will tell. I removed some tiny bone fragments. I was able to preserve most of the muscles in your hand. Your biggest problem is infection. I stitched your hand but left a small hole for the wound to drain. Get someone to change the bandage daily. I'll give you laudanum, but use it sparingly. If it gets redder or develops a bad smell, come to me immediately."

"Will I be able to go on the cattle drive?" Bart's words were emotionless, but his eyes pleaded with her.

"I wouldn't recommend it. Using your hand too soon or getting it dirty could result in gangrene. I've placed your hand on a wooden splint and wrapped additional bandaging to secure it. Keep that splint on your hand for two weeks. Our hope is the wound drains well this week."

Evangeline put bandaging, laudanum, and a bottle of carbolic acid in a parcel for Bart. "Cookie has the wagon ready to take you back to the Farleys' place." She held up her hand against his protests. "Don't even try to ride your horse until the chloroform has completely worn off. Tomorrow will be soon enough."

Jake escorted Bart to the waiting wagon.

Evangeline went back to clean up the surgery table but stopped to touch Isabel. Her skin was clammy, yet warm. Too warm for someone who was supposed to be dead.

"Lord," she prayed. "I sure hope no one else was the wiser."

CHAPTER 25

E vangeline sat at the dining table with her journal.
May 6th
The house is empty this morning. Juliet is helping Manny in the barn, and Selena is in her garden. It has been difficult to find the private time to give an account of the past few days while it is fresh in my mind.

We found a place to hide Isabel. Jake's family homestead served nicely. It is hidden in the trees, and overgrown weeds disguise the entrance.

Artie's coffin was laid to rest in the family cemetery yesterday much to the objection of the community. There were those who wanted his body placed on public display at the undertakers. Tony managed to deliver his cousin's body to his family, depriving the community of the opportunity to display and photograph the local bandito in his coffin. Although it had only been a day since Artie's death, people came from miles away for the wake, mostly the curious. It could have been a carnival sideshow the way people stared and commented.

Mrs. Hanks was one of the few people who reached out to touch the corpse, but Duke stood guard and wouldn't allow it. He had no idea how much he was not only respecting his friend but protecting the ruse. People really hate cattle rustlers out here. They are second only to horse thieves. I think murders come in a distant third.

A few hours before the funeral, Jake and Cookie managed to smuggle Isabel out while she was still unconscious. The coffin was nailed shut, weighted with rocks, no one the wiser. Fortunately, the funeral was short and attended only by the Double M crew. Apparently, the curious had their fill at the wake, including the Farleys.

Having no minister present, all the men had many kind words for Artie, and Duke tried hard to hide his tears. Bo's emotions ranged from bitter sobs to silence. The others aren't speaking to him because of his friendship with Bart. My heart breaks for the young man. Bo needs a friend right now. Jake sent him to check the North Slope for strays, giving him time alone to grieve.

Instead of two, it took almost three days for Isabel to wake from the drug, leaving me frightened to the bone. Mr. Wong came at my request and reassured me she would revive soon. Isabel was rather flippant when she regained consciousness, declaring it had been her finest performance. She insisted I tell her every detail since her death scene. She delighted in it all.

Theatrical people are an odd lot. Isabel told me although the drug paralyzed her body, her mind remained alert. She heard everything that was said around her, but could not respond. What people say to the dead intrigued her. How she could remain lighthearted about it amazes me.

Dog is walking around rather well with only three legs. He attempted running when all the wagons came down the lane for the wake. Juliet is thrilled her friend can get around. She told everyone I performed the lifesaving surgery. A Mr. Carter approached me about seeing to his ailing hogs. I told him I knew nothing about livestock, and I had done the surgery on the family pet only for the sake of Juliet.

I am blessed by Jake's encouragement to resume my medical practice. I am still not confident to begin again. I should be drawing my confidence from Jesus, but I find myself losing the battle with doubt more often than not. Besides, there is still so much to learn about this man and this place.
It is time to tell him my secret. I am praying Jesus will show me how and the truth will be freeing as the Scripture says it is. My heart has one burning question—will Jake reject me as Richard did?

I think I see love in his eyes. I know I see desire, but such is the way of men. I thought I could bear it if he turned from me. Had I told him my secret the first day in Hardyville, I could have. After all, I had a plan for going on alone. Now I know it would be death to my heart. Here with Jake is where I want to be. Jesus will have to give me words and wisdom.

Evangeline paused from her writing when she heard Dog's excited yelps. She looked out the window to see Jake riding into the yard. A smile formed on her lips as the dog circled happily around the patient Traveler. After putting her pen aside and sprinkling sand on her journal entry to dry the ink before closing the book, she rose from the dining table and quickly returned the book to her trunk.

"Anyone home?"

Evangeline emerged from their room. The longing in Jake's eyes caused a flutter up the back of her spine. "Why are you here?"

"I live here."

She dropped her eyes and looked about for something to busy herself. The words she had just written burned in her mind. As much as she wanted to revel in the joy of them, she condemned herself. What right did she have to be loved? Guilt wrestled with her pleasure. His closeness reminded her of the wall she struggled to tear down.

"Can't a man come see his wife?" Jake wrapped his arms around her. Evangeline placed her head on his shoulder to hide the emotions in her eyes. She found comfort in his habit of breathing in her scent and kissing the top of her head. Aromas of the outdoors and hard work surrounded him. "I wanted to spend time with you since I leave tomorrow."

"Tomorrow?" Evangeline pulled back to look in his face. "I thought you weren't leaving until the end of the week."

"I've come from a meeting with the other ranchers. We don't see the need to wait. I hired six extra men this morning." The sunlight shone on his black hair and accented the scar running down his cheek. "Besides, the sooner I leave, the sooner I get back." Jake pressed her closer. Leaning down, he kissed her gently at first, her lips encouraging him. As the kisses became more intense, her body stiffened without thought, and her hands pushed him away.

"Woman, I came home to be with you."

She tried to swallow around the lump that formed in her throat. The hurt in her husband's eyes stabbed at her heart. "I'm sorry. It's not what you think."

"Then explain it to me." Jake took a step toward her, but she kept her arms wrapped around her body.

"It's hard to explain."

He stepped away, his eyes pleading for answers.

"I want to tell you." Evangeline walked toward the parlor window trying to calm the panic inside, praying for peace. *Father, this is too hard.* She stared out the window at nothing.

Jake's presence felt distant as he stood behind her.

"There are things I have kept from you. I needed to know I could trust you, know you accept me for me."

"You should know by now I accept you." His gentle voice drew her from the window.

"I believe you, but I'm fighting the old battle of accepting myself." She sat in her chair, focusing on the brocade curtains behind his head. When Jake sat and leaned forward, his elbows resting on his knees, she said, "There are questions you need answers to—secrets I have kept from you." She looked down at her hands. "I'm uncertain where to begin." *Lord, help me.*

"I'm listenin'."

"I suppose telling you about the money I brought with me would be a good place to start." *Oh, Lord, I'm sorry I can't be bolder. This is safer. Safe is what I need right now.* "Grandmother Olson gave each of her six granddaughters a dowry in a trust when we turned three. There it collected interest until we married." Evangeline relaxed with the telling. "I forgot about it until Greta had it deposited in my bank account in Missouri when she heard I was to be a mail-order bride. The bank was robbed on more than one occasion, so I sewed the money into my traveling suit to keep it safe."

"How much was the dowry?"

"Ten thousand dollars."

"You wore ten thousand dollars on the train all the way from Missouri?" Jake's low whistle lightened the mood.

"As you know, I'm no spring chicken. The dowry collected a lot of interest."

"None was wages from doctorin'?"

"People tend to pay female doctors less. My credibility was always in question." Evangeline's finger traced the pattern on the chair fabric. "There was an altercation shortly before I found out about your letters." Again, she grew quiet, searching for the right words.

"Take your time. I ain't goin' nowhere."

She drew strength from his voice. "Winston Duncan died from gangrene. The family blamed me. They waited too long to seek medical help for his leg. Had my dear friend and mentor, Fiona, still been alive, it would not have happened."

"What did Fiona have to do with it?"

"She would have encouraged Winston to come to the office right away. Fiona nursed most of the community long before Shamus set up his practice. The Duncans revered Fiona, relying on her for direction. Shamus was on a house call a day's ride away. Winston's brother Cosgrove brought him in and was furious to find only me. The leg was full of gangrene. I warned Cosgrove that it may be too late."

"Did you amputate?"

"Yes, and he died anyway. If not for Shamus reaffirming my original diagnosis, I would have been tarred and feathered by those backward people." She knew all her hurt and anger reflected in her voice as she held back the tears. "After Fiona died, not only did the townspeople lose confidence in me, I lost confidence in myself. She was my rock."

"Go on."

"Shamus saw my doubts and hired Dr. Marshall fresh out of medical school. That sealed my fate. If he considered me a failure, so would my patients." Her voice broke.

"No doc can save everyone. What's that got to do with, you know, us?"

She turned away from his probing look, wishing he would quit trying to read her thoughts. "Nothing, yet everything. It's about trust and acceptance." *Father, give me the right words.* "Jake, have I ever asked for details about your relationship with Nora?"

"If that's standin' in your way, I'll tell you whatever you want to know."

"Fiona encouraged me not to live in the past. Nora is the past, and I am content to leave her there. The Jake of the present is all I care about." She leaned forward and laced her fingers together. "There are things in my past I want to let go of. Things God has forgiven me for, but others could not."

There was no condemnation in Jake's eyes as he waited for her to continue.

"I was engaged for a short time. I met Richard in a field hospital. He was a Union officer from New York. I thought he loved me. When I told him the truth, he rejected me. I swore I would never open my heart to another man, and until now that has been true."

Jake stepped over to her and ran his hands down her arms before taking her hands in his. "You're too fine a woman not to have had other suitors."

"Jake, my sister made new clothes for me for a reason. Until I came here, I wore only black and pulled my hair back in a severe bun. Trust me, any would-be suitors got a sharp tongue for their trouble."

"You must have had to work mighty hard to look unattractive." He stroked her fingers with his thumb and kissed her hand. "That man hurt you deeply."

Evangeline resisted the urge to fall into his embrace. Though still fearful of his response, she had to finish her story. "Wait here." She went back to their room. With her stomach in a knot, she opened one of her trunks. As she returned, his eyes fell to the journal she clutched to her side. "I want you to read this."

He held out his hand for the book.

"Not yet." She held it to her breast for a moment before extending it to him, her fingers still grasping the edge. "Promise me you will not read this journal until you are in Abilene, then and not a minute sooner."

"I promise. But why? What in this book has got you so upset?"

Placing her free hand on Jake's face and running her finger along the scar reminded her of his pain. The stubble tickling her fingertips caused her heart to race. "I want you to know, Jacob Marcum, I care deeply for you. I never thought I could love another man. But you need to read this journal, and then you will understand. If after reading it you don't want me, I will leave." Tears formed in her eyes.

"I'm sure there's nothin' in this book to change my mind about how I—"

Evangeline put her fingers on his lips. "Don't make any declarations you may regret. Read the journal, then make your decision."

"Why can't you just tell me what it says?"

"This journal contains what I tried to tell Richard. After he rejected me, I worried over that conversation for months. The only way I gained any peace was writing every detail. I don't trust myself to speak of it. You'll keep your promise not to peek inside until you are in Abilene?"

"It'll be hard, but I promise." Jake drew her to him as he spoke, and she returned his embrace. He stroked her hair and kissed it. In that simple gesture, she felt his intense love.

Then she pulled away and wiped her eyes. "Shall we go check on Isabel?"

CHAPTER 26

Jake pulled the wagon behind overgrown trees not far from the Marcum homestead. He grabbed the picnic basket and followed Evangeline to the cabin. She waited for him at the front door, holding another basket. Her lavender fragrance lingered in the air as she passed inside. A frustrated sound escaped his lips as he closed the door behind them. Spending time with Isabel was the last thing on his mind.

Evangeline laid her burden on the table and rushed to her friend. As the women embraced, Jake noticed the familiar blue dress that had been altered for the shorter, more petite Isabel. The stitches had been removed from her cheek, leaving only the tiniest scar. He was still amazed she had lived in his bunkhouse as Artie Weaver for months.

"Hello, Mr. Marcum, it is so good to see you."

Jake fidgeted with his hat. "Mrs. Weaver, ma'am, it's good to see you too."

"Please call me Isabel. Mrs. Weaver is too formal for a friend. In fact, my brother used to call me Izzy."

"I think Isabel will be hard enough to get used to." Jake scanned the cabin. The living room, though sparsely furnished with a table, chairs, and the old rocker, had homey touches. A vase of wildflowers and yellow tablecloth were on the table, one of Selena's braided rugs on the floor, and a glance through the bedroom door showed one of the bunkhouse beds covered with a yellow quilt. Evangeline had found all sorts of uses for the yellow material she had purchased. He sat in one of the chairs staring at the new Artie.

"It's so good to see you both. Tell me all the news. How are the fellows?" Isabel asked in Artie's voice.

Jake found Artie's voice coming from this elegant woman disturbing. His stare evidently amused her and caused her to laugh.

"Please, Boss, you are embarrassing me," she said as Artie, dropping the accent as her face reddened. "And I do not embarrass easily."

Jake ducked his head as heat started at his collar.

Evangeline laughed at Jake's expression. "You two can continue this conversation at the table. Lunch is served."

"If you will allow me, ma'am." Jake escorted Isabel to the table.

"I know it is quite a shock to see the transformation. Thanks to your wife's abundant wardrobe, I am myself again. Once my hair grows out, no one will know me. I plan on purchasing a hairpiece until it does."

Jake focused on his plate to avoid staring at his former ranch hand. "The men are packin' up for the drive. We leave tomorrow."

"So soon? I was looking forward to my first cattle drive, but alas, it shall never be." Isabel raised her fingers to her forehead for dramatic emphasis.

"I wonder if you wouldn't mind answerin' some questions."

"I am sure you have many."

"Where did you learn to ride and shoot? I know Tony taught you a lot of things 'bout ranchin', but he said you were a natural in the saddle and with a gun."

"My mother's family owned a fine estate back in Chesterfield, England. She was quite the horsewoman. When she married my actor father, her parents disowned her. Once we children came along, Grandmamma persuaded Grandpapa to recant his oath. My brother and I lived with them when our parents toured Europe. Grandpapa had been a sharpshooter in the British army. He loved to teach my brother to shoot. It didn't take much effort to charm him into teaching me."

"How long you been in America?"

"Since Israel and I were fourteen. My brother and I were twins." Her words were slow and measured. "Oh, how I miss him.

We used our riding skills to secure our family a place in a traveling variety show. Along with theatrical productions, my family put on exhibitions. My brother and I put together an act. He would show off his fine marksmanship and challenge all to beat him."

Isabel's posture straightened as she told her story. "I would be seated in the audience. When he asked for volunteers, I was the only woman to challenge him, of course. After he dispatched all other contenders, I would step forward." Isabel's voice created the mood. "The audience would scoff, and some of the men shouted out vulgar remarks." Pointing her finger like a gun, a tinge of excitement in her voice, she finished her tale with a flourish. "Then I would hit every target and shoot the hat off the man who had been the most repugnant. I never missed."

Jake could only imagine. "I'd like to have seen that."

"Once my father established himself in the theater again, we stopped what he referred to as sideshow tomfoolery. My father was the finest actor I ever knew." Her eyes misted, and her hand rested over her heart.

"I assume he has passed?" Evangeline inquired softly.

"My parents died in a flu pandemic a few months after I married Arthur. I didn't get to say good-bye. We had moved to Illinois. They died in New York, and as the new pastor of a church, we had no funds for train fare. My brother came to live with us after their death. He abandoned acting and became a schoolmaster. His theatrics made him an excellent teacher. He also inspired me to get my certificate. My brother and husband joined the Union army together. As I mentioned, my husband died of diphtheria and my brother at Fredericksburg." Isabel's shining eyes held unshed tears. "Friends, it is so good to finally speak the truth."

Evangeline drew out a lace handkerchief and handed it to Isabel.

Jake's curiosity had piqued. "So the Confederate hat was all part of the act?"

"As was constantly fighting with Duke."

"Tony always said you fought like a woman." Jake's remark

brought peals of laughter.

"When may I make my appearance as myself?"

"I figure once you're well enough, we'll take you to Hardyville and put you on a train."

"Not without Amelia." Isabel's tone turned serious. "I will not leave without my sister-in-law. A promise is a promise."

"I forgot about her." Jake rose to his feet and stared out the window. Just what he needed with the cattle drive moved up—another crisis. Before he could formulate a plan, Isabel spoke.

"I need someone to go and see her for me. She needs to know I am not dead. I fear she could take her own life." Isabel dabbed her eyes with her handkerchief. "Could you do that?"

"I could, but I ain't been in that place since I come to the Lord." Jake scratched his chin. "If we want to do this on the sly, I may not be the best choice."

"Can we send Tony?" Evangeline asked. "Selena told me he used to frequent Rose's Place. Would it look suspicious if he went there tonight?"

"We could send him with a note. Tell him Amelia was Artie's girl."

"Or we could tell him the truth," Isabel spoke firmly.

"Could be mighty risky." Jake was thinking more of Tony's response to being fooled than his keeping their secret.

"I'm willing to take that chance. He could go to her and tell her in person. I want someone to be there if she needs a shoulder to cry on. I trust Tony to do right by her. I don't think he is the lady's man he says he is." Isabel spoke with confidence. "I heard the things he said not only when he visited Artie's deathbed, but over his coffin."

Jake stared out the window for several minutes. When he sensed God's peace, he turned to the women. "I think you're right. I'll go get him now. We need to take care of this right away. Evangeline, we best leave together. Otherwise, I got to explain why I left with you in the wagon and come home alone."

"Please don't be long, Mr. Marcum."

"I'll do my best to get back here pronto."

As they rode back to the ranch, his wife seemed to read his mind. "When are we going to tell Juliet the truth?"

"I been debatin' that myself. You know Juliet tends to blurt things out."

"I can't bear to see her grieving and looking at me like I am heartless because I am not weeping all the time."

"None of us is grievin'. It don't look natural to her. She remembers when her momma died, and her pa. I think we should take a chance."

"I'll tell her after you leave for the cattle drive. That way there will be no one for her to tell right away. Her sorrow has kept the secret more real to the men."

"Frankly, I wish the whole crew knew. Maybe the bad feelings toward Bart would go away? They might even like knowing the joke's on him. Be easier on the cattle drive."

"Are you expecting someone to kill him?" Evangeline shivered with the question, placing her hand on Jake's arm as if to steady herself.

"There is the possibility. If it wasn't more practical for all the local ranchers to work together on this drive, I'd go it alone. I don't cotton to spendin' a month or more on the trail with Farley and his men."

"What about Bo?"

"I'm plannin' on leavin' him here. He's so dedicated to Bart, if someone would challenge him, he might take Bart's side. Besides, the men are none too happy with him."

"How will you explain to him?"

"I need everyone on this drive to protect the cattle and my men. I need Cookie's eyes on things. Which would leave you women here alone with only Manny for protection. I figure Bo would do whatever he needed to keep you safe."

"You do realize Manny had his hopes on going this year."

"I promised Selena I wouldn't take him till he was grown. I've taken many a man his age on drives before, and he knows that. But his ma ain't ready yet."

"You know Juliet will tell Manny Isabel's secret."

"Yes, but he'll keep it and make sure Juliet does as well."

Jake was silent until they arrived back at the ranch, wondering what would really happen when the truth came out.

CHAPTER 27

Horatio Hanks arrived on horseback as dusk was settling over the ranch. "Jake, I brought a telegram for the missus."

"Come in." Jake led the way to the parlor where Evangeline was reading.

"Ma'am, I brought the telegram. I had a devil of a time keeping my ma from reading it, but I promise, no one but me saw it."

Evangeline went to her room and returned with a twenty-dollar bill. She read the telegram and handed it to Jake.

"Give us a minute, Horatio." Jake signaled to Evangeline to follow him. He led her to their bedroom and closed the door. "Are you sure your cousin is not mistaken?"

"Ida was engaged to Robert Farley for a brief time. If she says Thomas Farley died in infancy, we can believe her. Now what do we do?"

"Ask her to invite Robert Farley to pay us a visit."

They reentered the parlor, and Jake spoke to Horatio. "You do realize if what's in this telegram got out, there could be trouble. And if our reply leaks out, you could endanger your family."

"I'll wait until Ma closes the store to send the reply." He stood by while Evangeline composed the telegram. Jake was watching over her shoulder, and she passed him additional money.

"No charge." Horatio held up his hand and gave Jake back the twenty. "Farley cheated me on a horse trade. Seeing him get his is payment enough." Horatio tipped his hat and departed.

"Well, ain't that somethin'. Never seen a Hanks do anythin' for free."

"Is it safe to go on the cattle drive with that imposter?"

"Don't think I have a choice." He pulled her close, and she put her head on his chest.

Before he could draw her into a kiss, Tony entered the room.

"What'd you find out, *amigo*?" Jake signaled for Tony to sit in one of the parlor chairs while he took the other. Evangeline sat on the arm of Jake's chair.

"I went and saw Miss Amelia. Delilah is the name she goes by there." Tony fidgeted with his black hat. "It has been a long time since I have been to Rose's Place. This is the first time I have ever felt sorry for those women. I am ashamed. They keep Amelia locked up because she is not willing to … you know." Tony coughed. "When I asked to see Delilah, they gave me a key and charged me double. At first, she did not believe me. Just like I did not believe Isabel when she said she was Artie."

Tony stood and started pacing. "I still cannot believe how Artie—I mean Isabel—fooled me. I was angry at first, and my pride was wounded. But when I saw the frightened *Senorita* Amelia cowering before me, I understood why Isabel did it. My heart hurt to see all she has suffered, and I asked God to forgive me for taking advantage of such as her in the past." Tony bowed his head and clenched his fists. "Now I am determined to help her. I left my silver spurs as payment so she is not molested while I am away. When we return from the cattle drive, I will rescue her somehow. It is foolish, I know, but Isabel cannot do it alone. She is still too weak. And Amelia did not trust me enough to rescue her today."

"Does she believe Isabel is alive?" Evangeline asked.

"Yes, after she read the note. But she trusts no man. And Isabel promised in the note she would come for her after the cattle drive."

Jake leaned his head back and stared at the ceiling. "That gives us more time to plan."

"Are you sure Amelia will be safe until you return?" Evangeline asked.

"Rose promised me when I handed over my spurs that Delilah would only deal cards." Tony walked toward the window. He stared outside for a moment before turning toward Jake. "I overheard something in the cantina."

"About Amelia?" Evangeline looked alarmed.

"No, about Bart. Jim Griggs and a few others were playing poker and whiskey loosened their tongues. I overheard Griggs telling the others Farley hired Bart to rustle cattle and hired my cousin to help. The plan was to connect me to the cattle rustling."

"Which would connect the Double M. You sure about this?"

"Griggs told his men that Bart was drunk and bragging. But then Griggs said Bart tried to claim the five-hundred-dollar reward for killing the cattle thieves and Farley refused. Claimed because he worked for him, he was not eligible to collect."

"Go on." Jake moved to the edge of his seat.

"Farley has some plan that involves Bart taking the fall during the cattle drive."

"What does that mean?"

"The men never spoke the plan out loud." Tony flopped back in the chair. "Boss, what you want to do?"

For the first time, Jake was conflicted about going on the drive. It was hard enough leaving his new wife. Now, with the possibility of unknown danger ... "We have no idea who or what is the target. We can't really make a plan. But we can pray."

A peaceful rest came over Jake after their time of prayer. Tony had asked to stay, and Selena and Cookie had joined them. Evangeline had prayed God would keep Bart from death and the loss of his hand. She even prayed for his salvation.

"It took a lot of faith to pray for that varmint," Jake said to his wife.

"God spoke those words to my heart. I had no choice."

When the others left, Jake and Evangeline moved to the porch steps and sat close, gazing at the stars.

"I will miss you more than you know," she said.

"Makes a husband feel real good. This is the first time I been reluctant to leave."

"Thank you."

"For what?"

"You have been so patient and trusting with me. Other than Fiona, everyone else has wanted to control me, tell me what to do and how to act. It cannot have been easy for you letting me discover my own place here." She looked up at him. "In case I haven't made it clear, I like your company more every day."

Jake kissed the top of her head, breathing her in, memorizing the scent and the feel of her for the long nights on the trail. His voice was husky. "Darlin', you are worth waitin' for."

Desire stirred in him as he held her. He stroked her arm and hugged her close. Before he was tempted to break his promise, he released her and stared up at the stars to still his emotions. After a moment of silence, he spoke more casually. "It's 'bout time for me to get some shut-eye. The sooner I sleep, the sooner I leave, and the sooner I come back to you." He stood and extended his hand.

Evangeline took it and walked into the house with him. "Jake, I can't wait for you to come home." She kissed him gently on the cheek, the first she had initiated. "I will pray every day for your safety." She released his hand and headed into the bedroom.

Jake went to his chair in the parlor to remove his boots. His promise to read her journal in Abilene kept him from following her into their room and making her his wife in every way. He longed for the cattle drive to be over and any wall between them torn down.

Father, I ain't sure how much more patience I have. Keep her safe while I'm gone, and don't let any doubts about my feelin's enter her heart.

He turned out the lamps and headed to his pallet on the floor.

CHAPTER 28

Jake dismounted Traveler, pausing to stretch all the kinks from his back before heading to the chuck wagon. Cookie was limping more than usual. Jake knew the trail was tough on his friend, but he never heard him complain. He needed Cookie's powers of observation as well as his calming manner. The man was also the best cook on this cattle drive. Jake admired the precision with which Cookie sliced bacon.

"Got any coffee?" Jake's words caused Cookie to jump.

"Tarnation, you oughta know better than to sneak up on a man when he's wieldin' a knife." Cookie wiped his hands on his grungy apron and picked up a tin cup. "There's fresh coffee brewin' over on the campfire. Any man with eyeballs can see that." He turned back to his meal preparation with a snort.

Jake poured coffee and returned to stand beside his friend. "Your leg painin' you? Evangeline put some laudanum in with the medical supplies."

"I'll take some afore bed."

"That's a long way off. You're hobblin' more than usual."

"Now I'm hobbling, am I?" He scowled in Jake's direction.

"Might surly there too, my friend."

Cookie's scowl remained as he reached into the wagon for the medical supply box. He took the bottle out and stared at it.

"That stuff's not gonna take hold of you. You've always been careful."

"That ain't what I was thinkin'." Cookie opened the bottle and took a small swig. "Bart stopped by a while ago lookin' for this for his pain, and I lied." He moved to his chair. "I cleaned his wound and put on a fresh bandage." He stretched his leg and began rubbing it. "I told the Lord a little pain might be good for his soul."

"So now you figure you deserve to suffer for them words."

"I know God forgave me, but I still felt guilty." Cookie rose from his chair. "That sidewinder has no business on this drive. I don't trust him."

"It's probably good you didn't let him have any laudanum. Knowin' Bart, he wouldn't stop at a little, and then he'd be even more useless." Jake threw the remains of his coffee on the ground. "Can't figure why Farley let him come."

The jingle of harnesses interrupted them as Javier Morales pulled the second chuck wagon up beside Cookie's. "*Señor* Marcum." He tipped his chin forward in greeting as he dismounted. "*Señor* Cookie, I am sorry for being late. The patron is very slow, and I must wait before breaking camp."

"Washing fine dishes and putting away that prissy little table takes time," Cookie said.

Jake felt sorry for Morales. He came along as second cook and received the extra job of Farley's personal servant.

Cookie pointed his knife at the prep table. "We still got lots to do before the men arrive."

"*Sí.*" Morales put on his apron and pulled out a bag of flour. "I will make biscuits just like you showed me."

"You might make a decent trail cook yet." Cookie snickered and went back to slicing bacon.

* * *

Lunch on the trail was always quick. Jake sat with the other ranch owners while Farley's men grabbed their grub and sat apart from the other ranch hands, gathered under a lone shade tree. They shoveled their food, guzzled their coffee, and headed out in short order.

"Lookee there." Abernathy, a red-headed Irishman, pointed his fork toward the departing crowd of men.

"Yep. Seems they remember how to work a cattle drive when Griggs ain't around." Cookie carried over a pot of beans.

"I think they are up to bad." Morales had just finished pouring coffee for the other cowhands and held the pot for the ranch owners. Jake lifted his empty cup.

"What do you know, Morales?"

"You can speak freely," Abernathy added. "We're all friends with a common enemy."

"Griggs, he tell the fat one, Danby, it won't be long." Morales placed the now-empty pot on the ground.

Skywater grunted as he finished his beans. "What does that mean?"

"I do not know. But I see Griggs caress his gun like a beautiful woman he must wait to possess. His eyes full of passion. This is not good."

"Do you think he's of a mind to shoot someone?" Abernathy asked.

Cookie grunted. "Bart might be the target. He can't do much with that lame hand. Farley's men have been goadin' him. You know how easy Bart gets riled."

"Maybe it has somethin' to do with all these trips to town." Jake placed his dirty dishes near the empty pots. "He never brings back supplies. I figure he's stayin' overnight in a hotel."

"Yeah. Too delicate for sleepin' outdoors without a bath." Cookie's remark brought laughter from the group.

Abernathy finished his coffee in one gulp. "I, for one, have had enough of Farley's bossy ways and his men treating me like I'm garbage. I left New York to get away from the likes of men like them. Me temper's just about ready to explode."

"If they're not careful, a raidin' party could capture 'em." Joseph smiled, apparently pleased at the prospect. "Farley's too foolish to realize what could happen to him."

"As much as he baits all our tempers with his arrogance, we don't want any convenient accidents to happen," Jake said. "We got our hands full as it is."

"You go speak to him for all of us." Joseph's suggestion elicited agreement from the others.

"You're the only one who won't bloody his nose," Abernathy added.

Jake knew that wasn't true. But he also knew the conversation with the haughty snake had to take place, and he was the least likely to shoot him for a misplaced word. "I'll speak to him if you'll back me up."

If the others were there, it would present a united front and perhaps keep Farley—and for that matter himself—from doing something stupid.

* * *

Dusk was hovering on the horizon when Jake returned to camp. Farley's men were playing cards while Farley reclined in a chair before his campfire with a brandy and a book. It got in Jake's craw how he set himself apart from everyone else.

Jake dismounted from the trail horse. Being covered in dust with a parched throat put him in a churlish disposition. He slapped his hat against his thigh, removed his kerchief from his neck, and wiped his face and the inside of his Stetson before shoving it in his back pocket. The action reminded him of all the kerchiefs Evangeline had packed for him. Never had he had so many changes of clothes for a cattle drive. He hadn't the heart to argue with her. He'd refrained from changing his clothes too often lest he be accused of being like Farley.

Pleasant thoughts of Evangeline faded with the prospect of confronting the rancher.

Cookie handed Jake a warm plate of stew and biscuits. His wink told Jake he had his friend's support, along with the other ranchers.

The coffee washed the dust out of his throat, and the food put him in a better frame of mind. Savoring a second helping of stew helped him think through the best way to confront Farley. The stares of the others made him uncomfortable.

Best get this over with. Lord, go before me.

Jake wiped his mouth with his sleeve and handed the empty plate to Cookie before he turned to Farley. "A word?"

Farley finished his brandy and closed the book. "Come, sit. Morales, bring another chair for the gentleman."

The Mexican drew another wooden folding chair from the wagon and set it up where his boss indicated.

"Take a load off, Marcum."

Jake sat down, noticing his chair was in a low spot, causing him to look up at Farley. He sat a little straighter. "I'll get right to the point."

"Please do." Farley casually lit a cigar.

"The other ranchers have asked me to speak for them." Jake noted a slight flash of irritation flicker in the other man's eyes before his face became unreadable once again. "I have no idea why you decided to come along on this drive when you usually stay home and let your foreman handle it."

"Since my old foreman left my employ, I felt it was a good idea to see what the drive entailed. Protect my interests since the cattle rustling incident."

"Let me put it all out there. We—that bein' all the ranchers— want to see you start pullin' your own weight around here. We all take our turn drivin' the cattle and doin' whatever needs doin'. You're not the king here. You have more cattle in this drive than the rest of us, which to my way of thinkin' means you ought to be more concerned about our success."

"I am concerned." Farley puffed a few annoying smoke rings in Jake's direction. "That is why today I went into Suttersville, or Suttenberg, or whatever that backward town named itself, to send a telegram to New York. I am keeping my buyer abreast of our progress. He will be sending his representative to Abilene." He stood up abruptly. "Are we done?"

"Not quite." Jake stood and locked eyes with the man. "We expect you to be up in the mornin' ridin' the trail with the rest of us. You'll not take more breaks than anyone else, and you'll get no fancy treatment. Frankly, I been at this too long to believe you have some special connection with cattle buyers in New York City."

The air between the men became thick with unspoken accusations. Jake wanted to say the man was a liar, but it would serve no purpose without proof. A brawl breaking out in the camp would not end well. "If you haven't noticed, none of us particularly trust you. But our main concern is gettin' these cattle to market and gettin' home without mishap. Know that we're watchin' you from here on out."

The ranchers had gathered around Jake in solidarity. Farley dropped his half-smoked cigar and crushed it under his foot. "Well, gentlemen, I need to retire if I am to greet the sun." He retreated to his tent.

The ranchers stared at each other in silence. Cookie and Morales began cleaning up the last of the supper dishes. Farley's men had retired by the time they finished, and Jake's crew was well into the first watch of the night. Jake stood by the water barrel quenching his thirst. He was on his third dipper when Cookie and the other ranchers joined him.

"Boss, got a minute?" Cookie signaled for him to follow away from camp. Sound carried easily on the night air. Cookie glanced behind him. "That character is fixin' to start a range war right out here on the drive."

"I'd bet on it," Abernathy said loudly, causing Joseph to signal for silence.

"He's not that foolish, but he's definitely up to somethin'," Jake said. "If we cut through Indian territory, we can cut a week off the trip and rid ourselves of Farley sooner."

"Is that safe, laddie?" Abernathy asked.

"We give Indians cattle, they let us pass," Joseph said.

Cookie snorted. "Farley won't pay out any of his cattle for passage."

"I'm willin' to give more than my share to get this drive over." Jake knew it would cut into profits, but that was better than possible gunplay later.

"We make fair trade, have no trouble," Joseph added.

Abernathy clamped his hand on Jake's shoulder. "Marcum, you must be anxious to get home to your new bride if you're willing to give up some of our profit."

"True, and his highness is gonna make me do somethin' I'll regret."

Cookie scrubbed the stubble on his chin with the heel of his hand. "Persuadin' him to see things your way might be a challenge."

"I ain't askin'. We're just goin', and if he wants to divide the herd and go the long way, he can."

"But he won't." Cookie's smile reflected in his voice.

"He knows he'll get more per head if we get the cattle in before anyone else," Abernathy chimed in.

"The idea of losin' money is what I'm countin' on," Jake said.

"If the weather holds and nothin' spooks the cattle, we should get there in two weeks instead of three. Suits my leg just fine." Cookie shifted and slapped his leg with his hand.

"Best we hit the hay. Got a long day ahead of us." Jake kept a slower pace with Cookie as the men headed to their bedrolls.

CHAPTER 29

Evangeline smiled as Isabel admired her new pink dress with full sleeves and a fitted bodice. Her rosy cheeks reflected her restored health.

"Evangeline, you spoil me. This is the third dress in as many weeks."

"We must give you a traveling wardrobe. You can't come back as Isabel Weaver with only the clothes on your back."

"How do you find the time?"

"Anxiety works wonders at keeping my hands sewing. Hard work numbs my mind and helps me sleep a little at night." She took out a simple lunch of cheese and bread.

"You needn't worry about me. I have peace in my heart," Isabel assured her. She set out two place settings and strawberry jam.

"I'm sure our plan to introduce Isabel Weaver will go smoothly." Evangeline bowed her head as she blessed the food.

Isabel mentioned the dark circles under Evangeline's eyes. "It's Jake. You miss him."

"Yes, I worry something could happen in the company of Mr. Farley. He is not who he says he is."

"I am not surprised."

"Really?"

"Well … it takes a fake to know a fake."

"What made you suspicious?"

"While in my *coffin*, I overheard Farley mention selling his place to foreign investors. Don't know who he was talking to, but the voice sounded familiar. Part of the craft of acting is paying careful attention to others' speech patterns. It will come to me."

"Why establish himself as king of the cattlemen only to sell out?" Evangeline pursed her lips. "Are you sure it was Farley you heard?"

"I'd know that voice anywhere." Isabel's imitation of Farley was near perfect.

"Here you are about to reappear as Isabel after fooling everyone into thinking you were Artie. Aren't you afraid of being found out?"

"Of course, but good actors can fool any audience. However, my trust is in the Lord, not my own abilities. He will guide me in helping Amelia. I can trust Him to blind the eyes of anyone who may think something is suspicious. As long as I sound American, everyone will believe I am Artie's elder sister."

Evangeline longed to have Isabel's confident trust when it came to Jake's return. Her mind went back to Richard's betrayal. The truth of her past had pushed him away. "Absence doesn't always make the heart grow fonder."

"What a strange thing to say. I imagine those words had no reference to my plight at all." She rose to pour the steeped tea. "One lump or two?"

"You know I don't take sugar in my tea."

"I was referring to the beating you are giving yourself."

"You can't know—"

"He will, jolly well, care for you more, I'd wager." Isabel set the full teacups on the table and took her place once again.

Evangeline remained silent.

"Dear one, what are you so worried about? Anyone can see Jake is a man in love."

"There is a voice in my head telling me once Jake knows the truth, his feelings will change."

"Evangeline, if you believe God has forgiven you, why do you insist on believing Jake will respond so differently?"

"I promised Jake would be the first to know the whole story."

"I don't know what this truth is, but as a man, he took my pretense in stride and has kept my confidence." Isabel drew a handkerchief from her sleeve and handed it to Evangeline. "Jake shared his testimony with the men one Sunday after I first arrived. He told us all the sinful things he had done and how the Lord had forgiven him, made him a new man. I am sure he will offer you the same grace the heavenly Father offered him."

"Thank you, Isabel. I pray you are correct." *Father, I am trusting her words are from you.* Concentrating on her tea gave a break in the conversation which she directed back to Isabel's wardrobe.

"I am teaching Juliet to sew. She is making you a handkerchief and should finish it today. Selena helped me redo a bonnet, and I have a few dresses my sister gave me I will never wear. I have altered them for you."

Isabel had a faraway look as she rose from the table. "When do I leave?"

"Tomorrow. Selena and Manny will come for you. You'll hide in the wagon bed until they pass the Farley's ranch, then on to Hardyville."

Isabel's voice dripped with melodrama. "There I shall board the stagecoach to Charleton where I will meet you as Isabel Weaver, Artie's distraught sister."

"Selena and Manny will visit with her cousin outside Hardyville for a few days before returning home. When you get to Hardyville, send a telegram to me so Mrs. Hanks will be expecting you."

"Alerting the whole town to my arrival." Isabel clapped her hands in delight.

"I hope to receive a telegram from Mr. Robert Farley soon. Ida had ample time to receive my letter detailing the action of the so-called Thomas Farley. Surely, the real Mr. Farley would want to come in person and deal with this matter."

"I would think he would bring the law to deal with him as well." Isabel took her place at the table again and nibbled on a piece of cheese.

Evangeline broke her cheese into small bits, no longer hungry. "Don't you wonder how this imposter managed to fool a respectable and intelligent businessman?"

"After my experience with Prentiss Davis, I am not surprised at the lengths men will go to for greed."

Evangeline froze. Hearing that name pulled her back to a time of tears, pain, and fear.

"What's wrong, my friend? You're white as a sheet."

"How old is this Prentiss Davis?"

"Somewhere in his thirties. Do you know him?"

"Of course not." The sharpness of her own voice startled Evangeline. She took a moment to school her emotions before speaking again. "No, the name reminded me of someone with whom I had an encounter long ago. He has since passed on."

"Don't let the evil from your past color your future."

The words pierced Evangeline's heart like a surgeon removing the last piece of buckshot from an old wound, allowing it to heal. She realized she'd painted her future with the same black brush of her past. The black dresses, the severe bun. Her whole demeanor had reflected her mourning over sin that God had taken from her long ago.

Cleansing tears began to wash away the guilt. Dabbing at her eyes with the handkerchief, she felt joy rising up. Dare she allow it? Sadness had wrapped her heart like a shawl for so long. She ached to be the carefree person she knew herself to be deep inside. A smile spread across her face as the weight of her self-imposed punishment dissolved.

"Isabel, you are a wise woman of faith. You have no idea how much God has used you today to open my eyes."

"I am humbled at your compliment. If you had not been here when this crisis occurred in my life, I am confident I would have been hanged. Without you, I would not be returning to my own life." Isabel sat a little taller and held her cup with her pinky finger extended. "My next goal is to free Amelia. But unlike you, I have no plan or relatives back East to help me."

Evangeline tapped her lips with her finger. "I have a plan."

"When did it come to you?"

"As I heard your story, God reminded me how I could provide the funds necessary to release her. I had my bank in Missouri set up an account for me in Hardyville." Excitement rose in Evangeline as her thoughts unfolded.

"In case your mail-order groom was less than desirable?"

"I may be bold to come to the West, but I am not foolish. While you are there, go to the bank. I will give you a letter of introduction."

"Will there be enough to redeem Amelia?"

"More than enough. I want you to withdraw all of it."

Isabel's brows shot upward. "All of it? I cannot take all your money."

"Don't worry, more is deposited every month. It will be replenished soon enough." Evangeline's heart was racing with the prospect of helping her friend.

Confusion was evident on Isabel's face. "When you spoke of your family, I never got the impression they were wealthy."

"They were not. I promise someday I will explain it to you. For now, trust me and follow my instructions. Together, we must trust the Lord to use the money to free your sister-in-law."

Evangeline longed for Jake's presence. Placing her head on his shoulder had become a source of safety for her. The ache in her heart for her husband was a new experience. Fear no longer held her paralyzed. She hoped when he returned she could explore these new feelings and see if God had placed His stamp of blessing on their union. She took Isabel's hand. "My dear friend, I leave you to do whatever last-minute packing you need. When Selena comes tonight, she will bring the rest of your things."

Isabel rose and hugged her tightly. "You are the sort of friend the Scripture speaks of who is closer than a brother. Thank you for being so faithful."

* * *

Violet's arrival was uncanny. *She must have passed Selena and Manny on the road.* Putting on her best smile, Evangeline opened the door and moved aside to let her neighbor enter.

"What a pleasant surprise. Please come in and have some tea. Have your driver make himself comfortable in the bunkhouse."

Violet made no objection. "Evangeline, are we still friends?"

"Yes, of course we are." She took note of the uncharacteristic attire—a simple day dress and bonnet. No one would take her for a woman of means.

"Good." Relief filled her voice. "Thomas has forbidden me to leave the ranch while he is away, but I had to come." Leaning toward Evangeline, she spoke quietly. "Can you tell if my baby is healthy? I'm worried."

"Certainly." Evangeline escorted her to the infirmary. After a thorough examination, she went to make tea while Violet dressed.

As Violet entered the parlor, the young woman's face was etched with worry. "Is anything wrong?"

"No, I told you everything is fine. Please, sit down."

"I feared your offer of tea was to prepare me for bad news."

"You needn't worry so much. The baby seems fine, but you are much too nervous, which is not good for either of you."

"I am so afraid and so alone."

Evangeline's heart broke for the timid woman before her. Reaching up, she took Violet's hand and pulled her down beside her on the settee. She suspected Violet was in the dark about her husband's dealings. Getting away before she was confronted with the awful truth seemed the best course of action.

"I would suggest you go stay with your family back East until the baby comes."

Violet wrung her hands. "I'm afraid that won't do. Thomas would never approve."

"Why not go for a visit? You could see a specialist there, and it would put your mind at rest. And if the doctor felt you should stay, well, surely your husband would not object to doctor's orders."

"Thomas has never let me visit my family since coming here. They are not in the same social circles." Her face reflected anxiety as her eyes misted over. "For now you have set my mind at ease. I shall go home with a lighter heart. Thank you for being a true friend in my hour of need. Do come visit me soon."

"I'm afraid it will have to wait until the men return. Jake left only a few men while he is away. I would feel wrong asking them to interrupt their work to drive me." Evangeline patted Violet's hand. "You are here now, so let's enjoy the time we have." She picked up the teapot. "Now was that two sugars and lots of cream?"

"Yes, please. You are very kind. How I wish we didn't live in such a godforsaken place. I long for the city where it is safe to walk the streets. Perhaps I can stop by next week?"

"I have a visitor from Illinois coming. Artie Weaver's sister."

Violet's face paled. "Perhaps I shouldn't come. It could be awkward."

"I think Isabel will be very forgiving. If you should decide to come, you are most welcome." Evangeline had mixed feelings about future visits from her neighbor with all the drama afoot. But the poor woman needed a friend, especially now. "Violet, I would love to hear about your family. Have you written them about the baby?"

"No. Thomas would rather I not talk about them." Violet stared at her hands in her lap.

"Well, I'm not Thomas, and I would love to hear about them."

Violet appeared flustered. "Why don't you tell me about your family instead?"

Trying not to look surprised, Evangeline smiled. "With pleasure." She spoke of her brothers and sisters and told a few stories from her childhood. She could have sworn she saw envy in the woman's eyes.

Violet left soon after, exacting a promise from her to visit as soon as the men returned.

Evangeline gathered up the tea things and took them to the

kitchen, wondering about her visitor. What social circles kept Violet from her parents? And why would Thomas Farley marry outside his own social class unless even his marriage was a sham? Thinking back on previous conversations, Evangeline recalled that Violet's comments often sounded memorized. Maybe Evangeline had misjudged her. Maybe she was almost as good an actress as Isabel.

***

Isabel exited the stage. "Mrs. Marcum, I presume."

Evangeline tried not to laugh at the exaggerated greeting. "Miss Weaver, it is a delight to meet you. However, I wish it were under more pleasant circumstances." Evangeline turned to Bo. "Please collect Miss Weaver's things and take them to the wagon." Bo tipped his hat at Isabel, not a sign of recognition on his face.

Mrs. Hanks stopped sweeping the steps of the Mercantile and called out loud enough for the whole town to hear, "Hello, Mrs. Marcum, how are you today? Who's your visitor?"

"This is Miss Isabel Weaver from Illinois. She has come to inquire about her brother's death. You remember our ranch hand, Artie Weaver."

"Yes, I believe I do." Mrs. Hanks paused and leaned on her broom as if she were trying to recall him. "You do resemble your brother a great deal."

Isabel smiled but said nothing.

"We must be off, Mrs. Hanks. My husband returns in a few days. I received a telegram, but I'm sure you know that. I'm most anxious to get home."

As Bo maneuvered the wagon along the main road, Evangeline followed her friend's gaze toward Rose's Place. Neither spoke their thoughts in Bo's presence.

Isabel's anguish showed in her eyes as she turned her face away from the saloon, but in moments, her face transformed to her new role. "My dear Mrs. Marcum, I do look forward to seeing the place where my little brother spent his last days and view his grave." Her voice sounded more educated than Artie's, but there was no trace of British heritage.

Lord, I believe this is going to work.

CHAPTER 30

Jake woke from his strange dream, almost forgetting he was on a cattle drive. This dream had no battle scenes. Instead, he stood on a hill overlooking his ranch as a black cloud overshadowed the house. It engulfed the outbuildings, growing in intensity to cover the land. Just as it was about to consume the ranch house, a voice from heaven spoke like loud thunder. "The Lord protects the righteous and hears their prayers." The last vibrations of the celestial voice dissolved the clouds.

Jake was completely awake now. Leaving his bedroll, he found a place outside the camp where he could pray. "Lord, I don't understand. Are you trying to tell me something? Give me wisdom."

He walked and prayed as the night turned to dawn. Peace rested on him as he headed back to camp. Not since he surrendered his life to Jesus had he sensed God's presence so strongly. Whatever was coming, he knew God would take control.

Back in camp, he set his mind on the tasks at hand. They would have the cattle in the pens in Abilene today. Farley had disappeared again. Whatever the man was up to, Jake knew he needed to let God handle it.

Reflecting back on the cattle drive, Jake realized God had really kept all the men in His hand. Farley had been agitated by the path through Indian Territory but surprised Jake by not complaining about surrendering a few head of cattle to the Indians as payment. They lost fifty head in the swollen river and another thirty of the weaker ones to the elements.

The biggest problem had been the growing animosity between Farley's men and the others. Farley's men refused to help with any injured or lost cattle that didn't have the Triple Diamond brand.

The free-flowing whiskey Farley allowed definitely turned the river crossing into a nightmare. Quick thinking on Tony's part had averted a stampede, and God's peace had kept Jake through all of it. He knew his wife's prayers were making a difference. By noon they should be herding the cattle into the holding pens and collecting their pay. He looked forward to the letter waiting for him in Abilene as Evangeline had promised.

***

Jake waited for Cookie in the hotel restaurant. A long, hot bath had soothed away the aches and fatigue of the trail.

Cookie sat down and squinted at the menu. "I'm hungry 'nough to eat a bear. Can't decide if I want roast beef or a nice leg o' lamb."

"Thought you were a cattle man," Jake said in surprise.

"My folks were sheep farmers for two generations. I miss a good leg o' lamb from time to time. 'Sides, who's gonna tell?"

"Certainly not me, friend. But I'd take beef over lamb any day. Ain't nothin' as good as a nice piece of beef."

"'Course, if you didn't believe that, you'd be outta business."

"Absolutely."

Their pleasant exchange turned to silence as Thomas Farley approached. "Mind if I sit down?" He was dressed in a cream-colored suit with a red satin vest.

Jake motioned to the chair beside him. Cookie stared at the menu.

"I want to speak to Mr. Marcum in private. It will only take a few moments."

"Speak your mind, Farley, or wait till we're done eatin'." Jake snapped. "Cookie's mighty hungry, and I don't think he should have to wait."

"I've come to inform you I am taking possession of your ranch. I'll give you thirty days to vacate the property."

"Farley, what kinda crazy talk is this?" Jake's laugh was cut short by Farley's sneer.

"I have been inquiring as to the details of how you took possession of the Double M." Farley's speech was haughtier than usual, and Jake wanted to dump his coffee on the cream-colored suit.

Cookie slammed the menu down on the table. "Everyone knows Ben willed the ranch to Jake. No mystery there. What you tryin' to pull?"

"Unfortunately for you, the will was not legally filed. I have been in contact with his brother, Lord Byron Mitchell or rather, McKay. He has agreed to sell me your ranch for a fair price."

"You liar!" Jake's voice rose along with his tall frame, knocking over the chair. Patrons at the adjoining tables stared. Righting the chair, he gripped it hard and spat out his words. "You will take my land over my dead body ... if I don't put you in the ground first."

"And you, a Christian man." Sarcasm oiled Farley's words. "You prove once again every man has a price."

"A price?"

"To sell his soul to the Devil. Yours is your land." Farley rose and straightened his fancy jacket. "You have thirty days." He placed a large envelope on the table before leaving.

"He's bluffin', right?" Cookie asked.

"Probably, but we're gonna have to go through these papers to be sure. Must have been what he was doin' all those days he left the drive."

"You gonna open it?"

"Right now I'm goin' up to my room to pray." Jake's appetite was gone.

"Don't let Farley get to you. The man's a cheat and a liar."

"He's right, though, the Double M could be a mighty temptation to take matters into my own hands."

As Jake turned to go, Cookie abandoned the menu. Together, they headed to Jake's room.

***

Jake stared at the sunset out the window of his hotel. Cookie had been gone for an hour. The prayer time had calmed him, and his friend's reminders that God is in control lifted his spirit. Cookie had returned to the restaurant to eat, but Jake still had no appetite. He lit the lamp to read the letters from home. He laughed as he read Juliet's description of Dog trying to herd the horses in the corral on his three legs. Juliet was becoming quite a good writer. Evangeline's letter filled him in on Isabel's recovery and preparation for her journey to Hardyville. The last line caught his attention.

I do not know if you have read my journal yet. I am praying God will use it to help you sort out your feelings for me.

Jake removed the journal from his saddlebag. He loved her, and nothing from her past could change his feelings.

July 12th, 1865
Richard's lack of compassion wounded me. How could he be so callous toward what happened when I was a mere girl of thirteen? Such a fraud. Upon hearing my story, he spoke kindly to me, saying it made no difference. The coward then sent his sister to deliver the news he'd wed another. He had agreed to an arranged marriage to a woman more suited to dreams of wealth. I am ashamed to admit I actually fainted. My soul is bitter and remorseful. My God is far from me. I wonder if He has ever been near. Therefore, I resolve to write upon these pages the whole story of my thirteenth year. If ever I give my heart to another man, he may read this and know the truth. If his love is true, it will not matter. How could it be otherwise?

In truth, I fear if I do not write this account down on paper, it will fester in my soul for all eternity, and I will never be free of it. Somehow, I hope to find a way to make amends, but until then I will continue to hope God will return to me and bring His forgiveness.

Jake read of a frightened girl sent to live with her wealthy relatives in New York to be taught how to be a lady. She wrote of her eagerness to please them and of her older cousins who loved to dress her up in fancy gowns. The first few pages described the innocence of a young girl preparing to take her place in the world as a woman. But as he read further, anger stirred within him.

My cousins refused to accompany my uncle when he did business with Mr. Davis. To Aunt Dorothy's credit, she was persistent in her efforts to dissuade my uncle from taking me along. Uncle Carl insisted all would be fine. He needed Mr. Davis to have a nice evening in order to close the deal. I have always wondered why he did not protect me. He left me with Mr. Davis while he spoke with an old friend. During that brief interlude, he whisked me away.

Jake wanted to pummel her uncle for using this innocent girl to expand his business. Learning the details of the business associate's actions sickened him. As he read on, the night shadows deepened. Seeing the woman he loved as a terrified young girl wrenched his heart. Several times, he placed the volume down, but he knew he had to finish it.

Infuriated by the cover-up her uncle had insisted on, Jake threw the book across the room. He stewed for some time before retrieving it. His anger grew as he felt her pain of rejection and humiliation. His heart broke when he read how she cut off her beautiful hair in an attempt to rid herself of that man's hands and his unspeakable deeds.

There was a note to him on the last page.

My Dearest Jake,

God has done much healing in my heart since I was thirteen. He has healed both my heart and my mind. I still mistrust myself and, of course, men in general. But by God's grace, I know I can learn to trust you.

God has taken the hate from my heart for Uncle Carl and Prentiss Davis, freeing me to open my heart to love again. My uncle died last year. Enclosed you will see the letter begging my forgiveness. I forgave him when I let Jesus heal the hurts and fears buried inside. I know God has forgiven his greed and has received him into heaven. Over the years, Aunt Dorothy and my cousins Ida and Rowena have corresponded with me. Each has taken Jesus as Savior and found joy in serving Him. This brings me a measure of comfort. As for Prentiss Davis, he has gone before the judgment seat of Christ, and I leave his eternal fate in my heavenly Father's hands. As for the child I was forced to give away, my heart longs for him every day, and I pray that one day we might be reunited. That, too, is in the Father's hands.

I hope this journal has helped you understand. God has used the difficulty in putting these events on paper to begin my healing process. I am praying you find it in your heart to forgive my past and love me for the woman I am now.

Your wife,

Evangeline

Jake closed the journal, blew out the lamp, and lay exhausted on the bed. Thoughts of Evangeline flooded his mind.

She was betrayed, abused, humiliated … and there was a child.

An intense desire to be with her overwhelmed him. Now he

understood those times when she seemed warm and affectionate only to suddenly turn cool and stiff. Even now, Jake could feel her gentle fingers removing stitches from his head. He had felt foolish when first taking the lace handkerchief, but as he pulled it from his pocket and breathed in the lavender scent, the small cloth brought her close. He longed to run his fingers through her thick hair.

A vision of her joyous smile when he uncrated the sewing machine brought with it a resolve to do everything in his power to make her happy.

"God, help me love her as she deserves to be loved. Increase my patience. I need your grace to wait for her to come to me. This day has brought more heaviness than one man can bear. The ranch—my wife—whatever the future holds—I give it to you. I can't do this on my own."

Jake prayed until sleep overcame him. The words of the previous night echoed in his mind. *The Lord protects the righteous and hears their prayers.*

CHAPTER 31

Dog's persistent barking alerted the household to Jake's return. Evangeline peered out the window as he raised Juliet in a swinging hug and planted a kiss on her forehead.

Her eyes took in his haggard, dusty appearance and stubbly chin. He looked wonderful to her. She longed to run to him and bury her face in his chest, but fear froze her in place. Perhaps there would be no smile for her. His telegram had said he was headed home early. There was no explanation or words of affection in the small missive. But Jake was frugal, and telegrams were expensive. Did he keep it short in case Cordelia read it? Did his early arrival mean he missed her, or did he want her gone before his crew returned home? Evangeline smoothed her dress as the happy pair headed toward her. Pulling her shoulders back, she stilled all the emotions his presence stirred within her.

He was in the middle of answering Juliet's questions. "Traveler rode on the train with me."

"You got him a ticket?"

"No, he rode in an empty cattle car." Jake chuckled, and the sound caused Evangeline's heart to skip a beat. "Cookie and the others should be arrivin' in a few days."

"How come they didn't take the train too?"

"They weren't in as big a hurry as I was." Jake's voice sounded cheerful, giving Evangeline hope. He stopped at the porch steps and turned to look at Juliet. "You look like you've grown a head taller since I been gone."

Juliet hugged him hard once more. "I missed you so much. We prayed for you every day." Smiling up at him, she loosened her hold. "Isabel's here now."

"What do you think of her?"

"She's as nice as Artie, but better 'cause she's a girl, of course. I'm so glad she didn't really die. We been ridin' every day since she got here. Isabel's been workin' on Aunt Evangeline to come with us."

"Has she now?"

"Isabel has her talkin' to Sage and groomin' her so she won't be afraid."

Evangeline warmed at the exchange between the two. Leave it to Juliet to tell all the secrets. As the two approached the door, she drew away from the window, her face aflame from eavesdropping. She hurried back to the kitchen and busied herself helping Selena.

* * *

When Jake spotted Evangeline, she was setting the table for what looked like a dinner party. His favorite green dress hugged her curves and deepened her green eyes. "Darlin', you're the most beautiful thing I've seen in a month."

"Cattle and cowboys are the only things you've looked at in the past month," she said playfully, keeping her eyes on the table.

Jake crossed the room in two steps, wrapped her in his arms, and kissed her thoroughly but gently. He held her for several moments, breathing in the lavender smell he'd come to love. "Woman, I've missed you."

"I'm so glad." Her words were a whisper as she relaxed in his embrace.

"If I were Artie, I'd be *so* jealous," Isabel said as she entered from the parlor.

Evangeline cast a pleading look at Jake. "I never mentioned anything to her."

"I'm a woman. We know these things. It was quite obvious how you felt, Jake. You gave Artie every disagreeable job on the place and sent him on wild goose chases at the far ends of the ranch." Isabel's laugh filled the room. "Welcome back, Boss."

"Sorry about all that." Jake ducked his head as he shook Isabel's hand. "I better get washed up. Need a bath and a shave, I'm thinkin', to sit at such a fine table."

"No need. You look fine. You can bathe and change after you eat. I'm sure you are famished," Evangeline said.

"We all been workin' on a special meal for you from one of Aunt Evangeline's cookbooks. So hurry up and wash your hands." Juliet ran to help Selena in the kitchen.

***

"Cookie might be a bit jealous when he hears about this."

"I see the *Señor* was wise to come home early to his new wife and leave Cookie to tend to business." Selena seemed even happier than usual as she brought in dishes of food. Evangeline followed with a large bowl.

"I don't know about wise. I feel a mite guilty, but not too much." As he seated himself, he fixed his gaze on the woman he loved, taking in every movement as she fussed with the arrangement of the dishes on the table.

Selena and Juliet brought in the remainder of the food. To Jake's delight, Selena joined them at the table. "It is permitted, *Señor*?" she asked meekly.

"Absolutely. It's an honor, Selena. What other miracles has my wife performed during my absence?"

Seeing the womenfolk grinning at each other made Jake even happier to be home. He led the blessing and then enjoyed every mouthful of the delicious meal. He amazed himself by having three helpings and two slices of cake that melted in his mouth.

"The *Señor* enjoyed the chicken and dumplings, I see," Selena said proudly. "I have not made them before. I worry you would prefer beef. But I can see how you love the chicken."

"And you've outdone yourself with this cake." Jake scraped the last bit from his plate.

"The *Señora*, she made it." Selena smiled at Evangeline.

"Darlin', I had no idea you could bake." Jake held up his empty cup. "I could sure use another cup of your fine coffee, Selena. It's just not the same on the trail."

As they enjoyed their coffee, Jake's description of the cattle drive brought a response from Isabel. "How I wish I could have accompanied you. It is my one regret in ending my greatest performance when I did."

"How can you say that?" Evangeline asked. "The whole trip sounded more harrowing than I would have cared for."

"Well now, Mrs. Marcum, I thought you came out west for adventure," Jake said.

"Believe me when I say I've had quite a lot of adventure right here at home." Evangeline gave his hand an affectionate pat as she rose from her place. The women joined her in clearing away the remains of the meal. Selena took the last of the plates to the kitchen where Isabel and Juliet were doing dishes.

Evangeline stood near the table, her hands smoothing back her hair as her eyes wandered around the room. "Do you want me to fill a bath for you?"

"Not yet. Let's sit a spell on the porch."

They settled on the steps, facing the setting sun and enjoying companionable silence. As the purple and red hues filled the horizon, Evangeline took his hand. "Did you read my journal?"

"I did."

"Really?"

"Why do you sound so surprised? It's what you wanted."

"My past doesn't upset you?"

"It upset me plenty. I wanted to shoot those varmints. Fortunately for me, they're already dead." He stroked her hand, enjoying the softness of her skin. "It was the hardest thing I've ever read. I wish I could have been there to protect you."

"Oh, Jake." Her voice cracked.

"Before I left, I knew I loved you and nothin' in your journal was gonna change that." Cupping her chin in his hand, he turned her head to look at him. "It did change one thing, though. I understand now that you been strugglin' with everythin' in you to overcome what happened."

"God has truly blessed me with an understanding man."

Jake placed a kiss on her lips that he hoped would prove just how much he did understand. "I promise, my love, to never hurt you. I can wait as long as you need me to. I want to love you the way you deserve to be loved, and by God's grace I will."

After Jake bathed and put on clean clothes, he sat with Evangeline in the parlor. Her stiff posture and the way her teacup rattled against its saucer indicated some of the former awkwardness had returned. Her eyes no longer reflected the secret she held, but the moment for intimacy had passed. She set her cup on the table and looked concerned.

"You look exhausted. Please go to bed and sleep as long as you need."

"I will, but first, there's somethin' I need to show you." Jake handed her an envelope. "I figured you could make more sense out of all this legal stuff."

She read through the pages as he waited. "If we didn't know he was not who he says he is, this could be very disturbing. Let's wait to see what the real Mr. Farley says about it."

"Have you heard from him?"

"Yes, Horatio came out with a telegram this morning."

"When's he comin'?"

"He is waiting for the investigator to secure more evidence. He will send a telegram when all is ready."

"We can only wait and leave it to the Lord to work it all out."

"I agree." Evangeline rose with the papers in hand. "Mr. Thomas Farley, or whatever his name is, makes my blood boil. He has some nerve trying to take your ranch. Surely, judgment is forthcoming."

The feisty side of Evangeline pushed the troubled side into the background. Jake loved the transformation. Her eyes flashed, and her hands moved to emphasize her words. Her strength buoyed his confidence. She stopped pacing and pointed in the air for emphasis. "Let's not forget the scriptural exhortation to be anxious for nothing."

"And to pray about everything," Jake finished. "That's what we're gonna do before I fall asleep in this chair."

CHAPTER 32

Sleeping until midday helped, but Jake's fatigue lingered. He stretched and glanced toward the pallet. His heart argued with his tired body about the time wasted in slumber that could have been spent with his wife. He ignored his aching muscles as he dressed, knowing it would take a few days to recover from his marathon ride. It had been worth it to spend those private moments together the night before.

Jake combed his hair and took time to shave before he sought out Evangeline. He found Isabel at the table, assisting Juliet with her schoolwork. "I see you have a new teacher."

"Miss Isabel is much better too," Juliet blurted out.

"Don't let your aunt catch ya sayin' that." Jake tried to sound firm.

"She's the one said it first."

"As I mentioned before, I taught school. This has been delightful," Isabel said.

"Where's my wife?" Jake started for the kitchen.

"Violet sent Javier around for her."

Jake said nothing.

"I can see by your confused look you had no idea Mrs. Farley is with child."

"Aunt Evangeline went to check on her," Juliet added. "She sent a driver 'cause Aunt Evangeline told her we was too shorthanded to have someone drive her over."

"Miss Juliet, you are a fountain of information." Jake reached over and yanked her braid. "I brought you somethin'. Wanna see it?"

"'Course I do." Juliet opened the small box he set on the table. She held up a delicate silver chain. "It's beautiful. It's for Ma's locket ain't … I mean, isn't it?"

"Yep, I think you're old enough to wear it now—for special occasions anyway."

Juliet kissed Jake's cheek, then ran to get the locket. On her return, Jake helped her with the clasp. "Thank you. I'll take really good care of it. Lookee here, Isabel, there's pictures of my ma and pa inside." She opened the locket to show her friend.

"Isn't that wonderful?" Isabel gave her pupil a warm smile. "Enough studying for today. Go finish your chores, and perhaps we will ride again after dinner."

As Juliet started to gather up her books, Evangeline came in carrying her black bag.

"How's Mrs. Farley?" Jake greeted her with a kiss, and she gave him a playful swat on the arm.

"Physically, she is perfectly fine, but I'm very worried about her emotional state."

"Did you try persuading her again to go back East to her family until the child is born?" Isabel asked.

Evangeline handed Juliet her slate. "Do you have your chores finished?"

"No, ma'am, but I will. Look what Uncle Jake brung, I mean, brought me. A chain for my mama's locket. Ain't … I mean, isn't it beautiful?"

"Yes, it certainly is." Evangeline admired the locket before hugging Juliet. "Now, put it away in your room and do your chores. Those chickens won't gather their own eggs."

"The chickens won't gather their own eggs. You are so funny." Juliet giggled before she scampered away.

"That's another thing I love about you," Jake said. "Now, tell me about Mrs. Farley."

The women shared the details of Violet's pregnancy and her husband's strange reaction.

"What kind of man wouldn't let his wife visit her own people if she felt the need?" Jake said in disgust.

"That's not the only odd part. After you went to bed last night, I connected Farley's papers with something Isabel told—"

Isabel interrupted. "Farley said some interesting things over my dead body. He plans on selling his land to investors. I think he might have some connection with Amelia's dilemma."

"Explains why he's goin' after my land. It's rumored Farley has some connections with Rose's Place. He owns several businesses in Charleton, but the saloon don't fit with his upstandin' image." Jake raked his hair back with his fingers, and Evangeline reached up and smoothed a lock that fell back over his eye. His irritation melted with her touch, but her hand moved away as fast as it had appeared, leaving Jake wishing she hadn't started her pacing.

"Perhaps I'm overreacting, but it seems Violet might be using a false identity too. As long as we talk about trivial things, the conversation feels ordinary. But as soon as we talk about her family, everything becomes vague and confusing, like she's trying to hide something."

"I thought perhaps she might be ashamed of her family," Isabel said.

"Today, it seemed like she had forgotten her story. Before, she mentioned her family lived in Boston. Today, she said Illinois. I didn't press the matter." Evangeline stopped pacing and nervously tapped her foot.

"Sounds like we have a fine mystery on our hands." Isabel's eyes sparkled. "It would make a wonderful play."

Evangeline grinned. "Only you could find a silver lining in our trials."

"Indeed. I think I would like a spot of tea." Isabel excused herself from the room.

Jake grabbed his wife's hand as she began pacing again, pulling her into his lap.

"Jake, please," Evangeline said but did not resist.

"I brung you somethin." He opened the palm of his hand.

Evangeline gasped at the mother-of-pearl cameo. "It's beautiful.

Thank you." She pinned it to her blouse. "So lovely." The peck on the cheek she offered in appreciation left Jake wanting more. Before he could turn her face for a more thorough kiss, Isabel returned with a tray.

"I brought you some coffee." She poured Jake a cup, but her smile disappeared like the grains of sugar in a hot cup of tea when her eyes rested on him holding his wife in his lap.

Jake felt Evangeline stiffen under his caress but couldn't resist kissing the back of her neck before releasing her. She quickly stood, twisting her shoulders in response to the kiss. He picked up his coffee while she took the chair beside him, sorry he had embarrassed their guest. "Yep, need to stay awake till it gets dark. Otherwise, I'll be up in the middle of the night. My whole body aches like a wagon run over me."

"When do you think the others will get here?" Isabel asked.

"In a few days, but they may be movin' slower. Cookie was feelin' poorly."

"I put some laudanum in the medical bag. Didn't he use it?"

"Till someone stole it the day after he used it."

"How awful for him." Evangeline fixed Jake with a disapproving look. "How could you leave him behind if he was feeling poorly?"

"Insisted I come ahead. 'Sides, he don't like being treated different 'cause of a bum leg."

Evangeline wrinkled her nose before picking up her cup. "Did you find out who stole it?"

"We figured it was Bart since he'd asked for some earlier. Cookie didn't let on like he had any."

"Did you confront the varmint?" Isabel asked, reverting to her Artie vernacular.

"Cookie did, but Bart denied it. I spoke to Farley. He denied any knowledge and claimed he would investigate, but if he let whiskey flow every night, he don't care about stolen medicine." Jake took another swallow of the hot brew.

Isabel fiddled with her napkin. "Is he always obnoxious on a cattle drive?"

"Never went before."

"How is that possible?" Evangeline asked.

"When he came six years ago, the elder Mr. Farley's foreman was still there. Troy Smith always headed the drive. Last year he up and quit. At least that's the story. I figured he must've left town, but now I wonder. A man as capable as Smitty could've had a job anywhere in these parts. I'd a found a place for him myself."

"Doesn't Farley trust his new foreman?" Isabel asked.

"Griggs has got gunslinger written all over him. Half of Farley's outfit seems cut from the same cloth."

Evangeline appeared deep in thought as she traced the rim of her cup with her finger. "Soon, Farley and all his men will get what they deserve, and we will be done with them."

Isabel agreed. "Speaking of being done with people, I want very much to be done with the evil man who has my dear Amelia."

"Tony told me he was goin' right to Rose's Place before he even comes back to the ranch. He's worried Rose ain't kept her word."

"I wish Tony had returned with you. But at least it will be soon." Isabel looked troubled. "When can I go and redeem her?"

"Do you want to do this thing publicly or quiet-like?" Jake asked.

"Is there a way to do it quietly? We had discussed marching in there and paying off her debt—perhaps knocking over a few tables." Bitter sarcasm tinged her voice. "Chase the men out of that den of iniquity."

"Why not let Tony handle it? He's willin' to pay to redeem her. Seems she made quite an impression on him."

"That won't be necessary. The interest on the debt is quite high now. Evangeline has given me the money to redeem her, and I think Amelia would be uncomfortable if a man paid off her debt."

Jake felt his eye twitch at the mention of Evangeline's money. "I can see your point. We'll talk to Tony about it. Men are dumb as posts when it comes to understandin' women."

"Before Juliet comes back, I promised I would explain to Isabel about my bank account in Hardyville."

"Bank account?" Jake tried not to appear as shocked as he felt.

"Did you read the letters in the journal?"

"Didn't care to read what your uncle had to say."

"But they explained about the blood money."

Isabel looked confused. "*Blood* money?"

"Last year, my Uncle Carl died. My Aunt Dorothy sent me a letter explaining my uncle's wish. He had calculated how much profit he had made from his association with Prentiss Davis and made that my inheritance." Evangeline's voice cracked, and tears coated her eyes. "The second letter was from my uncle begging my forgiveness." She stopped to compose herself. "I didn't want the money at first. But the last counsel my friend Fiona gave me was to keep it. Turn it into something redemptive. She said every time I used it for good, it would remind me of the blood Christ shed for me."

Jake worked to keep his voice calm. "All this money is in a bank in Hardyville?"

"Well, most of it is still in a bank in New York, part of it in investments, I suppose. All I really know is money is deposited into my account every month. It became a bane to my existence back in Missouri once the neighbors found out I was an heiress."

"Did anyone ever find out the truth behind the inheritance?" Isabel's voice was sympathetic.

"I hope not. The fear of my shame being discovered weighed heavily in my decision to come here. Before we left Hardyville, I met with the banker I had contacted through my banker back in Missouri. I had an account set up in Hardyville because there is no bank in Charleton."

"I understand why you never mentioned it till now. So the money in your petticoat is your dowry, and the money in the bank is your inheritance." Jake repeated it to be sure he had it straight. The conversation he'd had with Farley accusing him of marrying for money pressed into his thoughts.

"Yes, the money sewn into my petticoat was my dowry from my grandmother. I want to use it to build up our ranch."

"Your petticoat. How very clever," Isabel said.

"As a nurse during the war, I had to keep people from stealing medicines. I created a petticoat with heavy, reinforced pockets."

"You are clever and very caring, dear friend," Isabel said. "Making you the perfect keeper of the blood money."

"Thank you."

Jake stood before his wife started pacing again. "How 'bout a walk around the ranch before dinner? I want to see what things need doin'." The discussion of her wealth left a dry feeling in his mouth and an ache in his heart. *Lord, you kept this secret from me because I am so prideful and pigheaded. Help me.*

Evangeline took his arm. "I'd love to walk with you."

Isabel started placing the cups back on the tray. "I'll clear the table and help Selena prepare dinner."

"She lets you in her kitchen too? Another miracle." Jake chuckled and took his hat off the hook.

"Yes, and she is trying another recipe from that fancy cookbook. Sometimes the directions are confusing, so I translate them into Spanish for her."

"I should have realized you speak Spanish. *Artie* did."

"We don't need her to translate for us, do we?" Evangeline winked mischievously.

"No, ma'am, we surely don't."

CHAPTER 33

One week later

E vangeline groaned in frustration as Violet Farley's carriage pulled into the yard. There were so many things to attend to, none of which included a visit with Violet.

She met the woman on the porch, hoping to make it short. Jake would be home for lunch, and she didn't want to be entertaining company. Since the cattle drive, their relationship had grown deeper, and she looked forward to the time they shared together. Jake's men had returned, and time alone with her husband was precious.

Her neighbor immediately began applying her charm. "Please come with me. I am headed to town to buy baby things. I loathe shopping alone."

"I have a houseguest. It would be impolite to leave her." Evangeline hoped the excuse would satisfy.

"Bring Miss Weaver along. We can make a party of it," Violet pleaded.

Evangeline went into the house to interrupt Juliet's studies. "Mrs. Farley would like us both to accompany her on a shopping trip to buy things for her baby."

"I think not. Juliet and I must press on. Please, don't stay on my account. If you recall, today I go to collect Amelia."

"Maybe I can dissuade her." Evangeline found the porch empty. She feared she might have offended her troublesome friend by not inviting her in. Katie wasn't here to lecture Evangeline on her lack of hospitality, and she preferred not to waste the day shopping.

She found Violet standing near her carriage. As she strolled closer, her mind filled with possible excuses she could give to discourage further pestering. Javier was inspecting the horse's hoof, and Violet stomped her foot to emphasize her vexation.

"My servant says the horse has thrown a shoe." The woman started to cry.

"We can always go another day."

"No, it must be today. It took every bit of persuasion I could muster to get Thomas' consent to go today. He was very cross with me. I doubt he will be so willing to give permission again." Violet's tears gave way to a very unladylike wailing.

A woman in Violet's condition was prone to tearful outbursts, but this display reached epic proportions. Solomon came to the door of the blacksmith shop, and others stopped their various chores to stare.

Evangeline couldn't believe the words coming out of her own mouth when she looked at Violet's downcast expression. "Solomon can shoe your horse. Let's hitch Sage to the wagon. She could use the exercise."

**

Jake saw the dust from a lone rider as he left the stable. Several of the ranch hands stopped their trek to the bunkhouse to watch with him. One of the men walked toward the palomino as the rider dismounted—a tall, stocky man whose leathery skin most likely disguised his true age. Jake approached as the stranger extended his hand.

"Jasper Sims, U.S. Marshal."

"Jake Marcum." He shook the man's hand. "You investigatin' Thomas Farley?"

"Yes. Mr. *Robert* Farley should be here in a few days."

"You expectin' trouble?"

"Always expect trouble. This man has given me the slip on more than one occasion. It's as if he knows I'm coming."

"I don't think he suspects this time." Jake escorted Sims into the house.

"I hope you're right."

"Selena, please bring some coffee," Jake called as they sat at the table.

Selena entered moments later with the coffee and two pieces of Evangeline's cake.

"Sims, you'll enjoy this. My wife makes some mighty fine cake. She'll be sorely disappointed to have missed this meetin'. She's shoppin' with Violet Farley for baby things."

"Her lead is why I'm here." Sims sliced into the cake. "Congratulations are in order then?"

"Uh … no." Jake felt his face warm. "It's Violet who's expectin'." The idea of a child with Evangeline sent feathers tickling his gut. Jake worked to school his features. "Tell me what you have in mind. No, wait. Selena, call Cookie in."

Cookie joined them immediately. "Should I fetch some of the other fellas?"

"Tony left with Isabel a bit ago. Call Walters and Duke. I want some of my crew to hear the marshal's plans."

The others gathered in the room, and introductions were made. Sims outlined how the men could help by watching Farley's place and questioning his crew. "Now that we have our plans set, I have to ask a question. How close is your wife to Mrs. Farley?"

"She feels compassion for Violet. The woman's latched onto my wife. Seems to need her friendship, especially now."

"The fact his wife is sneaking around behind his back could be used to our advantage. When are they expected back?"

"I worry. They should already be here by now." Selena frowned from the kitchen doorway.

"I saw the carriage with the ladies on my way over here. I also saw two riders trailing them."

Panic grabbed Jake's heart as he looked at his men.

Duke jumped to his feet. "Boss, we'll find the ladies. Don't worry none."

"I'll get the wagon." Cookie went to stand.

"No, Cookie, you need to rest your leg." Jake ignored his friend's protests. "I need you to stay here and pray, watch over Juliet. If the womenfolk show before we get back, send Manny after us. Walters, you get whoever is handy and head toward Farley's place."

Walters hurried out the door without a word.

"Duke, we'll head toward town." Jake tried to sound like he had things under control as he pushed down the fear in his heart.

As they headed to their horses, Sims joined them. "You'll need a level head around."

"Thanks." Jake knew the man was right.

They were almost at the gate when Bo rode up. "Boss, I got a note for you."

"Who's it from?"

"Bart. He told me to bring it to you. Said he wanted to apologize for how he done acted."

Jake read the note and handed it to Sims, who scrutinized Bo. "Where were you when you got this note?"

Bo turned to Jake and whimpered. "Mendin' the north fence just like you asked me to. Why's he lookin' at me like that? I ain't done nothin'."

"Bart gave you a ransom note," the marshal said.

"Ransom note?" Bo looked confused. "But he said—"

"It's okay. We know you had nothin' to do with this. Take Pete with you and get this note to Farley. Tell him we'll meet him at the north fork. When you catch up with Walters, bring him with you." Jake hoped that would be the route Bart took after delivering the note. "Wait here, Sims. I need to go back for somethin'."

Jake raced back to the house, ran to the bedroom, and rummaged through the wardrobe until he found Evangeline's infamous petticoat. He pulled his hunting knife from his boot and ripped the lining loose. Money poured onto the floor. He pushed aside the overwhelming sensation that he was invading her privacy or stealing her money. It galled him to think he would be using her money to redeem her, but her safety outweighed his pride. He grabbed a pillow case and stuffed it with the money, retraced his steps, and leapt on Traveler's back. Once he had rejoined Sims, he prayed for God's peace and whipped up his horse. Sims kept pace at his side.

At the fork, he was surprised to see Griggs and Danby. "Where's Farley?" Jake demanded.

"The boss decided we could take care of this better 'n he could. He's got more important things to do." Griggs smirked like an idiot.

"What about the ransom?" Jake could almost anticipate the answer.

"He ain't payin' it. As I said, he figured we could take care of this better."

"What kind of man leaves others to rescue his wife?" Sims asked.

Griggs shot a suspicious look at the marshal. "And just who are you?"

Jake went to answer the man. "This is Jasper S—"

"Saunders," the marshal interrupted. "Jake and I served together … in the war."

CHAPTER 34

Violet's prattle about the latest fashions matched the rhythm of the wagon's traverse over potholes. The heat from the sun only added to Evangeline's discomfort. Half-listening, her mind drifted to thoughts of Jake. *What possessed me to trade lunch with my husband for ...*

Violet's hysterical scream jerked Evangeline back to the present. She recognized the sound of gunfire as Javier fell from the wagon. The horse bucked then began to gallop. Evangeline climbed over the seat to grab the reins and bring Sage to a halt. Violet sat frozen, her face a ghostly pallor. There was no time to comfort her. She grabbed her bag and raced back to Javier's body. Evangeline wiped blood from the young man's face as riders approached.

"You're wastin' your time, missy," Bart taunted. "I'm a dead shot, and at that range with this fine sniper rifle, that Mexican is meetin' his maker right now."

Evangeline rose and glared at him. "Why was it necessary to kill this man?"

Bart's smug expression stood in contrast to his disheveled appearance. His companion wore a bowler hat and a stained suit vest over his worn flannel shirt. A well-chewed cigar revealed where his mouth hid underneath a thick beard. His eyes told Evangeline he was enjoying her dilemma.

Bart smiled wickedly as he grasped Evangeline's arm. "It's you ladies I want."

"Whatever for?" Violet's eyes widened as she leapt from the wagon, catching her voluminous skirt on the wagon brake.

"Hitchcock, see to that." Bart's friend went into action, reaching the wagon as Violet ripped her dress. He brandished his rifle, causing Violet to once again go into hysterics. He slapped her, and she quieted to heavy sobs.

"Get back in the wagon," Bart growled. We're gonna take a little ride together."

Violet boarded first, giving Evangeline time to reach for the rifle Javier kept under the front seat.

"I wouldn't even think of touchin' that rifle. By the time you did, our snobby Ms. Farley would be dead. Now pick it up gentle-like and toss it away."

Evangeline did as he commanded.

Bart tied the two horses to the carriage while Hitchcock stood guard. Evangeline sat in the front seat with Bart while Hitchcock joined Violet in the back.

Violet's trembling voice seemed to feed Bart's mood. "Why ... why are you doing this?"

"Shut up! You know what you women done." Bart swatted Sage hard with the reins. She whinnied and jerked, racing forward. He pulled on the reins, but the horse would not slow.

"You must be gentle with her," Evangeline said in the calmest voice she could muster. "She'll overturn the wagon if you don't loosen your hold on the reins."

"Don't need no woman tellin' me how to drive." Bart's surly tone changed as he loosened the reins and spoke softly to the horse. "Easy girl, settle down now." As Sage calmed, Bart winced in pain. He held the reins in his good hand and remained silent.

Hitchcock seemed to take pleasure in resting his rifle on the back of Evangeline's neck or turning it toward Violet's face.

"You ladies best be quiet lest my partner here gets distracted by your chatterin' and pulls the trigger." Bart kept his face forward while his words chained the women to their places.

Evangeline took careful note of the terrain during their silent ride. She sorely regretted her fear of riding. By now she might have figured out an escape route if they could free themselves from their captors.

After a few hours, Bart stopped the wagon. "We get out here."

Evangeline reached below the seat, and Bart grabbed her wrist. "Hey, what you after now?"

"Please, may I get my medical bag?"

"What for?"

"Violet is with child, and she looks very pale."

Bart held his injured hand on the elbow of his gun hand. Pain reflected on his face as he eyed the bag. "Tie it to my saddle horn."

When Evangeline was finished, Hitchcock unhitched Sage. "Climb aboard, ladies." Violet grabbed Sage's mane and swung up without hesitation, offering Evangeline her hand. Hitchcock kept his rifle aimed as they settled on the horse's back.

Evangeline prayed as her anxiety increased. *Father, help me stay on this horse. Deliver us, please deliver us.*

The men took positions in front and behind. As Evangeline patted Sage, the horse's calm seemed to pass to her. *Thank you, Jesus, for the wisdom to have Sage pull the wagon.*

Violet whimpered as they rode. "If he kills us, your bag will do us no good."

"But there are sharp objects in my bag," Evangeline whispered from her position behind her friend. Her grip around Violet's waist turned to a brief hug of assurance as the men picked up the pace.

"You all shut your mouths. No talking!" Bart barked.

They rode for over an hour before coming upon the soddie Jake and Evangeline had stayed in their first night. From the direction they had approached, it was virtually unnoticeable except for the chimney protruding from the sod roof.

"Get on in there," Bart ordered. "Hitchcock, I'll watch the women while you go back and cover our tracks."

The coolness inside gave them relief from the late afternoon sun. Bart hadn't bothered to take the picnic lunch or water from the carriage. He ordered the women to sit on the floor near the wall. His silent vigil at the lone window blocked much of the light and gave the soddie an even more dismal feel.

Evangeline worried for Violet, who was sagging against her.

How different it had felt sharing the soddie with Jake. His presence had made her feel safe and the darkness merely part of the journey. *Jake, I'm sorry I didn't stay home. Please, Father, don't let me die.*

Hitchcock returned within the hour. "Backtracked in a few different directions. Oughta confuse anyone tryin' to find us."

"You better be right."

"I'm a tracker so I oughta know how to cover tracks."

"Mr. Vickers, may we have some water?" Evangeline asked.

"Where do you suggest I get it?"

"There should be a rain barrel outside. May I check to see if there is water?"

"Just remember, if you don't come back, your friend dies." Bart's threat formed a shiver down her spine, and Violet whimpered again. Neither Bart nor Hitchcock left to accompany her. She momentarily thought of running, but Hitchcock would probably relish shooting Violet. She resolved to be as cooperative as she could while still trying to find an escape. Her body quaked as the familiar helpless feeling tried to surface. *Please, God, keep us in Your care.* She took deep gulps of air, forcing her feet forward.

Evangeline checked the barrel. The last rain had filled it. She put water in the bucket and set it down. Before going back inside, she climbed the hill until she reached the roof. Ripping a long piece of petticoat, she stuffed it into the loose chinking of the chimney. It waved as a salute in the breeze. She hurried back down, grabbed the bucket, and reentered the soddie.

Bart shoved his gun in her face. "What took you so long?"

"I had to relieve myself," Evangeline blurted.

He grunted and signaled for her to join her friend on the floor. After taking the dipper and drinking his fill, he passed it to Hitchcock, who took a long draft and spat tobacco on the floor. He refilled it and drank again before passing the dipper to the women.

Evangeline took her finger and carefully cleaned the tobacco residue from the edge of the dipper before drinking, then wiped her hand on her dress. Violet's face registered disgust as she handled the dipper. Evangeline shot her a warning look, and Violet drank without complaint.

"Which one of you *women*," Bart spoke the word like a curse, "knows how to cook?"

"I imagine I can do a fair enough job with the supplies on hand," Evangeline said. She glanced at Violet as a plan formed in her mind. With shaking hands, she lit the fire. As she reached into the box of provisions, smoke filled the room. She ran to Violet and pulled her out the door. As they ran, a shot blasted past their heads. Violet froze, sobbing hysterically. No amount of persuasion could get her to move.

Hitchcock reached them in two long strides and punched Evangeline hard in the face.

She held her footing.

"Open the damper and the window," Bart instructed Hitchcock as he pushed Evangeline back into the soddie. He jerked Violet by the arm, causing her to wince and stumble. His eyes flashed anger as he hissed at Evangeline. "Try somethin' like that again, and you won't live to tell about it." He looked at Hitchcock. "You do the cookin'."

"I ain't your servant." The man swore under his breath as he prepared the meal.

Violet grew more and more agitated, which fueled Bart's manic state. He paced like a caged animal, looking out the window one moment, glaring at Violet the next.

Insects moved from the wall onto Violet's dress. She jumped up, desperately trying to dislodge them.

Hitchcock slapped Violet to the floor. She remained motionless while tears ran down her face. Evangeline crawled over and pulled her close. She rested Violet's head in her lap and stroked her hair while she prayed silently. *Please, Lord, make a way of escape. Don't desert us in our hour of need.* She wondered how long it would take Jake and the others to find them. *Please, Lord, show Jake where we are.*

Hitchcock glared. "Now that we're done with the grub, you two can clean up."

The women started the chores. If the tin plates had been breakable, Violet's shaking would have created a pile of shards and more trouble from their captors. She dropped two plates and a cup before the dishes were clean.

"What exactly have we done to you?" Violet asked in a timid voice.

Bart remained silent and glared.

Evangeline returned his stare. "Even a condemned man knows why he is being hanged."

"You women are all alike. You connive to get your men to do what you want and then pretend you had nothin' to do with it. A man serves his country because his wife tells him it would make her proud. When he comes home, she treats him like he's some evil thing—cryin' and accusin' him of changin'. Your high and mighty husbands are gonna pay for your return, but I ain't returnin' ya." A malicious smile appeared on his face. "They'll be better off without ya." Bart's wild-eyed expression brought Violet to hysterics again, and Hitchcock raised his hand to slap her as before.

Choking back the tears, she sat down and huddled on the floor.

Evangeline finished the dishes while silently praying for deliverance.

***

The sound of a single gunshot echoed in the distance. The men kicked their horses into a gallop. It seemed like an eternity to Jake until he spotted the white flag flapping in the breeze. Somehow, he knew Evangeline had put it there. *Thank You, Lord. I need Your wisdom and peace. Keep her safe. Don't let these men take her from me.* Signaling to the men to stop, he dismounted. They joined him behind a boulder.

"Do you think he shot one of them?" Duke asked.

"Sounded like it," Sims responded. "If that's the case, it won't be long until he shoots the other."

Duke began to inch away. "I'll sneak down and see what I can do."

Jake stopped him. "No, I'll go." He couldn't let anyone else do his job. He angled his way down the hill until he leaned near the door. From this vantage point, he saw three horses tethered nearby. Sage whinnied recognition. Jake stood still until he heard movement inside.

When Evangeline opened the door, he could tell she was startled, but she kept her composure and adjusted her stance to block the view of the men inside. She emptied the dishwater at Jake's feet. Her cheeks were bright red, and his hands fisted.

Swearing emanated from inside. "What are you doin', woman? Come in and shut the blame door."

As Jake crawled back up the hill toward his men, he heard Hitchcock threaten to put a bullet in the women's heads if they tried any more nonsense. He resisted the strong urge to go back. "They're safe, at least for now. Sounds like Vickers has an accomplice."

"If we hadn't seen the piece of cloth, we'd have ridden right past," Walters said.

Duke removed his hat and wiped his brow with his forearm. "What's the plan, Boss?"

"It'll be dark soon. We'll wait." Jake instructed each man into position around the soddie.

"You're taking a risk, Marcum," Sims said. "How do you know he won't kill your wife and her friend before we can get them out?"

"I think Bart's more interested in the money than shootin' the women. What would you suggest?"

"Same as you, I'm afraid. If it was only Vickers, I'd block the chimney and smoke him out. He'd either come out or die in there." Sims scanned the area to see if the others were in position. "I'd keep a close eye out for Farley's men."

"I know not to trust any of 'em."

"More than that, they're wanted for murder and bank robbery in Missouri and Indiana. Funny how they got hooked up with Paine, aka Farley." Sims refrained from saying more.

Jake's blood ran cold as he thought about what could happen. They could rescue the women and still end up in a gunfight with these two. And what if more of Farley's men showed up? Everyone could die. Again he prayed.

When the sun finally melted behind the horizon, the men went into action. Bo secured the horses so they couldn't escape. The others took their positions near the door and window.

＊

Inside the soddie, Evangeline had a prayer vigil swirling in her mind. Relief flooded her that Vickers and Hitchcock had tired of tormenting them. They'd settled into a not-too-friendly game of cards.

"Hitchcock, you're the worse cheat they is. I seen you palm that ace." Bart slammed his fist on the table.

Violet jumped and clung more frantically to her friend.

Evangeline thought she heard the clink of spurs over the sound of Bart's violent outburst.

"No one calls me a cheat." Hitchcock gathered up the cards and flung them into the fireplace. Embers ignited the cards.

Bart leapt to his feet to put out the fire. "Idiot. Tryin' to send smoke signals?"

"I still don't like the idea of you goin' for the money." Hitchcock spat a stream of tobacco toward Violet, landing the glob near her feet. She flinched but made no sound.

"It's my plan. I come up with it. I go get the money while you take these two over to Baxter Hill and take care of 'em."

Hitchcock grumbled under his breath. "Yeah, I know. I get to do your dirty work."

"And your share will make you a rich man." Bart flexed his right hand. In his rush to put the fire out, he'd used it without caution. Evangeline saw sweat forming on his brow.

"You got any laudanum in that bag?"

Evangeline's heart raced. Every fiber of her body tensed while her mind cried out in prayer. Where was Jake?

"Woman! Did you hear what I said?" When she didn't respond, he stuck his gun in her face. His angry tone captured her full attention. "Do you have any laudanum in that bag?"

"I don't think so. I ran out and have not been able to get more." Evangeline quelled her rising fear for the sake of Violet. Bart's nearness caused nightmarish memories to play in her head. A cold chill overtook her. She tried harder to breathe. *God, hide me under Your wing.*

"Dump it out on the table and let's have a look," Bart ordered.

Evangeline did as she was told.

Bart scanned the contents. "Which one is laudanum?"

"I told you there is none."

"Then what is all this stuff?"

"Those are for headaches, stomach disorders, and nerves. I brought those items along for Mrs. Farley. I had no need for painkillers."

"What is this?" Bart held up a small brown bottle. He obviously misread the expression on Evangeline's face. "So ... you do got somethin' for the pain."

"That is not a painkiller."

As he tipped the bottle back, several drops fell on his tongue. "Hey, what is this?" Bart cursed and heaved the bottle toward the women.

Violet screamed as she scrambled out of the way. The bottle crashed into the wall as Bart fell to the ground, paralyzed.

Hitchcock knocked his chair over as he turned his head to get a better look. He pointed his gun toward the ground. "Bart, you okay?"

As Violet screamed again, the men came running. Griggs crashed through the door, dispatching Hitchcock with a single shot to the back of the head.

"What happened?" Sims stood over Bart. "Is he dead?"

Evangeline shrugged as she looked at Jake. "No. He's gone the way of Artie."

"Take this varmint and lock him up in one of the sheds," Jake ordered Pete and Walters. He hugged Evangeline close as her chilled body trembled. He grabbed a blanket from one of the bunks and wrapped her in it as she broke down and cried uncontrollably.

Jake's embrace soon broke through her fears, and tears changed from terror to relief in his arms. When they walked outside, Hitchcock's body was tied to his horse. Sage whinnied and nuzzled Evangeline. She relaxed as Jake drew her closer.

Violet looked on as tears trickled down her face. "My husband didn't even bother to come to my rescue. He sent these despicable characters instead. Please, may I stay with you?"

Evangeline sniffled, still clinging to Jake. "Of course you may."

"Andy promised me if I'd come West with him, he'd make me rich. I had no idea it required me to be someone else. My name is Hester Stanton. My parents own a dry goods store in Shelton, Illinois."

Griggs raised his gun at her confession, and a click sounded. Sims's peacemaker lay against the gunslinger's head. "I wouldn't." Sims turned to Danby. "That goes for you too. Drop the guns."

The men complied.

"I'll be needin' that shed for these two, as well."

"Who do you think you are?" Danby protested. "Griggs and me are on your side."

"I'm U.S. Marshal Sims." By the men's reaction, no other explanation was necessary. "I'm arresting you both for multiple bank robberies. The last two were well played, I must say. Hiding out on a cattle drive was ingenious."

Jake gave Evangeline one last squeeze. "You're safe now, darlin'.

Let's go home."

CHAPTER 35

Jake helped Evangeline from Sage. She held to him for a moment as Juliet and Selena came to greet her. As the women embraced, Manny took Sage's reins.

Evangeline caught the relieved expression on the boy-man as he spoke encouraging words to the horse. "Sage, you have brought the *Señora* home safely. Glad to have you home, my friend."

Selena touched Evangeline's face. "Let me tend to your wound."

Juliet held tightly to her waist as they stepped up on the porch. "I was so worried. I prayed and prayed for you." A trembling smile formed as her eyes glistened with joyful tears. "Tell me all about your adventure."

Jake handed the reins of the other horses to Manny and helped Violet down. She meekly followed the other women into the house. Evangeline paused, waiting for her husband to join them. When he took her hand, she felt her weariness once more.

"Adventure is probably not the word I would use." Evangeline wrapped her arm around Juliet. "But let's go have a seat in the parlor, and I'll tell you all about it." Cookie and Manny joined them as Evangeline and Jake shared details of Bart's thwarted plan.

Violet's silence reminded Evangeline of her confession. At least the woman's face was regaining color. Not once did this otherwise talkative friend add to the story. Tears trailed down her cheeks. Evangeline offered her a handkerchief, and Selena patted her like a protective mother. Violet's head hung lower with each offer of kindness.

Finishing her story, Evangeline looked at Selena. "Has Isabel returned yet?"

"She left early afternoon and we have no seen her and *Señor* Tony since. I fear it was not easy to redeem Miss Amelia."

Jake frowned and scratched his head. "The marshal took my crew and headed into town. If there was any trouble, they'll get to the bottom of it. Duke told Sims all about Amelia's problem. Sims told us how he'd been in Rose's Place a few times investigatin'. He heard lots of suspicious things while we were on the cattle drive."

The sound of horses brought the entire group to the porch. Duke and Isabel dismounted as Tony helped a tiny woman from his horse. The woman shrank back and covered her chest with her arms, hiding her immodest apparel.

Evangeline and Juliet ran to hug Isabel, who beamed at them. "Allow me to introduce Miss Amelia Weaver."

Evangeline embraced the young woman. "I'm so glad you're safe. God has truly answered our prayers."

As Amelia began to cry, Evangeline tightened her embrace, cooing words of comfort. Together, she and Isabel helped the distraught woman into the house. Selena brought out a warm meal of tortillas and beans. While they ate, Jake and Tony exchanged information from the day's events. Isabel's description of her ordeal was far more colorful than Tony's.

"Isabel has many skills, *jefe*." Tony grinned around a forkful of beans.

"And Antonio Garcia Sanchez is a very brave man." Isabel's use of his formal name caused Tony to duck his head. "Without him I would not be alive."

"I think we make a good team."

Juliet squirmed in her chair. "You said this Mr. Davis locked you up and planned to kill you?" Her tone was intense. Leave it to Juliet to find intrigue in a fearful situation.

"Tony pushed his way into Davis's office. Such a menacing glare he gave that reprobate. I was very impressed." Isabel recalled the entire scene for her listeners. "I knew him immediately. His was the voice from the funeral. Prentiss Davis, alias William Cramer, the man who had seduced Amelia and brought her to this place. When he asked how I found him, I said, 'Quite frankly, the odious scent of greed led me to you.'"

Tony joined in. "When he refused to give us Amelia, I say, 'Davis or Cramer or whoever you are, you will do this, or you will die.'"

Juliet's eyes widened. "Then what happened?"

"Two brutes subdued us both, I'm afraid," Isabel said. "They knocked Tony unconscious and tied us up in a room. Their plan was to kill us at sundown."

"But we were *mucho* clever." Tony described how they managed to loosen their bonds and Isabel picked the lock.

"After we found Amelia, Tony broke the window in the hallway, and we climbed out."

Tony grinned. "I whistled for Bonita, and she waited below the window for us."

"Don't forget I was there in the nick of time," Duke added.

"*Sí*, Duke drew on a big man who came out the saloon door just as the marshal, the sheriff, and his deputies came upon our plight."

Isabel patted Duke's hand, causing him to flinch. "We four fled town with haste."

Duke filled a plate as Tony took up the story. "Once we were clear of Charleton, I asked my friend, 'What took you so long?'"

Duke swallowed a mouthful of food. "I told him I was busy rescuin' other damsels in distress." He shot Isabel a smile. "The marshal sent me to tell the sheriff to head to Rose's Place."

Evangeline caught Amelia staring at Tony. He smiled back at her. "*Señorita*, you are safe now. No one will hurt you again."

"Thank you, Antonio. If not for you, my sister-in-law and I might be dead," she said through her tears.

Tony turned his gaze to Jake. "*Jefe*, what's next?"

"Sims got the full story from Mrs. Farley—I mean Miss Stanton—before he left. She told him the silent partner at Rose's Place was Matthew Paine, our fake Farley's real brother. One of his aliases is Prentiss Davis. His job was to lure women."

When Amelia began to sob, Tony leaned over and took her hand. Evangeline studied the interaction between the two. Tony's touch seemed to comfort the wounded woman. Amelia took the handkerchief Evangeline offered and breathed deeply as she wiped her tears.

"I'm sorry, ma'am, Didn't mean to cause you more pain." Jake's words were gentle.

"These are tears of relief, Mr. Marcum. I have been rescued from hell and am eternally grateful." Amelia picked up her fork and began to take small bites.

Isabel finished her coffee and picked up another tortilla. "Where is Marshal Sims now?"

"He's gone to meet the sheriff and his deputies. They're makin' plans for bringin' in the Paine brothers. He promised to send word if he needed our help. A bunch of other lawmen should be here by mornin'. Seems the Paines are wanted in a lot of places."

***

Evangeline brought a nightgown for Hester. It would take time to get used to Violet's real name. Juliet was happy to give up her room for the adventure of sleeping in the hayloft. Evangeline had persuaded Marshal Sims not to take Hester into custody just yet.

Shame covered the woman's face. "Do you hate me for deceiving you?"

"Now that you are Hester, not Violet, I like you much better."

"I want to raise my child the same way I was raised. My parents taught me about the Lord, but I went after money and what I thought was the good life. I need to send them a telegram tomorrow to see if I can come home. That is, if I don't go to jail."

"What will you say when your *husband* comes looking for you?"

Shame crossed her face again. "Andy said he wasn't the marrying kind." A tear spilled down her cheek. "I thought my life in Shelton was so boring. I wanted excitement. Now I just want to go home.

Do you think it would be wrong to say my husband died?"

They sat in silence until Evangeline offered a suggestion. "May I pray for you?"

Hester bowed her head.

CHAPTER 36

At the stagecoach, Evangeline hugged her friend one last time. "Remember, Hester, the truth will set you free."

"I appreciate the reminder. Marshal Sims wants me to testify against Andy and Matt. Then he says I will be free to go because I was a pawn in the whole affair. God has shown me mercy. I honestly had no idea Andy was a con man. He told me he was a businessman and, like any woman in my position, I asked no questions. The trial will be in Hardyville, at least for his crimes here. Then he and his brother will be taken back East for another trial. I won't need to be there. Once I get to Hardyville, I'll write a letter to my family. After the trial, I plan on going home. I'll write and let you know how I'm doing. Pray for me. And thank you for the money. It will make it easier to raise my child. I won't have to worry about finding a job right away."

* * *

Jake studied the two men who exited the stagecoach as Evangeline was saying good-bye to Hester. One was short and stocky, the other extremely thin and dressed in the latest East Coast fashion. They patted the dust from their expensive suits as Marshal Sims approached them. After shaking hands, he assisted with the luggage and led them toward Jake.

"Jake Marcum, let me introduce the real Farley." Sims pointed to the shorter man. "This is Robert Farley and his assistant, Whitney Smithton."

Jake shook hands with the men.

"Why are you looking at me in that manner?" Farley protested.

"Sorry, I'm tryin' to decide if I remember you."

"You have an older brother, Clevis, isn't that correct?"

"He died in the war."

"My sympathies. I lost many dear friends in the war. I do recall something about your brother that might assure you I am the real Farley."

Jake hoped so. "Go on."

"When I was a boy of ten, I came to visit my father for the summer. I rarely left the house, but on one particular day, my father took me with him to visit his neighbor, Mr. Mitchell. Your brother was there and, along with the Mitchell boys, sold me a rock, insisting it had magical powers. They convinced me this rock would make me taller if I slept with it under my pillow. Your brother told me he, too, was ten and it had worked for him."

"I remember hearin' about that."

"As you can see, it did no good."

They both laughed.

"Forgive me for doubtin' you."

"Perfectly understandable under the circumstances." Farley turned to Sims. "Now, tell me, when do we confront this imposter?"

"The sheriff and his men raided Rose's Place last night and arrested Matthew Paine. I had a few other marshals in place already. My report of the young lady being kept against her will seemed to turn the sheriff's sympathies away from Paine. Having a bunch of marshals on his doorstep didn't hurt either. When Paine's henchmen tried to stop the rescue, my men went into action. With the aid of the sheriff, his deputies, and some honorable cowpokes, we rounded them all up. Rose's Place is shut down, and Matthew Paine and his men are locked up. He's being held on attempted murder charges for starters. Once we have his brother, they'll both be taken to Hardyville for trial." Sims recounted the kidnapping just as Evangeline joined them.

With a look of admiration, Robert Farley spoke to Evangeline. "Mrs. Marcum, I must say you look well for someone who has been through such an ordeal."

"Looks can be deceiving. I'm still unnerved by it all. But God's peace and the presence of my husband have been my comfort." Evangeline held firmly to Jake's hand. "Thank you, Mr. Sims, for removing Griggs and Danby from the ranch."

"I still don't think keeping Vickers is wise, even if he is unconscious."

"My wife's a doctor, and she wants to be sure Bart recovers from the drug he took." Jake did not miss the smile his confession brought to his wife's face.

"You are a *doctor?*" Robert Farley looked at her, his face registering surprise for only a moment. "I am sure the town values your services to them."

Jake ignored the remark. "My wife also has other reasons for keepin' Bart."

"I have discovered that anyone under the influence of this particular drug, although unresponsive, can hear everything that goes on around them. I have a plan to encourage Bart to confess his sins when he regains consciousness. I refuse to be held captive by my own emotions. I'm working on forgiveness and praying for him."

Robert nodded solemnly at Evangeline. "You are far nobler than I, madam. I wish to see this man prosecuted to the full extent of the law."

"Mr. Vickers will get what he deserves. He shot Javier in cold blood. But I know the Lord would desire to give him eternal life."

"You sound like your cousin Ida."

"You're welcome to stay at our place," Jake offered. "The hotel here is owned by that Paine fella, and it ain't much to speak of."

"Our home is humbler than you are used to, but it's clean, and Selena is a wonderful cook," Evangeline added.

"We would be delighted."

* * *

Jake's buckboard entered the yard, followed by Farley's rented one. Manny and Bo left the barn and stood by the fence as the wagons pulled to a stop.

Bo's head was bowed with shame as he pulled Jake to the side. "Boss, I need to talk to you. It's real important."

Jake turned to his guests. "I need to tend to business. My wife will show you to your rooms. Manny, take in their luggage."

Bo led Jake into the barn. "I got to confess somethin'."

"Go ahead."

The young man's hands were shaking. "I stole them cattle, me and Bart."

"I suspected as much." Jake's calm response apparently surprised Bo.

"You did? Why didn't you say somethin'?"

"I was waitin' for you to tell me."

"You gonna turn me over to the marshal?" The shaking intensified.

"Do you think I should?"

"Well, I done wrong, that's for shore. I got Mrs. Marcum kidnapped and almost killed. I never told when I heard Artie was killed, 'cause Bart said he done it." Bo's confession flooded out in one breath. "I kept quiet, and my momma always said if you do wrong and no one finds out, you're guilty anyways 'cause God knows all 'bout it. An if you know the truth and don't tell it, same as lyin' ..." His voice trailed off, and he hung his head.

"Your momma is a wise woman." Jake put his hand on the boy's shoulder. "Tell me, Bo, you ever steal anythin' before?"

"No, sir."

"You plan on stealin' in the future?"

"No, sir—I done learnt my lesson." Bo fidgeted while Jake pondered a response.

"Tell you what. Let's handle this like the Bible tells us to. It says if a man steals, let him steal no more but work with his hands. I figure if I make you work for me a few months without pay, it would make things right. How about you bein' available to help any neighbor that has a need as well? Should square us up, don't you think? After all, the cattle are all accounted for, and Mrs. Marcum is home safe."

Bo's brows drew together. "What about Artie's sister? Won't she turn me in when I tell her what I done?"

Jake considered telling Bo the truth about Artie but decided that with Bo's new resolve for honesty, it wasn't a good idea. "I'll discuss it with her, but I don't think she's the kind of woman to hold grudges."

Bo's face reflected his relief. "I'll start workin' off my debt now by finishin' the stalls."

Jake headed to the bunkhouse to check on Bart. He found him tied to the bunk with Cookie sitting nearby reading aloud from the Bible. "'The wages of sin is death, but the gift of God is eternal life through Jesus Christ our Lord.'" Cookie stopped when he saw Jake. He set the Bible in the chair and walked over.

"How's the readin' goin'?" Jake asked.

"Reckon it's goin' fine. The Missus gave me a list of Scriptures to read to him. Do you think he really hears me?" Cookie turned to look at Bart's still form on the bed.

"Isabel said she heard every word said over her coffin. Evangeline figures Bart is kind of a captive audience for God's Word. She was in here early this mornin' prayin' for him."

"Bo overheard her tellin' Bart she forgave him and that Jesus would too if he'd ask. The kid left blubberin' like a baby."

"The real Farley and his lawyer are here. Sims plans on movin' in on Paine and his men later today."

"Well, Boss, I reckon it'll all be over sooner than later."

*　*　*

Sims appeared at the ranch just before dusk and accepted Jake's dinner invitation. "We got the whole bunch," he said while heaping food on his plate.

Every muscle in Jake's body relaxed.

"Please enlighten us as to how you dealt with the villains," Smithton said.

"Most who work on the Triple Diamond are good men." Sims spoke between forkfuls. "Some of them helped at Rose's last night. They got word to the cowboys still at the Triple Diamond. They cleared out, leaving Paine with only a handful of men."

"Sure he loved that." Cookie chuckled as he stabbed a piece of beef.

"Without Griggs to bully them into submission, they could care less about Paine. All they were interested in was the stash of money from the robberies. Once those hombres got the money, they hightailed it. We caught 'em a few miles south of here."

"I feel mighty stupid I didn't catch on." Jake took a second helping of fried potatoes.

"Don't," Farley interjected. "He is very good at his profession. He approached me after I returned from a business trip in Europe, posing as a land speculator. My father had passed while I was away. The cad knew my hands were full with many ventures, so he persuaded me he would come here and check out my holdings and report back. He advised waiting before I sold the land. Claimed anthrax had taken some of the cattle and rendered the land unusable."

"That explains a lot. But it don't make me feel any less foolish."

Sims shoveled in a few more mouthfuls of food before adding, "Andrew Paine was apprehended dressed in Violet's clothes." Everyone at the table roared with laughter.

"When can I take possession of my father's home again? I would like to get this unpleasant episode behind me as soon as I can." Robert's face brightened as he tasted Selena's steak. "This meal makes the entire trip worthwhile."

"Told you Selena's food was first rate. Sims, what's next?"

"We take the whole bunch to Hardyville where they'll stand

trial. Then the Paines will stand trial again back East. At some point they'll be hanged."

"What happens to Farley's daughter Lily?" Isabel inquired.

"You mean, Lulu Paine, their baby sister," Sims corrected. "Her part was simple. She would come home from boarding school, and whatever money her brothers had accumulated went back to Boston with her. We found the bank account, at least one of them. The Paines come from a long line of swindlers and con artists."

"Are they going to arrest her?" Farley asked.

"Another marshal has been tracking her. She left the school for parts unknown."

"I can assume she has a large purse to keep her living comfortably for a long time," Smithton interjected.

"Well, you can paint a skunk white and call her a rabbit, but once she's riled, everyone knows she's a skunk." Sims laughed at his own joke. "When she does, we'll get her."

"If I may, now that my father's ranch is vacated, I wish to stay there. There is no need to impose on your hospitality any further." Robert lifted his coffee cup for Selena to refill it. "However, I will miss your delicious cooking, my dear."

"My cousin, Maria, she is the cook there. You shall not be disappointed, *Señor*. But first, you must have a piece of *Señor* Cookie's pie before you leave."

"Then I must." He picked up his coffee mug. "Smithton and I need to take a full inventory of what is there. Whit will review any legal papers. I want to make restitution to everyone who has been wronged. I'll have him take a look at all the documents, including the one you mentioned."

"Mighty decent of you." Jake was impressed with the man. "Your pa would be very proud. I recall him as a man who done right by others."

"I am remorseful for not spending more time with him. I would have avoided this whole unfortunate thing if I had not let my mother poison me against him." Robert sighed like a man who carried a lifetime of regret. "I cannot change the past, but I can try to make the future brighter for those this scoundrel has cheated."

CHAPTER 37

Double M Ranch, June 10, 1873

Jake was in the stable brushing Traveler when Evangeline found him. He had just returned from a visit with Robert Farley.

"Are you ready?"

"Ready for what? Your sisters send you more furniture?"

There was pure joy in his wife's eyes. "I do believe the last of my grandmother's things have found their place."

"Good to hear. I wondered if we'd have to build a bigger house to make more room."

"I have a surprise for you." She hooked her arm through his. He chuckled at the flirty way she looked at him. "You are forbidden to ask questions."

"Forbidden, am I?" He touched her waist, but she wagged her finger. "Oh, no, come with me." Her green eyes sparkled, and a giggle escaped her lips.

Jake followed her outside. Sage was hitched to the carriage Jake had purchased from Mr. Farley. The entire Double M crew was gathered around.

"What's this all about?"

"We are going on a little trip."

"How do you expect me to do that with all the work needs doin' around here?"

"*Jefe*, the ranch, she will not fall into ruin if you are not here." Tony loaded a bag into the carriage.

"We'll do the chores," Amelia said. She and Isabel had donned Artie's old trousers.

Isabel imitated Artie's voice. "Duke promised not to fight me while you're gone."

Duke rolled his eyes. "There ain't nothin' this bunch can't

handle while you're away." Bo and Manny simply grinned.

"Boss, have I ever let you down?" Walters asked.

Jake raised his arms in surrender. "I give up. Guess it's settled."

"Wait up a minute," Cookie hollered as he and Selena hurried with a picnic basket.

"You no get hungry on your trip." Selena smiled mischievously as she and Cookie stowed the basket. Juliet followed with another bag.

"I'll bring you somethin', sweetie." Jake said the familiar promise, causing Juliet to giggle. He turned to help Evangeline into the carriage.

Once aboard, she took the reins from him. "I told you I know how to drive." She clicked her tongue and Sage responded. Jake leaned back, wondering what his wife was up to.

"Where we goin'?"

"Not far—a place I heard you are very fond of."

"Do you want me to guess?"

Evangeline kept her eyes straight ahead. "No, just relax and enjoy the view."

Jake gazed at his wife, hoping she could see the longing in his eyes. "I am."

"Tell me about your conversation with Mr. Farley this morning. How is Mr. Smithton's progress in settling things at the Triple Diamond?"

"They've reviewed all the legal—or should I say illegal—papers served on all the ranchers and homesteaders. Fakes, ever last one of 'em. The eviction notice he gave us wasn't worth the ink to write it. Smithton told me Ben Mitchell's brother, Byron, passed a few years ago, and he was never Lord McKay. It's one of Paine's aliases."

"It's sad to see how an entire family would waste their lives cheating people."

"Now their sins have come back on 'em with a vengeance." Jake put his arm around her.

"You are distracting me from driving, sir."

"Good." He kissed her cheek. "There's somethin' else Farley told me. After givin' back the land that was stolen to its rightful owners, he still had a sizable piece of land, includin' the house. He sold it."

"I hope whoever bought it will be a good neighbor and not treat the servants like slaves."

"I think you'll approve."

"You know who bought it, don't you?" Evangeline looked at him suspiciously.

"I did."

Evangeline brought Sage to an abrupt stop. "You did? Why? I thought you loved the Double M."

"I do, and I got no plans for movin' right now. However, Robert made me a very generous offer." Jake gave his wife a little pinch.

"Jacob Marcum, you can be so aggravating. What offer?"

"He said if you would set up a medical practice in the house, he would sell me the land for one dollar an acre."

Evangeline stared, open-mouthed.

"Why, you ask, would he make such an offer? Because he's very impressed with my gal." Jake looked at her, hoping his eyes conveyed all the love and pride that was in his heart. "He admired your willin'ness to buy Rose's Place and the adjoinin' hotel to convert into a school for the area ranchers' children. I think what impressed him most was givin' the gilded ladies money to start new lives somewhere else."

Evangeline seemed overcome with emotion. "Isabel will be an excellent headmistress. The children here need a school. And the women from Rose's deserve a chance to start over. I didn't do these things for personal gain."

"He knows that. Everyone does." Jake's hand moved a stray hair behind her ear. "Darlin', you touched his heart. Seems you remind him an awful lot of your cousin Ida, and I think he regrets puttin' money ahead of his feelin's for her."

Evangeline finally signaled Sage to move on. Jake remained silent. He knew the look of deep reflection when he saw it on his wife's face.

She turned to gaze at him. "You want me to open a practice?"

"It's what you're meant to do."

"But I'm not sure I'm ready to practice medicine full-time again."

"So, have office hours twice a week. The Triple Diamond is centrally located, and the house is near the road. People can come to you, and now with this fine carriage, you can go where you're needed. Besides, we gotta have a place to put all the furniture that keeps comin' from your sister."

"Do you realize how much time tending the sick could take up? I'd need to hire someone to help me. I have no idea who."

"I married a woman with a callin' from God for healin'. I'd be a fool to hold you back."

"Beloved, your confidence in me means more than I have words."

Jake warmed to her term of endearment and leaned over to kiss her cheek again. Gently, he thumbed away her tears.

"I have an extra surprise for you." Evangeline's voice caught. "I was going to save it until we got to our destination, but I want you to have it now. Open the basket. There is a letter in it."

Jake retrieved the letter from the picnic basket. He stared at the envelope for several seconds. "You wrote Johnny?"

"I did."

Jake read every word twice and stared at the picture of his young friend, now all grown up with a family of his own. He was so engrossed in the letter, he didn't notice when the wagon stopped.

Evangeline touched his arm. "We're here."

When he looked up, the homestead stood before him. The house had been repaired and whitewashed, the grounds cleared, and as they entered, he was amazed at the transformation. "Darlin', this looks amazin'. When did you do all this?"

"The ladies and I have been working on this since Isabel returned as herself. Mr. Walters got the men to come over here whenever they had time to clear away the dead trees and such."

Jake put his arm around her waist. "Looks like when I was a child, but there is so much of you here too."

"I know this home has good memories for you. I wanted to make it a place of rest from your hectic days. It's not far from the ranch but yet secluded." Evangeline's voice softened as she took his hand and led him to the bedroom. It had been transformed by a beautiful four-poster bed with a lovely blue wedding ring quilt and sheer white curtains.

Jake's heart rejoiced. "So this is the end of the journey, my darlin' Evie." He held out his arms to his wife.

Willingly, she melted into him. "No, my love, it's only the beginning."

Acknowledgments

Now is my chance to tell all those who gave a helping hand in the story you now hold in your hands how awesome they are.

Gayle Haas went through every page of an earlier version with joy and careful eyes, giving editing suggestions even though neither of us knew what we were doing.

My sweet daughter-in-law, Maribel Huff, and her sisters Marbella Rucker and Leticia Millan helped me get the Mexican/Spanish phrasing right. You ladies rock.

Retired Chief Petty Officer Christopher Bryant, Civil War reenactor and lifelong friend, loaned me some wonderful out-of-print books about women in the West. Chris' vast knowledge of guns of the period amazed me and, thanks to him, I could get the details right.

Rowena Kuo believed in me enough to present me with the Editor's Choice Award. Her continued encouragement has been priceless.

Molly Jo Realy stepped in to do the first thorough edits. My thanks go to her for journeying with me to get it done. And thanks go to Andrea Merrell for doing the final edits. Her touches and encouragement have made all the difference. So grateful God brought these two wonderful editors in on this project.

Thanks to Lighthouse Publishing of the Carolinas for taking a chance on me.

Thanks to Jerry B. Jenkins' Christian Writer's Guild for providing writing courses to help me learn the craft of novel writing.

Thanks to Word Weavers International for starting critique groups in my home state of Illinois. My critique group has challenged me and helped me be a better writer.

Thanks to my first accountability partner, Tez Brooks, for his input. Knowing a guy's guy found my characters interesting was inspiring.

Thanks to Lin Johnson for letting me work off the tuition for my first Write to Publish conference. It was there I learned so much and began calling myself a writer. Attending Write to Publish every year since has helped me make all sorts of wonderful connections that led to the publication of this book.

Most importantly, thank you, Jesus, for giving me the gift of words. May they always honor You.

31902325R00186

Made in the USA
Columbia, SC
04 November 2018